Courting Lord Dorney

Non-fiction by Marina Oliver
Writing Historical Fiction
Writing Romantic Fiction
The Beginner's Guide to
    Writing a Novel
Starting to Write *by Marina and*
    Deborah Oliver
A Century Of Achievement
History of Queen Mary's High
    School, Walsall
Castles and Corvedale
Local guide to accompany new
    circular walk

Fiction by Marina Oliver
A Civil Conflict
Campaign for a Bride
Cavalier Courtship
Charms of a Witch
Courtesan of the Saints
Gavotte
Highland Destiny
Highwayman's Hazard
Lord Hugo's Wedding
Lord Hugo's Bride
Masquerade for the King
Player's Wench
Rebel Heart
Restoration Affair
Runaway Hill
Sibylla & The Privateer
Strife Beyond Tamar
The Maple Leaf Trail
The Baron's Bride
Wild Heather
The Cobweb Cage
At the Earl's Command

The Glowing Hours
The Golden Road
Veiled Destiny
A Cut Above The Rest

As Sally James
A Clandestine Affair
Fortune at Stake
Heir to Rowanlea
Lord Fordington's Offer
Mask of Fortune
Miranda of the Island
Otherwise Engaged
Petronella's Waterloo
The Golden Gypsy

As Bridget Thorn
A Question of Love
Fires in the Forest
Hospital Heartbreaker
Island Quest
Theft of Love

As Vesta Hathaway
Honor and Passion
Cupid's Shot

As Livvy West
Royal Courtship
Her Captive Cavalier

As Donna Hunt
Forbidden Love

As Laura Hart
Manhattan Magic

Courting Lord Dorney

Marina Oliver

ROBERT HALE · LONDON

© Marina Oliver 2007
First published in Great Britain 2007

ISBN 978-0-7090-8422-8

Robert Hale Limited
Clerkenwell House
Clerkenwell Green
London EC1R 0HT

The right of Marina Oliver
to be identified as author of this work has been
asserted by her in accordance with the
Copyright, Designs and Patents Act 1988

2 4 6 8 10 9 7 5 3 1

Typeset in 10.75/13.5pt Janson Text
Printed and bound in Great Britain by
Biddles Limited, King's Lynn

Chapter One

—◦◦◦◦—

BELLA TWISTED ROUND in her seat and looked thoughtfully out of the window at the black clouds gathering ahead. She hoped they would reach home before the storm broke. Then her thoughts reverted to her own affairs. What did she really want? She had to resolve her dilemma before arriving at home. They were almost at the top of the pass, and in a few minutes would be rolling down towards Trahearne House, the large, stone, square-built house set in a deep valley which sheltered it from the worst north winds. It had been in her father's family for hundreds of years, and named after them, although it had been sadly neglected since Mama died and Papa had retreated into his own world. Bella loved it deeply, however, as she loved the fells which surrounded it, and the river which flowed through its overgrown fields and woods.

As the chaise reached a stretch of level ground and picked up speed Bella came to a decision. With a brisk smile and a nod to her companion, she rapped on the panel and gave the postilion new directions. She would visit her cousin Jane before facing her father.

'There won't be time for visiting, Miss Bella, it'll be dark before we get home as it is,' Meg, the elderly maid, protested. She had been with the family long before her young mistress had been born, and didn't fear to speak her mind. She had done so continuously for the first twenty minutes of their journey, and had subsided into an offended silence only when she realized that Bella wasn't even listening to her tirade.

'Don't exaggerate, Meg. But we won't be going home tonight. We'll stay with Jane. Since Papa doesn't know we're coming he

5

won't worry, and Jane's groom can drive us over in her carriage tomorrow. Stop being so grumpy.'

Not that he'd worry if he did expect them, she thought with amused acceptance. He'd most likely forget all about them.

Meg sighed loudly, but clearly decided she'd wasted enough breath.

Bella grinned at her. Meg knew she wouldn't listen to anyone when she'd made up her mind to something. 'Don't fret, Meg, you'll be home tomorrow, and then you can tell Cook all about it.'

Bella sank back into the corner of the chaise and shut her eyes, the better to think. She hoped she was a dutiful daughter. Indeed Papa, when he infrequently emerged from his obsessive study of Greek literature, often remarked on her compliant nature.

Perhaps, she reflected a trifle guiltily, it was because he was so withdrawn from the real world that he scarcely noticed her occasional lapses. He'd never enquired into the real reason for her governess, Miss Watson's, sudden and unexpected departure five years ago, for instance. If he had, and Bella's action in forging his signature on her dismissal letter had been revealed, he would have received a severe shock. As it was, he'd accepted that at eighteen she had no more need of a governess, and since then she had run her own affairs.

This time the shock would not, she hoped, be severe. He could hardly fail to wonder why she was returning home so abruptly after a visit to Harrogate. He need not be told about the furious duenna whose lucrative employment had been abruptly terminated, the five disgruntled suitors whose offers she had rejected out of hand, and other hopefuls whose attentions she had equally briskly spurned.

If she had not been a dutiful daughter, Bella reflected, as the post chaise crawled up the steep Pennine slopes, she would have deeply resented her mama. If that lady had to die in giving birth to her, Bella heartily wished she had done so before settling on so ridiculous a name for her only child.

Rosabella, though a mouthful, was a pretty name, she conceded reluctantly, but she was not a pretty girl.

The name conjured up a vision of slender delicacy, golden hair which nature curled unaided, creamy skin with cheeks tinged a pale pink, and deeper pink lips. In fact, exactly like the portrait of Mama painted on her seventeenth birthday, a few months before her wedding.

Whereas she was dark-haired and brown-complexioned, too short, too plump, her eyes too large and her nose too small. Not even a besotted lover could call her pretty, let alone beautiful. And none of her would-be suitors had been besotted by her face or figure.

Her musings were halted as thunder crashed above them. The sudden April storm had caught them. Rain and hailstones clattered on the roof, and the coachman struggled to control the nervous horses who showed every desire to bolt. Meg clutched Bella's arm and moaned in terror.

'The horses will run away with us and overturn the chaise! We'll be killed!'

Bella peered out of the window. 'Nonsense, Meg! They're under control, they're slowing down and walking. And the sky's lighter ahead.'

As the pounding rain diminished slightly, Meg sat back, still muttering, and Bella sighed in exasperation. Meg was devoted to her, always had been, but she lacked common sense and Bella often resented having to calm her fears and control her sometimes annoying starts.

They were a mile from Jane's home and the rain was still heavy when Bella glanced out of the chaise window and exclaimed in dismay. Once more she rapped on the panel and this time commanded a halt. As the vehicle drew to a stop she gathered her skimpy skirts about her and leapt down nimbly, ignoring Meg's fretful demand to be told what in the world was the matter now.

Bella ran back a few yards until she could kneel beside a child huddled in the ditch. It was a boy, no more than six or seven, though his stunted frame might house an older lad. He was incredibly dirty and dressed, if having a few scraps of material clinging to his skinny frame could be called dressed, in a motley collection of indecent rags, and he was snivelling loudly.

'I won' go back, miss! I'm ascared of 'im.'

Bella lifted him bodily and thrust him into the chaise, ignoring Meg's indignant protests.

'Miss Bella! What are you up to now? What do you want with a scruffy urchin? And he's soaking wet, he'll ruin your gown,' she added, pulling her own well away from the child, who was indeed wet through, his curly hair slicked down and hanging over his eyes, and his clothing clinging to his body.

'It's little Jed Tanner,' Bella informed her maid curtly, as she scrambled in after him. 'He's miles from home, and appears to be running away.'

There was a despairing howl from the child, and Bella was just quick enough to seize his arm and prevent him from leaping out of the chaise.

'Stop that row and tell me what's wrong!' she commanded briskly, and recognizing a stronger will than his own Jed tearfully complied.

It emerged that he had been caught stealing hens' eggs from the garden of his employer, Mr Josiah Ramsbottom, when he should have been at work in the latter's mill mending the constantly breaking cotton threads.

'Why did you steal, Jed? You know it's wrong to steal,' Bella said sternly.

'I was 'ungry,' he replied simply. ''E don' gi' us much food, an' I didn't fink 'e'd miss a few eggs.'

'You're a naughty boy!' Meg chastized him.

'He's no more than six years old, Meg, and working twelve hours a day in that awful mill!' Bella protested.

'I 'as ter sleep there now, wi' the work'ouse lot,' Jed said, a sob escaping him.

'With the children apprenticed to Mr Ramsbottom? In the mill?' Bella asked. 'What about your mother? And your sisters?'

'Mam got caught in one o' they machines,' Jed whispered. 'It cut off 'er arm, an' they buried 'er last week. Sal and Bet were sent ter Preston, ter the work'ouse there, and I 'ad to sleep in. I'll not see 'em ever agin.'

Bella put her arm about his skinny shoulders. He shuddered, but swallowed his sobs and went on.

'At mill, they keeps us in a big 'ouse, an' mek us work all day. I 'ates the noise. An' they don't gi' us much food. We'm allus 'ungry! An' they meks us learn ter read an' stuff like that what's no good ter us,' he added resentfully.

'Well, you can't run away and live by stealing eggs. It's not so bad with summer coming, I suppose, even when it's raining, but what will you do in the cold weather? Your clothes are too thin. You'd soon die of cold and starvation.'

He looked at her, and the sheer misery in his eyes made her blink hard. He sobbed anew, and Bella, ignoring his filthy rags, gathered him to her and did her best to comfort him.

'We'll see about that!' she declared. 'You won't have to go back, Jed, I promise. I'll look after you, and we'll find Sal and Bet too.'

'But Miss Bella,' Meg intervened, 'what can you do with him? It's not lawful to take away an apprentice. He'll have to go back.'

'But when I did summat wrong 'e said 'e'd send me ter work fer a chimney sweep!' Jed burst out. 'I'm ascared o' chimneys. An' they lights fires ter mek climbing lads go up.'

'He won't do that, Jed. Don't worry. I doubt Mr Ramsbottom will take me to court,' Bella said cynically. 'He owed my uncle money, and still hasn't settled his debt. Jane's cook can feed you, Jed, and find you some decent dry clothes, then we'll take you home. You can help in the garden for now. You'd like that, Jed, wouldn't you? And we'll go and find Sal and Bet and somewhere you can all be together again. And you'll have as much to eat as you want.'

'Miss? Yer means it? Why?'

Because I'm sorry for you, she thought. Because I hate the idea of little children being forced to work twelve hours or more a day, and brothers and sisters separated when they have no parents and have to go to the workhouse.

'Can you read?'

Jed looked at her suspiciously. 'I dain't like lessons,' he insisted.

'But did you learn to read?'

'Bits, but what good's that?'

'It might help you to get a better job, when you're older.'

'Yer'll not mek me 'ave lessons?' he asked apprehensively, and Bella suppressed a grin.

'Not if you don't care for it. Come on. I'm spending the night with a cousin, and she'll give you some cleaner clothes, and a good supper.'

He smiled and sat up. 'Cor, I ain't never bin in a carriage afore,' he said.

'And ought not to be in one now,' Meg said, breaking her offended silence. 'Miss Bella, have you gone quite mad? He's no doubt covered in fleas and lice!'

'Then we'll give him a bath.'

''Ere, I ain't 'avin' no bath!'

'You will if you want me to find Bet and Sal for you. Or shall I take you back to the mill?'

He snivelled, but subsided. Meg retreated into a corner as far away from Jed as she could get, and Bella was free to fume silently about the iniquities of the mill owners who ill-treated young children.

Lord Dorney rode out of the short drive, thankful the rain had ceased, and pulled his horse to the side to let the carriage turn in. He hesitated and looked back at the house, wondering whether it was his friend's wife returning. Though Philip Grant had been married for several years, their various duties, Philip's in the navy, and his own in the army, had prevented meetings, and he'd never met Mrs Grant. He'd sold out after Waterloo, when his brother had died, but Philip was still involved in navy matters. A pity Mrs Grant had been out when he called to deliver a book his and Philip's importunate godmother had pressed on him when she'd heard he was visiting his small estate in Lancashire. She would have more recent news of Philip. It must be at least a year since they'd met.

He wondered whether to retrace his steps, whether it would be intrusive to call the moment Mrs Grant, if it were her, had just arrived home. The butler who had opened the door had seemed puzzled when he'd asked for her, but had simply muttered his lady was not there. Had he understood the message? He hadn't seemed particularly bright. Perhaps he ought to make certain. Lady Fulwood would not have hesitated, and would call him a poltroon for doing so, but just as he decided to go back and make a brief explanation of his call, he was startled to observe an elderly maid, followed by an elegantly gowned young lady emerge from the chaise. She was too far away for him to distinguish her features, but he could see that her gown was soiled, clinging to her legs as though it were soaking wet, and her dark hair dishevelled. She seemed quite unconcerned as she lifted a small ragamuffin boy down from the chaise. Who on earth could she be, and what was she doing with such an urchin? She was too young to be Mrs Grant who, in any case was, Philip had told him, a blonde. Intrigued though he was, he decided it was inappropriate to become involved in whatever drama was happening; it was none of his affair. It was late in the afternoon and he had to decide whether to accept the somewhat paltry offer he had received for his house near Lancaster, and he would have to make haste if he were to reach the inn where he intended to meet his friend and stay that night.

Jane Grant, Lady Hodder since her husband had unexpectedly inherited a cousin's title six months before, lived alone while Philip, an officer in the navy, was at sea. She had been out visiting a friend when Bella arrived, but reached her home almost immediately after Bella's many trunks and valises had been transferred to the hall and the post chaise dismissed.

She found Bella directing her harassed servants to pile the trunks near the door, explaining that she would be staying just one night and only needed her small dressing case.

'Bella! What in the world brings you here? I thought you were to be in Harrogate for another month? And who is this?'

Ignoring the first question, Bella rapidly explained Jed's plight, and he was despatched to the kitchen for food and a bath. Meg, disassociating herself from such goings on, retired to unpack what her mistress would require for the night. Bella went into the small neat drawing-room laughingly trying to stem Jane's avalanche of comments and questions.

'Have mercy, Jane! I'm cold and hungry. When do you dine?'

'In half an hour, but you know we can't talk freely then, Bella, for Bates insists on waiting on me, doing everything ceremoniously as though Philip were here. Though he didn't bother to discover the name of the gentleman who brought that book. Just said he looked a well-set-up cove who'd strip to advantage and was riding a bang-on horse.'

Bella grinned. She knew exactly what Jane meant. Bates was an old friend, a seaman Philip had taken pity on when he'd lost a leg as a result of an encounter with a French cannonball. Now he stumped round on his wooden peg, ordering the other servants about, and behaving as he thought a butler in a ducal residence would behave. But no ducal servant would treat his mistress as though she were a helpless child, or join in his employers' dinner-time conversation as with equals. Bella had even known him, when moved to vehement expostulation about conditions for the ordinary seaman aboard most ships, to pull out a chair and sit down with his employers.

'I wish I'd met your visitor,' she said. 'He sounds a pleasant change after the fops I've been seeing in Harrogate.'

Jane sniffed. 'Even the note Lady Fulwood sent with the book didn't say who she was making use of this time. For all she cared he might have had to ride dozens of miles out of his way. But let us forget him. Tell me why you've come home now, or I shall die from curiosity!'

Before they could sit down at the table, though, a harassed maid appeared to ask what Lady Grant wished them to do with Jed.

'Cook says she won't have the little varmint – beg your pardon, ma'am, but that's what she said – in her kitchen no more.'

'What has he done?' Jane asked. 'Bella, I won't have him upsetting Cook.'

'We filled the bath in the scullery, ma'am, but he wouldn't get in, and while Ann and I were trying to undress him, he kicked the bath over. Then he ran out into the yard and hid in the hay loft. He won't come down. He's got hold of a hay fork and won't let Walter get near him.'

Bella stood up. 'I'll make him come down. Get another bath ready, please, but in the yard this time.'

She marched across the stable yard and halted under the opening to the hay loft. She could see Jed peering down at them, and the prongs of the hay fork were visible at the edge of the opening. Walter, the groom, looked abashed as he stood beside the ladder.

'He'll come down when he's hungry,' he said, but without much conviction in his voice.

'He'll come down now. Jed, if you don't come down at once I'll take you back to the mill. I won't go to Preston and find your sisters, and somewhere for you to live together again.'

Jed protested that he didn't want no bath, but in the face of Bella's repeated threats he gave in. Bella's last view of him was of Walter holding him firmly as he squirmed, while the maids stripped his skinny body and dumped him unceremoniously in the hip bath.

'Bella, it's a mad idea!' Jane was sitting behind the tea tray in her elegant drawing-room, looking at Bella and frowning.

'Why? It's the only way I can see of finding someone to marry who doesn't want me for my fortune. Aunt Maria and Cousin Gareth made such a fuss when Uncle Peter left me everything, the whole country must know how much it was.'

'You could always give it to him. You're not poor. You have quite a respectable income from what your mother left you.'

'Why should I? I'm a Trahearne, he's not. And Uncle Thomas Carey left them both well provided for. Besides, if I did give him any he'd wager it all in a twelvemonth. I have a better use for it.'

'But if you married your husband would have control over it.'

Bella sighed. 'I know, but if anyone wants to marry me for myself, I'll insist he allows me to use the money as I wish. I want it partly to repair Trahearne House; there's so much needs doing and Papa never even notices if the chimneys smoke or the roof leaks. But Papa won't hear of using it for that sort of thing. Yet if I'm married and have a son who can inherit it after me he'd agree, I know he would. Besides, if I don't marry and have a child the wretched Gareth or his equally wretched children would claim it. He said he'd go to law if I tried to give it to the houses for orphans I'm setting up. He'd get a crooked lawyer and probably convince a court I was mad. Then he'd try to get control of my money.'

'Surely not! He can't do that. Your father would stop him.'

'But Papa won't live for ever. And Gareth's very convincing when he wants something badly enough. How do you think he persuaded Helen to marry him? She had far better offers. There's no one else I can leave it to but you, and you say you won't take it, and you're older than I am anyway. I have to have a child, and to do that I need a husband!'

Jane was persevering. 'Gareth is older than you are.'

'Only by a couple of years. But he could start to try and prove I'm mad as soon as Papa died.'

'He doesn't have any children. He only married Helen six months ago.'

'But she's increasing.'

'And you want to use the rest of money to house your orphans?'

'Yes. Most of it; I'm not saintly enough to give it all away. I found one house in Preston before I went to Harrogate, and left Papa's attorney to deal with the purchase, and hire a decent couple to run it.'

'Does the attorney approve?'

'He'll do what he's told if he's being paid for it! But, as it happens, he's all in favour, and so are his brother, who's a Wesleyan preacher, and their wives. They will find more children, supervise the house, start to raise money to finance it and, perhaps, find other people to help.'

'Can you trust them?'

'Yes, they're all good people. They're not of the Evangelical persuasion. They'll give the children a good Christian upbringing, but they won't be forever preaching duty and virtue at them, and not permitting innocent pleasures. I'll take Jed there and get his sisters out of the workhouse. It's iniquitous to split families like that, especially when their mother has just been killed in a horrible accident! They'll all go to school and get a better start in life.'

'What about their father?'

'He was a soldier; he died at Waterloo. They all had to work in that wretched mill just to earn enough to eat.'

'You can't rescue all the mill children,' Jane said.

'But we can persuade other people to help, to give money, set up decent small houses – so much better than those horrid, monstrous workhouses where families are split. We'll employ sensible couples, who are kind yet firm, to look after them and see that they are trained for decent trades.'

'Was it really so dreadful in Harrogate?' Jane changed the subject.

'I hated the whole business. The men were all odious. I could see their busy little despicable minds calculating exactly how much a year I'm worth. They wouldn't have cared if I'd been a hideous old hag with unspeakable diseases if only they could have laid their hands on my beastly money.'

'Were they all fortune hunters?'

'Yes, hateful ones. And the distressing thought is that now I can never be sure anyone wants me and not my money. So I determined on this plan and I need you to help me.'

'I thought you might,' Jane said, with a laugh that was partly a sigh. She'd been involved in the younger girl's exploits many times before, and although she normally enjoyed them in retrospect, at the time she was too apprehensive to appreciate them. 'What are you going to do?'

Bella grinned at her, knowing quite well what she was thinking. 'I mean to find a husband who doesn't know about my wretched fortune.'

'But how can you do that?' Jane asked.

'I know I'm not beautiful, tall and slim and blonde like you are, but I'm not a complete antidote, even if I am three and twenty!' she declared indignantly. 'Someone might wish to marry me. I did have two offers when Aunt Maria brought me out with Cousin Caroline.'

'Yes, and you told me one was a widower of fifty, a parson who had six children under ten and wanted someone to undertake parish duties.'

'No wonder his poor wife expired! And the other was boy only a year older than I was. How could I even contemplate marrying a boy of eighteen, even if he hadn't had dreadful spots he tried to hide with some sort of flour paste? Besides, you know how pretty Caroline is. She had a dozen offers, good ones.'

'And married a rake who gambled away his fortune and her portion too. No wonder her mother is eager to get your uncle's money. She must have been devastated when Gareth married so imprudently last year, and Helen had only a couple of thousand.'

'She was, and I'm sure she's hoping Helen dies when the baby is born. Then dear Gareth could offer for me. But let's forget them. I'm determined on my plan, Jane. And I suppose I can lose weight if I eat less,' she added more doubtfully.

'I didn't mean you were ugly!' Jane protested, laughing. 'You keep saying you're not pretty, but Philip says you're very attractive when you're animated.'

'Does he? Truly?' Bella asked wistfully. Since her only season in London she had known few people, apart from neighbours and her father's elderly friends, until her visit to Harrogate. No one had ever complimented her on her looks until she had unexpectedly inherited her uncle's fortune a year before. She had soon grown suspicious of compliments after the first few days in Harrogate when she'd found herself surrounded by attentive men, old as well as young.

'What I meant,' Jane went on, 'was that everyone here knows about it, and now everyone in Harrogate, too. How can you meet a suitable man who doesn't?'

'Yes, that's the difficulty, but if I change my name it ought to be possible to find someone, especially if I let it be known that I have a modest dowry. I have to do it soon or I'll never know whether a man can love me for myself. And soon I'll be too old for even a desperate parson or widower to consider.'

'Will you go to London?'

'I'd love to,' Bella sighed longingly. 'But how can I? Some of the people I met in Harrogate will be there for the Season, as well as some of our neighbours here in Lancashire, and they'd recognize me, even if the ones I met six years ago don't remember me. No, I mean to go to Bath.'

'Bella, do think! If you do as you say it will cause all sorts of complications. And there could be someone from Harrogate who'd know you.'

'No one I know in Lancashire goes there, it's not so fashionable now, and from what those horrid men in Harrogate said they regard it as dreadfully slow. I didn't meet many of the older people who went to take the waters, so if any of them move to Bath they probably won't recognize me. But I need you to chaperon me.'

'They can't all have been old.'

'Well, some of them were young, but they were mainly the sons of wealthy mill or mine owners who'd never been out of Yorkshire in their lives except to go to London.'

'And none you felt even the slightest *tendre* for?'

'Not a whit! But they all knew I was rich and it was almost a race to see who could make me an offer first.' She chuckled. 'Lady Salway was afraid her job would be over almost before it began. It was, but not the way she expected. Really, Jane, I didn't think even Papa would have foisted such a dreadful woman on to me.'

'She answered an advertisement, didn't she?'

'With all sorts of glowing recommendations. I imagine they said those things to get rid of her – if they were genuine and not forged.'

'So what happened?'

'It was when she left me alone with her nephew. He's a beastly creature, and he tried to kiss me. Ugh! His lips were wet and flabby, and he kept trying to paw me. I kneed him where it hurt, and then told her she wasn't fit to be a duenna, and she could pack her bags and go that very night. I don't know if she did. I didn't see her again before Meg and I set out early this morning.'

'Then it's unlikely she'll complain to your father?'

'She knows I'd tell him what happened. But Jane, I can't endure to be foisted off with another woman like that. Please won't you help me? Philip is away for several more weeks and you must be lonely here on your own, so why not?'

'It's being deceitful,' Jane said slowly. 'Your father would be horrified.'

'He won't even know. Jane, it could be fun!'

Jane shuddered. 'For you, no doubt! You have no shame.'

'If you won't do it I shall have to travel on my own and hire someone from an agency when I get there.'

Sir Daniel Scott clapped Lord Dorney on the shoulder.

'Well met, Richard. It's months since we last had a good talk. But what brought you up to Lancashire? I thought you only visited Fellside in the autumn, for the shooting?'

Lord Dorney frowned. 'I do, and so I decided it had to be sold. I've found a buyer but he has not yet offered a good enough price. He's a wealthy cotton merchant who wants a country seat, and if he can offer what I think it's worth it would allow me to carry on with the renovations at Dorney Court.'

'I thought Robert had made all good, after your father died?'

'He repaired the roof and the windows, but neglected to do anything for the farms. The rent roll is pathetically small. And Selina ruined the inside. I can't live in her monstrous extravaganza.'

'So you are selling the properties your mother left you to finance it?'

'I have little choice. They are my only source of capital. I still have the hunting box, and I've rented out the town house for the Season. I don't want to have to sell them if it's at all possible to keep them.'

'And you will be back in London soon?'

'I have to go to Bath first to see Alex.'

17

'Then save yourself the expense of hiring rooms and come to stay with me in Bruton Street.'

'Thank you, I'd like that. I've some good friends. Now tell me all about America.'

Soon he was listening enthralled to Sir Daniel, who had just returned from a few months at the British Embassy in Washington, and forgot all about his abortive call on Mrs Grant.

'So you think the matter of the boundary between America and Canada will soon be settled?' he asked.

'It's in everyone's interest to settle it. Wars are too costly. The Americans don't want another war with Britain, and we're too exhausted, we need a few more years to recover without indulging in more heroics.'

'Is that what you thought about our little disagreement with Boney?' Lord Dorney asked, laughing.

'We had to stop him, but peace with America will be good for trade. They have cotton, which we need, and they buy many goods from us.'

Suddenly he yawned. 'I must sleep. We've a long ride tomorrow to Cheshire, and I hope you'll stay with me there for a few days while I deal with matters at home before I go and report to the Foreign Office.'

'And I to see how the work goes on at Dorney Court before I go and see Alex and this chit he wants to marry.'

Chapter Two

—◦◦◦—

A T BREAKFAST ON the following day Bella was still trying to persuade Jane. 'I must spend a few days at home. I promised Jed I'd find his sisters, but we'll start as soon as possible. Papa won't want me there for longer than to ask what happened.'

'But Bella! I promised to visit Philip's godmother, Lady Fulwood, soon, and remain in London until Philip comes home on furlough. I can't go to Bath.'

'Tell her you'll come later. Just for a few weeks, Jane. Please! And Philip can come to Bath if he has leave earlier. Jane, you can't let me down! I mean to go, whatever you do. If you refuse me I'll find some way, even if I have to tell Papa Lady Salway is still with me.'

'You wouldn't dare! You'd never lie to him.'

'I will! I hate the very idea of deceiving him, but what else can I do when he won't listen? I've never actually lied to him. If he asked me I always told the truth, but I'm determined to marry someone who loves me, not my fortune. You married for love, Jane, you can't deny me the same chance.'

'But Bella,' Jane almost wailed. 'I can't!'

'Then I'll have to tell lies. I'll soon find someone in Bath like Lady Salway. I must go soon. Jane, have you any notion of how fast gossip spreads? And how determined some of these fortune hunters are? Only a few people know about me now, and I can be sure no one in Bath does. After the Season, though, with all those wretches from Harrogate spreading gossip, it'll be different. I'd expect to find coaches breaking down every day outside the gates, or riders waiting to rescue me from falling on every ride I took. I even heard of one man who deliberately crashed into a girl's coach so that he could meet her, and several heiresses have been abducted. Ravished and forced to the altar for very shame!' she declaimed in throbbing tones.

'You're not afraid of that, surely!' Jane was aghast, and with a secret sigh of relief Bella knew she'd won.

'We – ell,' she hesitated. 'One of the wretches hinted at something like that. But if I change my name and vanish from home, he can't do anything. You will help me, won't you, Jane dear?'

By the following morning they had decided to send Bates to Bath at once to hire them a house for two months before Jane went to London.

'That ought to be long enough,' Bella said, but doubtfully. She was assailed by a sudden bleakness, a total lack of confidence in her ability to attract potential suitors.

'I'll say I've determined to try the waters for the cure of a minor digestive disorder which I've ignored until now, but which seems worse of late,' Jane decided, entering into the deception wholeheartedly now she was committed. 'We'll hire servants there, who won't be aware of your change of name,' she added, 'and Bates must return to look after this house while I'm away.'

Mr Trahearne, although mildly surprised to see his daughter, accepted her carefully worded explanation that Lady Salway could no longer undertake her chaperonage, and she herself found Harrogate unpleasant. Her wish to accompany Jane to Bath seemed entirely reasonable, and absolved him from further effort.

On the following day, Bella went to Preston, taking an apprehensive Jed with her. He was clean and tidy, in respectable clothes which had been outgrown by the gardener's son, and he rarely stopped asking questions, and demanding reassurances that Bella would find his sisters. When they reached the office of Mr George Jenkins, her attorney, he told her that the house she had bought was fit for occupation, and a decent couple installed.

'Then let us go and I can meet them, and leave Jed to get acquainted.'

Jed clung to her hand as they drove to the house, in a poor but respectable district not far from the town centre. Bella subjected Mr and Mrs Lloyd to a barrage of questions about their plans for looking after the children who would be consigned to their care, and was soon satisfied that they were an ideal couple to take charge of her orphans. They had one son, a little older than Jed, but Mrs Lloyd had been injured when he was born, and had never started another baby.

'Much to our regret, miss,' Mr Lloyd added. 'We'd have loved a big family, and this scheme will give us one.'

Bella approved of them, and left Jed with firm instructions that he was to do everything they said on pain of being taken back to the mill. Then she and Mr Jenkins went to the workhouse.

After an acrimonious disagreement with the workhouse overseers, Bella succeeded in taking Jed's sisters away. She suspected that they were secretly relieved at having two fewer mouths to feed. Bet and Sal, seven and ten years old, were tearful in their thanks, and vowed they would keep Jed out of mischief. Bella went back to Mr Jenkins' office satisfied with her progress so far.

'You will keep me informed how they go on, and whether you find other children in need?' she said. 'I shall be staying for only part of the time in Bath with Lady Hodder, and it's best you send my letters through her. I'll send her direction as soon as possible. I mean to spend some time in Bristol, while I am in the area. Your brother recommended a fellow Wesleyan who is engaged in a similar project there, and I must meet him and see if we can help one another.'

And that, she thought with satisfaction, eliminated the possibility that Mr Jenkins might inadvertently give away her real name to Jane's servants in Bath.

When she reached home again and was sitting down after dinner with her father, Bella told him more of Jane's plans.

'So you didn't like Harrogate, my dear?' Mr Trahearne said, keeping his place in the book with one finger. 'What a shame, it seemed such a good opportunity for you to mix in wider society than we have hereabouts.'

Bella bit back her opinion of the opportunities her various suitors had seen, and smiled dutifully. 'Jane is planning to spend a few weeks in Bath, and she has asked me to go with her,' she said. 'I expect some of the people there will be – well, younger. And Jane is reluctant to hire a companion, someone she doesn't know. She would much rather have my company.'

'I've no doubt of it, my dear. When does she plan to go?'

'At the end of the week. So I may go, Papa?'

'Of course, child.'

'Thank you so much! I'll send a message to tell her you've agreed.'

His gaze strayed back to the book. 'I shall miss you, my dear, but I am nearly at the end of my translation, and it would be an opportunity for me to complete it without feeling I am neglecting you.'

'Of course,' she agreed, dutifully suppressing the thought that her father never permitted anything to distract him from his passion for Greek literature. He really should have been a university don, she thought, and no doubt would have been if he had not met her lovely mother and been swept up for a few pitifully short months by a different sort of passion.

She felt a moment's compunction. If she had not been born, perhaps he would have returned to Oxford. But he had come back to his home and made sure she lacked for nothing. He'd provided her with nurses, governesses, tutors for painting and music – everything except his undivided attention. She then reminded herself that she probably preferred it that way, being left very much to her own devices, and having far more freedom than most girls in her situation. She had roamed the hills, on foot or on horseback, since she was a child. She knew everyone in the farms and villages round about and was often invited to parties or to accompany other girls to the local Assemblies.

Mr Trahearne promised to keep an eye on Jed and his sisters in Preston. He insisted that Mr Jenkins was utterly reliable, and needed no supervision.

'But he would appreciate the attention, while I am away,' she said. She trusted George Jenkins, his brother and their wives implicitly, but she wanted to convince her father that she was using his brother's legacy wisely.

Mr Trahearne found it easier to agree, as Bella had known he would. Much as he loved her she knew he had never felt at ease with his motherless and impetuous daughter. He had no talent for dealing with children, and on top of his overwhelming grief for his young wife he had been afraid of the tiny baby's fragility. This awe had never entirely left him as Bella grew up, and he had consequently been far more lenient than most fathers. Now, she suspected, he was somewhat guiltily looking forward to the day when she would marry and depart to her own home, and the more she moved in Society the sooner that would be.

Bella shook herself, and seeing that her father was once more absorbed in his book, left the room. She swiftly wrote a note to tell Jane it was all arranged, and went to the stables to find a groom who would deliver it for her.

They left Lancashire a few days later, travelling post. They would hire a carriage in Bath. Bella had not bothered to unpack her trunks during her brief stay at Trahearne House, deciding that the gowns she had taken to Harrogate would do for Bath until she could acquire more. A disgruntled Meg had been left behind, volubly complaining and prophesying all sorts of disasters if she were not present to guard her beloved mistress from them.

'Jane's maid Susan can do all I need,' Bella informed her briskly. 'Besides, it will be cramped enough with three of us travelling in the chaise.'

Susan she could trust. Bella knew she didn't get on with Meg, because of some ancient quarrel between their families, and would never let her know what her mistress was doing, might even enjoy deceiving her about Bella's activities. And if Jane swore her to secrecy she'd know her own job depended on her discretion.

Bella had no intention of permitting Meg to know her real purpose. Loyal as the woman had always been, since she had taken over the care of the motherless baby, Bella knew she would heartily disapprove of her new plans, and might inform Mr Trahearne of them. That would be a disaster. Little as he normally noticed what Bella was up to, she suspected that this latest ploy might shock him out of his indifference. Susan was new to her job, a timid young lady who had replaced the elderly but now retired dragon who had been with Jane since she was a young girl. She was anxious to please, and would either not care or not know what to do if she did disapprove, though from what Bella had seen of her she doubted the girl had any opinions of her own.

'At last!' Bella exclaimed, as they left the village behind. 'How long will it take us to get to Bath?'

'Several days, for I don't mean to be cooped up in this chaise all day,' Jane replied. 'I've given way to you, since I suspected you would do something outrageous on your own if I did not, but I mean to enjoy the journey.'

Bella gave an exaggerated sigh. 'Dear Jane, I am so grateful to you, and of course we will go at the pace of a three-legged donkey if you wish. It will give us more time to decide on what clothes to buy in Bath.'

They spent several enjoyable hours doing this, in between looking at the countryside. Jane had been to London several times with her husband, but Bella had never been south of Liverpool and she was both fascinated and repelled by the flatness of the Cheshire plain.

'I couldn't live in this sort of country,' she exclaimed. 'If I find a husband who lives in a place like this I'll have to persuade him to buy an estate where there are hills.'

'He might not wish to,' Jane said, laughing. 'Bella, this is a mad start!'

'It's the only way I can be sure of finding a man who isn't more interested in my money than in me, and be able to use my money in the way I wish.'

Bella's enjoyment of the countryside increased as they drove through the Cotswolds, and she admitted, laughing, that it was tolerable scenery, though not so grand as Lancashire.

They had only a dozen or so miles to go, and were climbing back into the chaise, after having partaken of a light nuncheon at a posting inn, when they saw that the mail coach was partly blocking the archway to the street, and another chaise, crowded with half a dozen young men, was pulled over to the side, unable to leave. A couple of men who had just arrived on horseback were talking to an ostler, further blocking the yard.

The ostlers were changing the Bristol mail coach's horses, and a girl who had been waiting by the doorway to the tap room stepped forward. She was neatly dressed in a gown of dark-green serge, and a plain bonnet, and carried a bundle wrapped in a shawl.

Jane's chaise could not move and, as they settled themselves, Bella overheard the exchange clearly.

'You're not on the list,' the coachman said. 'I'm sorry, lass, but I'm full, there's no room for you. Mebbe the next will have room.'

'But I've asked two others, and they were full too! What shall I do? They told me I could get on a coach here!'

'You should have booked a ticket. I'm sorry, but there's nowt I can do.'

One of the young men leaned out of his chaise. 'Come with us, my pretty. We don't mind being a bit squashed. There's plenty of laps for you to rest on.'

The girl glared at him and turned away without replying.

'Hoity toity! Do you need persuading?' her tormentor asked, flinging open the door and leaping down on to the cobbles. He seized the girl by the arm and swung her round, laughing as he dodged the bundle she aimed at his head.

'Let me go!' she cried, her voice wavering in panic.

'No need to be frightened, we'll treat you well, and you'll get to Bristol,' he said, and loud guffaws came from his companions.

Another man had joined him by now, and between them they picked up the girl and started to drag her, crying and struggling, towards their chaise.

'Let her go!'

The first man turned towards Bella, who was leaning out of the chaise window, and raised his eyebrows. 'You'd best keep out of it, or we might decide to take you along with us as well,' he sneered, and then stepped back in alarm, letting the girl's arm go.

'I think not,' Bella said. 'This pistol isn't a toy, and it's loaded, and I'm accounted a tolerable shot. Though I might aim for your leg and hit somewhere a little higher. I can't guarantee just to lame you.'

The men still in the chaise laughed.

'A woman shoot straight,' one scoffed.

'Are you willing to hazard that?' she asked as she straightened her arm and flicked forward the safety catch.

'Oh, leave the wench, Lambert, she's not worth the trouble,' another said.

At that moment the mail coach pulled out of the yard and the archway to the street was clear. The two men, with shrugs, clambered back into their chaise and it moved off too.

The girl had dropped her bundle and as she bent, sobbing with relief, to pick it up, Bella jumped down beside her.

'Are you going to Bristol?'

The girl nodded. 'Yes, miss, or Bath, and thank you, miss. Would you really have shot them?'

'If I'd had to. Have you family in either?'

'No, miss, my parents live in Gloucester. I'm looking for work. My lady died, last week, and I thought there'd be suitable positions in Bath. There's none round here, and I can't go home, they haven't room for me.'

'You have references?'

'Oh, yes, miss. My lady's son wrote me one.'

Bella considered her. She looked clean and now she wasn't being threatened, she spoke up frankly.

'I need a personal maid. Come, we'll take you to Bath, and we can talk on the way. If we can come to an agreement, I could employ you for a few weeks. I left my own maid at home, and the post would not be permanent, but it would give you time to look around for something else.'

The girl was speechless, but the look of gratitude and the smile in her eyes were a good enough answer.

'What's your name?'

'Mary, miss. Mary Harding,' she managed.

'I'm Miss Collins, this is my cousin Lady Hodder, and her maid Susan. Get in, the way's clear now.'

Susan looked resentful as she was forced to move along the seat to make room for Mary, but one look from Bella made her bite back the protest she'd been about to make. She gathered up Jane's jewellery box and a couple of shawls which had been on the seat beside her, and nursed them on her lap. Mary sat beside her, muttered a shy 'Thank you', and tried to make herself as small as possible in the corner.

Bella sat in silence for the next hour. She had realized that Susan could not be expected to look after all her clothes as well as Jane's. She'd decided to find a maid once they reached Bath, but if Mary proved capable this would save her the trouble.

She began to question Mary, and discovered that the girl had worked for three years for the old lady who'd died, and before that had been apprenticed to a Cheltenham milliner. Mary handed her the letter, which praised her for her skill in sewing, and her patience.

'We'll try it for two weeks,' Bella said briskly.

'Oh, Miss Collins, I'm so grateful!'

'Well, you're just what I'm looking for, and we couldn't have let those despicable fools abduct you.'

Mary shuddered, and said no more, but looked eagerly out of the window at the villages they passed through. Bella knew Jane was itching to talk, both to demand an explanation of the pistol, now safely stowed away in Bella's capacious reticule, and discuss the wisdom of taking in an unknown girl as her personal maid.

Jane would have to wait until they could be private, until they reached the house which Bates had found.

'She beat you to it, old man,' one fashionably dressed gentleman said to another as they entered the tap room.

'I wonder if she would have fired it?' Lord Dorney gave a crack of laughter. 'That jackanapes thought so, in any event!'

'Your face was a picture, Richard! You'd started across to intervene when she did it for you.'

'And probably far more effectively. You and I, Dan, would have been hard put if all half-dozen of 'em had joined in.'

Sir Daniel laughed. 'Well, we don't have to worry about possible black eyes. Who'd have thought that dab of a girl had so much spirit.'

Lord Dorney nodded, and turned his attention towards ordering the best the inn could provide.

Sir Daniel was talking about his report to the Foreign Office, but Lord Dorney's mind kept wandering back to the scene in the inn yard.

He'd noticed the girl and her older companion while they'd been talking to the ostler, arranging for a change of horses. He tried to recall how she looked, but could remember only that her hair was dark, her eyes huge, and her figure plump but shapely.

'I wonder if we'll meet them again?' he said suddenly.

Sir Daniel glanced across at him and grinned. 'I don't believe that such a chit who had no looks to recommend her has caught your attention. Richard, Lord Dorney, the despair of countless mamas, the cause of innumerable languishing glances from all the debutantes, with the pick of them all for years, but so difficult to please, has found Cupid's dart at last!'

'Don't be an ass. But I'll wager none of this year's crop of hopefuls would have had the nerve to do what she did.'

'None of them would have possessed a pistol, let alone known how to use it. Are they an insipid lot, this year? Is that another reason why you left London so early in the Season? Apart from selling Fellside?'

Lord Dorney shrugged. 'It bores me, but I have to go sometimes. And I've no desire to wed. Besides, until I've brought Dorney Court back to decency I have to retrench. I can't afford a wife.'

'A girl like that might be an asset to you. She'd see off any creditors.'

'My situation's not quite as dire as that. After the experiences of my father and Robert at the hands of duns I've no intention of getting into their clutches. That's why the work at Dorney Court has to go more slowly than I'd like. The farms, in any event, are in better shape now, and the rents will improve next year. But I still wonder if she would have shot him, or whether she was bluffing.'

'I wouldn't like to have called her bluff! Well, if she's bound for Bath no doubt you'll meet her somewhere. I wish I was staying to watch, instead of paying this duty visit to my sister on the way to London. You'll come to me when you've finished with young Alex and his inamorata?'

Lord Dorney raised his glass to Sir Daniel. 'I'm wondering if his ardour will have cooled by now. He's not been very constant in the past, fancying himself in love with a dozen chits. But this is the first time he's asked me to approve of one.'

'It must be serious. So our ways part here.'

'Not for long. I doubt I'll be in Bath more than a week. My felicitations to your sister, and we'll meet again when I reach London. Then I will tell you what, if anything, happens in Bath!'

'And if you happen to meet that intrepid young lady. In some ways, I wish I were able to come with you,' Sir Daniel said, laughing. 'I'd like to know more about her.'

Chapter Three

———•❧•———

'WHERE ON EARTH did you get that pistol?' Jane demanded as soon as the drawing-room door had closed behind Bates, who had stayed to settle them into the house he'd hired.

'I've had it for years,' Bella said. 'It's one of Henry Nock's pocket designs, just the size to fit in a large reticule. I never travel without it, but I've never had to use it before.'

'Would you have shot him, really?'

'Of course. What would be the use of threatening if I didn't intend to carry out my threat? In some ways I'm sorry he was such a poltroon! He deserved to be shot!'

Jane closed her eyes. 'First you embroil me in this mad escapade, Miss Isabella Collins, and then you almost shoot someone!'

Bella strolled across to the window which looked out over Sydney Gardens.

'This really is a perfect position, with the gardens on our doorstep. You know, I'm not sure I like the name Collins. It's not aristocratic enough. Perhaps I should have chosen something that hinted at ducal connections.'

'Perhaps you should have been content with your own name,' Jane almost snapped.

'It's too well known, after all that fuss when Uncle Peter died. There was so much speculation about how many fabulous jewels and other treasures he'd brought home from India, everyone must have heard about Nabob Trahearne. Those country yokels in Harrogate certainly knew I'd inherited his fortune. But I kept as close to Bella as I could.'

Jane sighed. 'I think I was mad to agree to this masquerade.'

'No, darling Jane, you were kind and sympathetic, you want me to marry someone who appreciates me for myself, not for my fortune.'

'Heaven help the poor man, whoever he might be!'

Bates had hired this house in Henrietta Street, saying severely that it was better to be in a quieter part, away from the hurly burly of the town centre.

'But it's rather far from the Pump Room,' Jane commented. She had visited Bath once before, with an elderly aunt.

'Ye'll have to take a chair, then, and not try walking,' Bates replied uncompromisingly. 'Better for you than being kept awake with people walking past all night long.'

Jane knew better than to argue. They were country girls, used to walking, and Bates was departing on the stage early the following day, much against his will. He would be unable to complain.

'I've arranged for the butler, cook, maid and groom to be here this afternoon for you to approve,' he said now. 'Though why you couldn't bring your own servants instead of leaving 'em eating their heads off at home I don't know.'

'They can be occupied with a thorough spring cleaning before Lord Hodder comes home. It will be much easier with me out of the way,' Jane said briskly. 'Besides, I'm here for only a few weeks before going to London.'

'He'll have told them your real name,' Jane said worriedly later, as they waited for the new servants to arrive for inspection. 'I've only just thought of that.'

'Then we say your cousin was unable to come, so your husband's cousin came instead.'

Jane laughed. 'I think, despite everything, I'm beginning to enjoy this. I feel utterly irresponsible. Now how much a year are you supposed to have?'

'Don't say a precise amount.'

'That's sensible, I suppose,' Jane agreed.

'Good. Now tomorrow morning I want to go shopping. I feel dowdy, and I suddenly don't like the clothes I took to Harrogate. They remind me of things I intend to forget!'

Bates, as Jane had known he would, had chosen eminently suitable servants. Mrs Dawes was a rotund, motherly cook with a round face, bright eyes and clear complexion. She looked capable of endless chatter, but replied only to the questions asked. The butler was her husband, tall and thin, quiet but obviously experienced and reliable. The maid, Lizzy, was older than Jane would have liked, but was a friend who had worked in the same house with them before. Jackson, a small man who had once been a jockey, would look after the horses and drive the coach she intended to hire.

'We usually work each year for old Lady Sommerton,' Mrs Dawes explained. 'But she died last month, poor lady, and her daughter decided not to come this year, so we had to look for another place rather sudden.'

The next morning, wearing a walking dress she'd acquired in Harrogate, Bella sallied forth with Jane. Mary followed to carry the parcels. The dress was of a delicate primrose shade, with deeper gold ribbons at the high waist and gold Spanish embroidery round the hem and the edges of the short puffed sleeves. With it she wore a poke bonnet of the same colour, again trimmed with gold ribbons, brown sandals and elbow-length gloves in a supple leather. Jane was still wearing half-mourning for her husband's cousin, and had on a gown in a pretty shade of lavender trimmed with dark-grey braid.

Much as Bella would have liked to wear one of the necklaces from India, she bowed to Jane's advice that it would look crude.

'Save the jewels for evening, and even then, if you don't want to cause comment, you should wear very simple styles. Remember you're not a wealthy young lady.'

Jane having decided it was now time to abandon her mourning for a man she'd never met, they spent two absorbing hours selecting materials, bonnets and gloves, shoes and fans, and arranging for the dress lengths to be made up in the latest modes. Then they strolled towards the Upper Rooms where Jane signed the subscription book, and on towards the Pump Room.

'I don't think I'll drink the water,' Bella said thoughtfully. 'Let's just listen to the music rather than sample that.'

They had almost reached the doors when Mary, who had been casting anxious glances behind her for some time, turned to try and shoo away a small, scruffy-looking mongrel trailing after them.

'I wonder if the poor animal's lost?' Jane said doubtfully. 'I noticed him outside the Assembly Rooms.'

'He looks as if he's been lost for some time,' Bella commented. 'See how thin he is, poor little scrap.'

'What should we do?'

Bella's reply was lost in a sudden flurry of excited yapping, as a mincing poodle escaped from the leash held negligently by a small, dandified man, and rushed in to attack the stray.

Mary stepped hurriedly backwards out of the way, for the mongrel, although only half the size of the poodle and in much worse condition, was not prepared to suffer the indignity of being chased off by a pampered, coiffured, scented monster, however much larger it was.

'Beau! Come here at once, sir! Heel! Stop it, I say. Oh, do listen to me, you wretched animal.'

The dandy was hovering several yards away from the fracas, helplessly wringing his hands, while a quizzing glass danced unheeded on the end of a black velvet ribbon, and a cane slid from his nerveless grasp on to the ground. He was ejaculating feeble commands in a progressively weakening voice.

'Use your cane. For heaven's sake, hit him!' Bella exclaimed.

'Hit him? Hit Beau?' the dandy almost screamed at her. 'He's never been hit in his life!'

'He might have better manners now if he had,' Bella retorted sharply, and before he could prevent her she picked up the cane and turned towards the dogs.

They were growling ferociously as they circled and nipped each other in an attempt to find a grip.

The stray was weakening, though still game, but as the poodle went for his unprotected neck Bella brought the cane down sharply.

The poodle yelped, turned to face this new attack, and snarled as he gathered himself to spring at Bella.

Mary screamed as the dog hurled himself forwards, but Bella calmly thwacked the poodle across his nose. With another yelp, this time of real pain rather than surprise, the poodle decided he'd had enough and took off at speed in the direction of the river.

Jane laughed. 'Oh, Bella! You attract trouble.'

'How dare you!' The dandy was spluttering from surprise and

uncontrollable fury. 'How dare you attack Beau? A highly strung, delicate animal like that. He'll be lost. I paid a great deal for him. I'll make you pay for your interference, madam!'

'Don't be such a tedious fool! He'll find his way home when he's hungry!' Bella snapped, tossing the cane towards him and not looking up from where she crouched beside the mongrel.

'Are you hurt, ma'am?' a new voice intervened, and Bella glanced up to find another man bent over her.

Her eyes seemed unable to move, and she did not reply. He was a little above average height. Broad shouldered and narrow-hipped, he wore his discreetly elegant clothes easily. The thought went through her mind that he looked far more distinguished than the overdressed fop she had clashed with.

He was as dark as Bella herself, with short hair dressed in a carefully casual style. His eyes were a brilliant blue, wide apart and piercing. His mouth, lips curved in amusement, was – here Bella forced her errant thoughts to change direction.

'Your hand,' the newcomer said, reaching down to lift it from the head of the mongrel, which she had been stroking soothingly. 'There's blood on it. Were you bitten?'

'Miss Bella! Are you hurt?' Mary demanded urgently, trying to pull Bella to her feet.

'What? Oh, the blood. No, of course not, I wasn't near enough. It's this poor little fellow, that wretched poodle must have bitten his shoulder. Look, there's a tear and his leg obviously hurts him; see how he's holding it.'

'You've driven my dog away, beating him so viciously. If he's lost or injured you'll pay for it!' The dandy was still hovering on the fringe of the little group.

Bella was trembling, but she scrambled hastily to her feet, cradling the mongrel in her arms, and turned angrily on the dandy.

'I think it would be more to the point if you paid for your careless folly in letting that undisciplined, vicious brute attack this poor creature who was doing nothing at all to provoke him!'

'That miserable object? Who cares about him? He looks as though no one's claimed him for months. My dog is exceedingly valuable.'

'It's precisely because he's a poor, miserable object and clearly no one has cared about him for a very long time that he deserves consideration now, sir! Your pampered brute should be shot. All pampered, ill-tempered fribbles should be shot,' she added, flashing a contemptuous glance over him, from his red-heeled shoes, skinny legs encased in skin-tight pantaloons, and violet waistcoat beneath a deeper purple coat.

He spluttered in indignation, but Bella paid no heed. She heard a stifled laugh behind her as she stalked away towards Pulteney Bridge, Jane beside her, and the mongrel nestling contentedly in her arms, licking his wounds and occasionally the face of his rescuer.

Mary, apprehensive, caught up with her.

'Miss Bella, I thought he'd have apoplexy,' she gasped. 'I wonder who on earth he was?'

'A nonentity who tries to make up for nature's mistakes by causing himself to be a spectacle,' a deep, musical voice answered. 'Ma'am, pray let me carry the animal for you. He must be quite heavy despite his deplorable condition.'

Before Bella could reply the dog was lifted from her arms. It was the man who'd spoken before. After a brief moment of wariness the dog decided to accept this new arrangement and relaxed.

She looked up at the man beside her. Her head came only to his shoulder, and the thought came to her that it would be a very comforting shoulder to lean against, should she ever be in need of comfort.

'What do you intend to do with him?' he asked.

'I'd better take him home. Just until his wounds have healed. Perhaps Mrs Dawes knows of someone who wants a dog?'

'I doubt you'll get rid of him now,' the stranger prophesied, laughing. 'Perhaps we ought to introduce ourselves. I'm Richard Yates, at your service.'

'I'm Bella, that is, Isabella Collins. And my cousin, Lady Hodder. I'm most grateful for your assistance, sir. Jane, I wonder if Mrs Dawes likes dogs?'

Alexander Yates lived with his mother and two younger sisters in a small house on the London Road. When his cousin appeared he came into the hallway as the footman was opening the door, and tried to hustle him into the small room his father had used as a library.

'Alex, have patience! I must pay my respects to Aunt Emma before we can talk.'

Alex grinned ruefully. 'Sorry, Richard, but I've been waiting so long to talk to you.'

'Two weeks since I had your letter. Hardly a lifetime. And I understand that the lady of your heart will not be in Bath for a few days yet?'

He followed the footman up to the drawing-room where his aunt, the widow of his father's younger brother, sat near the window with some embroidery on her lap. She glanced at the footman and sighed. Lord Dorney had no difficulty in interpreting that sigh. She maintained that she could not afford a butler, and the footman was less than six feet tall, and his calves were less impressive than the calves of her wealthier friends' footmen. Despite his own monetary difficulties, his aunt frequently wondered why he was not willing to assist her to move to a better part of the town, and employ more servants. The truth was different: she was miserly and resented spending money.

'Well, Richard, it's been a long time since you deigned to visit your poor relations,' she said now. 'You may kiss me.'

He bent down and brushed her cheek with his lips. He'd been in Bath three months ago, but knew better than to argue with his aunt. She positively enjoyed complaining about her grievances, and she had a multitude of them. He wondered how Alex and his sisters could endure living with her. One day, one hour, was enough for him.

'I'm here now. I trust I find you well?'

She launched at once into a catalogue of her aches and pains, the snubs and slights she had received, and the disgraceful behaviour of tradesmen who did nothing but cheat honest customers. Lord Dorney exchanged a wry glance with Alexander. Eventually they escaped and Alexander led the way downstairs, letting out a huge sigh as he did so.

'Why don't you take rooms in London?' Lord Dorney asked abruptly. 'You can afford it. She has her jointure, and you're not nearly so poor as she pretends.'

'I can't leave Fanny and Anna to bear her ill humours all the time,' Alexander said, sighing. 'As it is I'm away more than she likes.'

'I honour you for it. Most young men would have fled long ago. But what will happen when you marry? Could you subject your bride to her constant complaints?'

'That's what I need to talk to you about. I wondered, that is, I hoped, you would allow me to rent Dorney Court from you, when I marry Felicity. That is, if she accepts me – I haven't actually asked her yet. Mama could move into the dower house. She's often said she'd like to live in the country. Then I'd still be near enough to look after her.'

Lord Dorney frowned. 'Alex, I need somewhere to live myself. I've sold almost all the property my mother left me, apart from Fellside, which I hope I'll sell soon, and a couple of houses in Highgate Village, which are let out. I only have the hunting box, and the town house is let. I may dislike what Selina has done with Dorney Court, but I used to love the place, and will no doubt appreciate it again when it's restored. It's my only proper home.'

'Are you planning to marry?' Alex asked swiftly.

'After Robert's experience of marriage, do you think I'm in a hurry to tie the knot?'

'You'll change your mind when you meet the right girl,' Alexander said, and Lord Dorney marvelled at the optimistic confidence of youth.

'Perhaps,' he said. 'You can have the dower house, but I don't think Felicity would care to share it with your mother. And what of your sisters? They are still young, they no doubt wish to marry, if only to escape from your mother. They'd have far less opportunity of meeting suitable men if they were living in the country. Dorney Court is isolated, there isn't much society nearby.'

Alexander sighed. 'I know. But I can't bring Felicity here. My mother would soon drive her to distraction. I can afford to buy a small house in Bath just for us, so that we could live separately, but not one in the country too, and Felicity likes the country.'

'You can come to Dorney Court whenever you wish. I won't object, and you can invite friends at any time. But if you ask your mother to stay, give me good warning and I will have urgent business in London! Now, when am I going to meet Felicity?'

'In a day or so, I hope. She is away with an elderly aunt at the moment, but she and her sister, Lady Andrews, will be returning home soon. Their parents are dead, and she lives with Lady Andrews in Lansdowne Road. I wanted you to meet her before I declared myself.'

Lord Dorney grinned. 'You don't need my permission. But if I don't approve? Will you abandon her?'

'No! Of course not! Oh, Richard, you know I want your approval, but I don't need your permission.'

'Then for your sake I hope I find her as attractive as you clearly do.'

Bella stood behind the curtains of the drawing-room staring at the retreating back of the exceedingly handsome Richard Yates.

'How attractive he is,' she said to Jane. 'There was no one nearly so good-looking at Harrogate. Did you see the way his hair curled over his ears? And his eyes – the lashes were as long as a girl's. And his mouth was so well-shaped.' She sighed. 'He doesn't need padding on his shoulders. Not like some of the fops I met in Harrogate. I wonder if he's married?'

'Bella!' Jane was shocked. 'You surely can't imagine you've fallen in love with the first presentable man you meet?'

'He's not the first presentable man I've met,' Bella argued. 'There were some even more handsome in Harrogate, even if I didn't like them. And I didn't say I'd fallen in love with him. I only wondered if he was married.'

'Then you must have been considering him as a husband, and I thought you wanted to marry for love?' Jane countered swiftly.

'Well, of course, I'm considering every reasonable man as a husband,' Bella changed tack slightly. 'That's why we came to Bath. It would be a ridiculous waste of time and effort getting to know someone who was already married, or falling in love with them.'

'Yes, but one doesn't normally talk about it quite so frankly.'

'That's a great deal of time wasted too, hinting and pretending not to be interested, when really it's all most girls and their mamas ever do think about.'

Jane abandoned the argument. Much as she often deplored her young cousin's outspoken views, when she stopped to consider the matter she had to acknowledge Bella spoke a good deal of sense, and it was only the conventions of society which made such frankness unacceptable.

'He'll almost certainly be in the Pump Room tomorrow morning,' Bella said slowly, 'and we'll soon discover all about him. It was a pity he wouldn't come in. And fortunate Lizzy took a fancy to the dog.'

'Yes, she'll soon have him looking sleek and fit; she and Mrs Dawes won't be mean with the scraps. And then what will you do with him?'

Bella looked at her speculatively. Jane knew that look and took a deep breath, ready to reject Bella's next plan.

'Perhaps Mrs Dawes knows someone who wants a dog,' Bella said, but without much hope.

'Lizzy asked her, and she doesn't,' Jane squashed that hope.

'Oh. Well, we'll be here for some weeks,' Bella said in a dismissive tone.

'And the dog will get more attached to you. What will happen when I have to go to London and you go home?'

'I can't take him back to Trahearne House. Papa's old Blackie won't permit any other animal in the house,' Bella said slowly. 'Jane, you ought to have a dog. Don't you think he'd be company for you, while Philip's away?'

'No, I don't!' Jane spoke with unusual determination. 'I already have those two cats you saved from drowning, because Blackie practically ate one of them. You'd have liked me to have little Jed, and I almost had to take the terrier you found in the woods, the one with a broken paw, who'd been caught in a trap, except that he was run over by a chaise.'

'Poor little thing. That wretched coachman was driving too fast and the poor lame animal couldn't get out of the way in time. Do you think some dogs are more likely to have accidents than others?'

'I don't know, and you're changing the subject. What are you going to do with this one?' Jane demanded severely.

'Jane, wouldn't you really like a dog to take for walks?' Bella asked wistfully. 'He'd be company for you, and he'd love it in the country.'

'No, I don't need more company, so one of the qualities you'd better insist on for your future husband is a boundless love of stray animals!'

'Mr Richard Yates got on with him very well, he seemed to know exactly what to do to make the dog trust him. We can't keep calling him the dog. He'll have to have a name.'

'Ask Mr Yates for suggestions. Go and change out of that filthy gown then come and look at these fashion plates. We must choose some more patterns ready for the dressmaker. She's coming this afternoon. Do you think this riding habit with the epaulettes and the tall hat looks too military? And do you like the braiding on the bodice of this walking dress?'

Chapter Four

THEY SPENT THE rest of the day discussing the latest fashions, arranging with the dressmaker which gowns she would make first, settling into the house, and before dinner strolling with the dog round Sydney Gardens. Bella looked eagerly about her in the hope of seeing her cavalier, but the only men in the Gardens were elderly, infirm, or in obvious attendance on other young ladies. Later she retired to bed, weaving secret, hopeful plans, for despite her reluctance to admit it to Jane she had found him amazingly attractive. Could she, plain, plump, dumpy Bella Trahearne, ever hope to attach such a man? She vowed to herself to do all in her power towards that aim.

On the following morning she urged Jane out early, despite the latter's protests that a fashionable man would be unlikely to stir at such an impossible hour. To Bella's chagrin Jane was proved right, and the only inhabitants of the Pump Room were elderly invalids and their companions.

'Well, I'm going to try the water after all,' Bella declared, after gazing round the elegant room. 'It's silly to come here and not.' She walked across to the fountain where the attendant supplied her with a glass of the warm liquid. Jane decided she might as well have some too, and they sipped cautiously, concluding it was not too disagreeable.

'I didn't taste the Harrogate water, but I'm told it's horrid,' Bella said over her shoulder to Jane as she handed back her glass.

'Did you like anything at all about Harrogate?' Jane asked, laughing.

'No, I don't think so.' Bella chuckled. 'Perhaps it's an omen if I like Bath. But what shall we do now? Do we have to sit here all morning?'

'We could go and visit the Abbey. Or do some shopping. Or – no. I've just seen one of my aunt's old friends. I met her when my aunt brought me here just before my come out. She lives here and knows everyone. I don't think she's seen me yet but let's go and introduce ourselves.'

'Will she know Philip doesn't have a cousin called Isabella?' Bella asked, catching Jane's arm as a sudden surge of panic gripped her, and she realized for the first time what disastrous consequences could result from her masquerade.

'No, she probably doesn't even know I'm married, for my aunt died the year after we came here and I don't think anyone else in the family knew her.'

Although slightly puzzled at first, Mrs Eversley soon recalled Jane. After voluble commiserations on the death of her aunt, exclamations and questions about Jane's marriage, and some embarrassing hints and comments about her lack of children, she ordered her to talk to her hitherto silent companion and turned to an unusually subdued Bella.

'Are you connected to the Bedfordshire Collins?' she demanded.

Bella gulped. 'No, I don't think so. Philip comes – and so does my family, of course, from Lancashire. But I don't really know very much about our other cousins.'

'Does he resemble you?' the inquisition went on.

Bella almost giggled as she thought of the tall, blue-eyed, blond giant who had married Jane.

'Not – not a great deal,' she answered hurriedly. 'I take after my mother's family,' she invented.

'H'm. You're a good-looking gal, Jane,' she said loudly, poking Jane with a bony finger to attract her attention, 'and I always said you'd get yourself a handsome husband. Are you betrothed, Miss Collins? You're no spring chicken, and soon you'll be thoroughly on the shelf.'

'No, I'm not betrothed,' Bella managed baldly, digesting the implications of Mrs Eversley's last remark. Had she intended to be deliberately rude, or was she one of those autocratic old ladies who considered it their prerogative to say anything they chose, however unpleasant or personal, relying on age and infirmity to protect them from retaliation? Was she, with her own excessive candour, liable to give similar offence?

'Money?'

'I beg your pardon?' Bella stiffened angrily. This was too much. At least she didn't ask impertinent questions, even if she did express her opinions freely.

Jane kicked her on the ankle and smiled sweetly at their inter-locutor. 'Bella has what I think you could call quite reasonable expectations,' she put in.

'Then you might make an acceptable match. I suppose that's why you've come here. Did you think it would be easier than London?'

'Jane has come to drink the waters!' Bella snapped, infuriated at the implication she could not hope to find a husband in London.

While Jane cast an anguished glance at her the old woman cackled with laughter.

'You're by no means a beauty, or as young as some, although you're not bad-looking. Jane, stop making eyes at her. Go and get me another glass of the loathsome stuff,' she ordered, and Jane went reluctantly away. 'You certainly have something when your eyes sparkle and you fire up like that,' she continued approvingly. 'I like a gal with spirit. But take my advice, don't aim too high. Settle for a solid country squire and don't languish after men like Dorney. Every silly gal in Bath's set her heart on him some time or other, despite his reputation, even before he got the title. He'll let his cousin succeed, mark my words. Still smarting from the way his brother's wife ruined him.'

Bella was no longer listening for Mr Richard Yates, accompanied by a younger man, had entered the Pump Room and strolled immedi-ately across to the fountain. Mrs Eversley had embarked on a catalogue of the current unattached male inhabitants of Bath, with pungent summaries of their many faults and occasional virtues, and the chances Bella might have of entrapping one of them.

Bella ignored her since she was regarding the newcomer more closely than she'd been able to the previous day. He was, she judged, in his late twenties or early thirties. His skin was dark, and she thought it came more from outdoor living than his natural complexion. He had a countryman's way of moving, steady and sure, none of the tripping daintiness of the poodle man. His figure was good, that of an athlete. And his eyes, bright blue and set deep under thick brows, she recalled as both penetrating in gaze and expressive of emotions he otherwise kept hidden. There had been a hint of laughter in them yesterday, directed, she was sure, at the fop even while he was talking contemptuously of him. His single-breasted, square-tailed coat fitted superbly, and Bella thought she could detect the rippling muscles beneath the dark-brown superfine. Pale fawn breeches were tucked into high hussar boots, and he carried a dark-brown beaver hat. Unlike his companion, whose dress betrayed a tendency towards dandyism, Richard Yates's shirt collar was modestly high, and his cravat tied in the simple Orientale. More than ever she longed to know whether he was married. She had this strange feeling that if he were her life would be for ever blighted. After such a short acquaintance she was already sure no other man could match his many perfections.

'We'd be delighted, wouldn't we, Bella?' Jane had returned.

Bella came to with a start at another kick on the ankle, and she turned to meet Mrs Eversley's amused gaze.

'What? Oh, yes, of course,' she stammered.

'Good, we'll see you both at eight tonight. Now I mustn't keep you from your other friends.'

'No. Yes. Thank you. Goodbye. Jane, what in the world was she talking about?' Bella hissed as they moved away.

'We're invited to a soirée tonight.'

Bella groaned. 'Not a soirée! You've no idea how excruciatingly tedious they can be! I swore I'd never attend another after I had to listen to a soprano who couldn't reach the high notes, and a poet whose verse never scanned or rhymed, and a dreadful harpist whose strings broke just when she was plucking away like mad.'

Jane laughed. 'Poor Bella, how dreadful for you. But everyone goes to Mrs Eversley's house. It's one of the best ways of meeting people in Bath. And that's what you wanted.'

Bella thought it hardly politic to announce she'd already met the only man she wanted to in Bath, but tried to steer Jane unobtrusively towards him. He was talking with a pair of fashionably dressed ladies, clearly mother and daughter.

43

The younger girl, whom Bella estimated as only seventeen, a few years younger than herself, was simpering up at him in a most repulsive way, while her mother gushed. Bella disliked them both on sight.

But he had seen them and swiftly, efficiently, and in a manner that left them with no intimation they had been dismissed, took his leave of the two women. Then he moved towards Jane and Bella.

'Lady Hodder. And Miss Collins. I trust you're not suffering any after-effects from that contretemps yesterday?'

'Not at all.'

'And the animal?'

'He seems to have settled into his new quarters remarkably swiftly,' Jane replied wryly.

He chuckled. 'He recognizes kind hearts,' he said. 'May I introduce my cousin, Alexander Yates? Alex, Lady Hodder, and Miss Collins, about whom I spoke yesterday.'

So he'd talked about her! Bella thought exultantly as she smiled at the younger man.

'I'm happy to make your acquaintance,' he said formally. 'Richard described how you vanquished that overfed poodle and his overdressed master. It's time someone told Dandy Ledsham a few home truths.'

They chatted for a few minutes and then Alexander, who had been glancing surreptitiously about him, coughed loudly. 'Dorney, excuse me, please. I must pay my respects to Miss Hollings and her sister. Ladies, forgive me, but I have an urgent message to pass on to someone.'

He bowed himself away and was soon in animated conversation with a lovely golden-haired girl, no more than sixteen, but enchantingly pretty with her delicate complexion and luxuriant ringlets.

Bella was frowning in puzzlement.

'Dorney?' she queried? 'I thought your name was Yates?'

'That's my family name, but I'm also Lord Dorney. Didn't I say so? How remiss of me. I do apologize. I've held the title for only a little over a year; I still sometimes forget it. But I value truth above all else and it could have been embarrassing for you not to have known.'

Bella was still frowning. Hadn't Mrs Eversley mentioned a Dorney? Of course, she'd warned Bella not to set her mind on him.

How could she know? But then she'd also said every girl had. And that he had a reputation. For what, she wondered? It was pure chance she'd picked on his name as an example, not the specific warning it must have been. Bella's heart sank, then soared at Lord Dorney's next words.

'Perhaps I might call on you one day?' he was saying politely, and Jane nodded acquiescence. 'Do you go to the concert tonight?'

'We're invited to Mrs Eversley's house,' Jane replied, oblivious of Bella's sudden pleading glance.

'Then I'll no doubt see you one day at the Assembly Rooms,' he said easily, and took his leave, strolling across to join his cousin who was talking urgently to the lovely Miss Hollings.

'What did Mrs Eversley mean by warning me away from him?' Bella demanded as they walked home. 'She said he had a reputation.'

'Perhaps she meant he flirted but didn't easily fall in love,' Jane replied.

'Then at least he can't be married!' Bella crowed, firmly disregarding the other information.

'But if he has a reputation, that's unpromising. And if lots of girls have set their caps at him, how can you do better?'

'Because they were certainly prettier? Is that what you mean? Oh, don't worry, Jane, I'm used to being plain.' She laughed as Jane uttered embarrassed denials. 'That's a challenge and, as yet, I don't know what I'll do. I wonder what sort of reputation she meant? I'll think of something, don't worry. But in a way,' she mused, 'it's more hopeful than if he were a man who fell in and out of love several times a year.'

She refused to elaborate on her schemes, and spent the afternoon walking in Sydney Gardens with the dog, planning how to set about her campaign to attach Lord Dorney. The animal, who was already looking sleeker after Lizzy had bathed and brushed him, was now dignified with the name of Rags, since Mrs Dawes claimed he reminded her of nothing more than a bundle of old clothes, with his multi-coloured coat, rough and torn in places, and straggly tail.

Despite her preoccupations, Bella had not forgotten her proposal to buy another house for orphans in Bristol. She had written to Mr and Mrs Tomkins in Bristol, and had that morning received a reply inviting her to visit them the following week. They said there was considerable interest amongst the Wesleyan people in the city, and they were confident a suitable scheme could be arranged.

She would take Mary to give her visit respectability, and Jackson, who was proving to be an excellent groom, could drive them.

There had also been a letter from Mr Jenkins, reporting that three more orphans had been taken in by Mr and Mrs Lloyd in Preston, and the local people were responding well to appeals for money to maintain them. Soon, he wrote, Bella's contribution to the upkeep of the house would not be needed, and she could put that money towards the establishment of similar houses elsewhere.

We, that is my wife and I, think the houses should be named after you, he wrote. *That would be a fitting memorial to your generosity.*

No, Bella rejected the notion. She had instigated the scheme, but the money had come to her through her uncle, who had been the one to earn it. She sat down to reply, suggesting that the houses should bear her uncle's name: *A pleasant idea, but it should be he who is honoured, not me. Can you arrange for a suitable, discreet plaque to be designed for the house and send me a drawing of it? When I have other houses I will ask you to have more made.*

For the evening she wore a simple pale-blue, high-waisted muslin gown, with short puffed sleeves and edged with darker blue ribbons. The hem was trimmed with ruffles and embroidery of the same dark-blue. Beneath the skirts peeped matching dark-blue slippers.

Jane had a more sophisticated gown of cream silk, with brown appliqued flowers round the hem and neckline, which was much lower than was considered suitable for a young unmarried damsel. Bella felt a moment's envy of Jane's taller, slimmer figure which the current fashions suited so well.

Mrs Eversley had a house just off Queen's Square, and Jackson drove them there in the carriage. Jane had insisted on hiring one, despite the preference of most Bath inhabitants for sedan chairs, due to the hilly nature of the town. Queen's Square was in the relatively flat area suitable for carriages, and as they intended to buy riding horses, Jane had decided that Jackson might as well earn his keep by driving a carriage too.

'Besides, it's so much more comfortable, and we can talk.'

Mrs Eversley's double salon was already crowded when they arrived, and after greeting their hostess they found places on two delicate gilt chairs at the side of the room, where they could see the musicians already disposed on a raised dais at the far end.

To Bella's relief the musical part of the evening did not last for more than an hour, and was of a far higher standard than she'd endured in Harrogate. Afterwards they were directed to another large room where a lavish buffet awaited them, and were soon seated at a small table chatting to a pair of elderly gentlemen. One had a distinctly military bearing, and seemed to find Jane irresistible. The other spoke with a northern accent and a blunt manner which Bella found refreshing after the meaningless society chit-chat of other people she'd met.

'From Lancashire?' the northerner, a Mr Kershaw asked. 'I'm in wool meself, in Leeds, but I'm thinking of moving over to cotton. Much more go-ahead in Lancashire, though I hate to admit it!'

'Go-ahead? How do you mean?' Jane asked, intrigued.

'Wi' they new machines, and the use o' power for driving 'em,' Mr Kershaw explained. 'The spinners and weavers can work in mills now, and be controlled far better than the wool workers can. Instead o' messin' about most of the day, working plots o' land too small to support 'em, and spinning or weaving only to get a bit extra, the whole family can work a proper day in the mill and earn a decent wage.'

'I don't call it decent when tiny children have to work twelve hours a day!' Bella exclaimed. 'They're not even fed properly, and were far better off running about the fields, earning a penny scaring birds, or helping to gather wood for the fire. Besides, it's unhealthy in those mills, with all the steam and the fluff.'

'And what do you know about it, lass?' Mr Kershaw, although taken aback by her vehemence, was prepared to indulge a little feminine sensibility.

'I found a lad of six, whose mother had just died from an accident with one of those wonderful machines, and he was being starved, living as a so-called apprentice in one of these dreadful places. Threatened, too, if he didn't submit to inhuman treatment. He was trying to run away, poor mite. And I went to see one of the mills a few years ago,' Bella informed him curtly. 'My godfather was inter-

47

ested in the machinery – he had some ideas for improvement – and I was horrified by what I saw.'

Mr Kershaw smiled benevolently. 'It's what you'm used to. They don't know any better, they haven't had the advantages of your position in life, my dear, and so don't miss it.'

'That's not entirely true,' Bella declared, her colour high. 'They did know a better life when they were not forced to slave in those beastly mills all day and half the night! They had fresh air, and good wholesome food, and spring water, as well as better places to live in than the attics of a mill or the hovels they have now!'

'The mill owners weren't forced to build good houses for their workfolk, but many of them did, out of the goodness of their hearts.' Mr Kershaw was growing heated and Jane, aware that the raised voices were attracting unwelcome attention from other guests, was doing her best to catch Bella's eye. But Bella ignored her warning glances.

'Good houses?' she exclaimed contemptuously. 'Two damp rooms for a family of eight or ten children? The only water from a tap a hundred or more yards away, and a privy shared with dozens of other families? Is that what you'd wish for your family, sir?'

'I hardly think this is a suitable topic for ladies at an evening party,' the military gentleman interrupted firmly, but Mr Kershaw was not content to let it rest there.

'You'd find your pretty gowns a sight more expensive, young lass, if we didn't encourage progress,' he said with an air of finality.

'Perhaps it would be a fairer world if we did pay more for such frivolities, and gave the people who produce them the chance of getting the necessities of life!' Bella retorted.

'Well said, Miss Collins,' an amused voice behind her commented, and with a gasp Bella turned to find Lord Dorney and his cousin standing by her shoulder.

She bit her lip, and felt her cheeks, already heated from the over-crowded room and the strength of her emotions, grow yet rosier.

With a curt bow, the military gentleman seized the opportunity of drawing Mr Kershaw away. Lord Dorney and Alexander took their places, but tactfully changed the conversation by asking whether the ladies had enjoyed the musical entertainment.

'I didn't see you there,' Bella exclaimed.

'No, I'm afraid I was late, I had another engagement first,' Lord Dorney said smoothly. 'But Mrs Eversley was so pressing with her invitation I promised to drop in for an hour or so later. She persuades some very talented people to play and sing at her parties, and I was sorry to miss it.'

After a while he enquired for the dog's welfare, and Bella was chuckling as she recounted the animal's encounter with a neighbouring cat.

'And when we walked him in Sydney Gardens he growled at a very large Dalmation. I fear he'll turn out to be a fighter,' she concluded ruefully.

'He's needed to fight to survive, no doubt. As do your mill children,' he added softly. 'I applaud your concern, and your courage in speaking out for them,' he added, and immediately rose to take his leave.

Chapter Five

———◦◦◦———

BELLA WAS WALKING Rags in Sydney Gardens early the following morning when Lord Dorney approached.

'You're abroad early,' he commented. 'This animal looks better already,' he added, bending down to pat the dog, who after an initial suspicious growl suddenly recognized a friend and began to wag his tail furiously.

Bella looked shyly up at him. Jane had scolded her soundly on the way home the previous night and, uncharacteristically, Bella had accepted the scolding as well deserved. She wondered if her behaviour, despite his words of approval, had made Lord Dorney despise her as an unsophisticated, provincial rustic unable to behave with proper decorum in Society.

'You simply must not argue so vehemently, especially with a man so much older, and in public,' Jane chastized her.

Inwardly rebellious, Bella wanted to ask why girls and even women were supposed to have no opinions of their own. Why must they accept what men said, however stupid and bigoted the men? She kept silent, knowing she had argued with unseemly heat. That was her real offence in her own eyes. She was mortified to realize she'd been unable to point out the evils of the crowded mills without allowing her emotions to trap her into rudeness.

'Jane was very angry with me,' she said impulsively.

'Lady Hodder angry? Why should she be?' he asked. 'Let's walk on, the wind is chill,' he added, turning to stroll beside her.

'I was too outspoken last night,' Bella sighed. 'I don't mean to be rude, but I cannot bear to hear foolish people saying things which are untrue.'

To her surprise he laughed.

'There may be more tactful ways of refuting what they say,' he agreed, 'but you spoke the truth, your sentiments are honourable. I passed through Preston recently and saw the dreadful conditions those mill workers have to endure.'

'I haven't learned to bite my tongue,' she confessed.

'It makes a refreshing change. Most girls are far too busy wondering what effect they're making to speak so candidly. They say what they think is expected of them rather than the truth. Which brings me to an apology.'

'You? Apologize? What on earth for?' Bella demanded.

'I should have told you before that I was in the yard at that inn and saw your very successful routing of those louts.'

Bella felt her cheeks grow warm. 'Oh, did you?' was all she could manage. 'But why do you need to apologize?'

'I'm not sure. I suppose I feel I ought to have told you that I'd seen you before, even though we had not met. That was one reason I had for asking Mrs Eversley to introduce us. I wanted to meet a young lady who owned a pistol and could face down those rogues.'

'I don't normally use it to threaten people,' Bella said, in a small, hesitant voice.

He laughed. 'I'm sure you don't! You have other weapons for routing people who offend you.'

She frowned. 'What do you mean? I don't understand.'

'Taking action to save a stray dog? Dandy Ledsham and his poodle. Not many young ladies would have acted with such promptness and decision.'

'Well, could you have watched this poor little dog being savaged by that ugly, overfed beast? I'm sure if you'd been nearer you'd have done the same.'

She stooped to stroke the dog, and Rags licked her hand with enthusiasm, then turned his attention towards a much larger dog which had approached within sniffing distance. He growled, and Bella spoke calmly to him. Rags looked up at her as if to ask permission to attack, then seemed to shrug and turn his shoulder to the intruder, who was called away by his owner.

Lord Dorney grinned. 'First Ledsham and his poodle, then Mr Kershaw and his manufactories.'

Bella blushed. 'You must think me very quarrelsome. But I know how badly those children are treated. I could not endure him saying such things, believing that the people were adequately housed, better off than before.'

'Perhaps you are a little impetuous, but always in good causes. I admire you for it. What did you do with the child?'

'What child?'

'The mill boy you rescued. How did you become involved with him?'

Guiltily, Bella recalled what she had said the previous night.

'I just found him, he was running away,' she said briefly.

'What did you do with him?'

'I took him to – to Preston,' she said. 'He's being looked after by – by a kind couple, some people I know.'

How nearly she'd given the game away, mentioning her home, and the house she'd bought in Preston, she thought in horror. Deception was not easy.

Lord Dorney didn't appear to have noticed her evasiveness.

'Do you mean to ride while you're in Bath?' he asked, and Bella explained they intended to buy or hire suitable mounts as soon as they could find the time to do so.

'I ride a great deal at home,' she said enthusiastically. 'But here I suppose we mayn't ride out without a groom.'

'I would be happy to escort you both,' he offered, and Bella hugged herself secretly. It really did look as though he was interested in her.

Within a week the rest of Bath began to think the same, and wonder volubly at the number of times Lord Dorney could be seen at Lady Hodder's house, riding or driving with the ladies, escorting them to balls and concerts, and behaving like an infatuated youth.

Jane was equally incredulous.

'I simply don't understand it,' she said one morning, as they drank tea and ate wafer-thin slices of bread and butter, before preparing for yet another ride accompanied by Lord Dorney. 'Mrs Vaughan was saying last night she believes him to be a somewhat reserved man, never more than ordinarily friendly towards girls. I can't imagine what Mrs Eversley could have meant by saying he had a reputation. It certainly can't be for trifling with their affections. She says the girls, and their mamas, pursue him relentlessly, but the moment it appears a girl is becoming fond of him he behaves with cold reserve and virtually ignores her in order to deter them. Not that it does, of course,' she added with a grin.

'Do you listen to gossip?' Bella asked scornfully.

'How else is one to know what goes on?' Jane asked, and Bella shrugged.

She was puzzled too. She'd laid many plans for bringing herself to Lord Dorney's attention, but needed none of them. He'd paid her marked attentions from the start and she could not imagine why. Surely it could not be because she had threatened Mary's would-be abductors with her pistol, or argued with Mr Kershaw? Most men would be disgusted with her, call her conduct unladylike.

'Why does he seek me out?' she asked now. 'I'm not at all pretty like Mama was. Papa adored her, and no wonder if that portrait is a true likeness. I must have been a severe disappointment to him.'

She'd always taken it for granted her father must have regretted her very different appearance.

'I'd have thought he might be grateful not to have a constant reminder of his loss by having a daughter who resembled her too closely,' Jane said thoughtfully. 'There can be different types of beauty.'

'I'm too small and too plump!'

'Some men might be tired of fashionable slender beanpoles.'

Bella grinned. 'They don't show many signs of it.'

'Well, your face lights up when you're animated, when you are passionate about urchins or stray animals,' Jane said with feeling. 'He must have noticed and liked that. He seems to have a serious, thoughtful disposition.'

'I just enjoy talking with him,' Bella said slowly. 'We talk of so many interesting things.'

Jane was cautious. 'You must not count on it coming to anything, Bella,' she warned now.

Bella smiled airily. 'We'll see,' she replied. Her hopes were too fresh and her fears too deep for casual discussion even with her cousin. In quiet moments she was already well aware of the bleak desolation which she would suffer if Lord Dorney lost interest in her. Firmly she dismissed her fears and concentrated on making ready for the excursion Lord Dorney had planned for two days hence.

Lord Dorney was confused. No girl had disturbed his serenity as Bella Collins did. He'd vowed never to marry, when he had seen the calamitous result of his brother Robert's venture into matrimony. He didn't need an heir, he had Alexander who would inherit the title. Yet here he was, lingering in Bath days after he could have left for London, and giving the gossips something to talk about by his attentions to Bella. He'd talked to Alex, met his Felicity, and though he thought them both too young, could find no other reason for objecting to the alliance. He should leave now, but somehow he couldn't make the effort.

However much he told himself that not all women were as rapacious, or as immoral as Selina, doubts remained. He did not wish to risk it, even if he were attracted to a woman. When he'd first met Selina, just before he'd enlisted and gone out to join Wellington in Spain, he'd thought her a pretty, and sensible young woman, whose behaviour had been unaffected, despite the fortune she would inherit from her wealthy father. That this fortune came from trade might be sneered at by some of the high sticklers in Society, but Robert had not cared, saying that Selina had been educated at a very good school for the daughters of gentlemen, and was prettily behaved. She would know how to go on as his wife.

'Besides,' Robert had said with a laugh, 'the money will restore Dorney Court. And it needs it.'

It certainly had. Their father had cared little for his ancestral home, and under his stewardship the land had been neglected and the house had fallen, if not into outright ruin, into the beginnings of it. The roof had leaked, some of the windows were broken, many of the rooms had been shut up, the curtains were falling into rags, and the place had been run with far too few servants. The estate cottages and farms were in even worse condition.

The moment he and Selina had married, Robert had set about bringing the house back to its former state. On his one visit home, on leave, Richard had been astonished and pleased to see his beloved home looking once more as he remembered it when he'd been a small child, before his mother had died and his father had set out on the road which eventually ruined him.

This had, however, been illusory. The exterior fabric was as he remembered it, but inside Selina had, in his opinion, ruined it. Much of the old oak panelling had been stripped out, and the small rooms decorated in the newly fashionable Chinese style. To his eye the clawed legs and elaborate carvings and exuberant decoration might be all very well in the spacious rooms of the Prince Regent's monstrosity of a palace at Brighton, but here they were oppressive, overwhelming.

If he ever married, would his wife turn out to be like Selina, wanting to change his home? The home he was only gradually restoring to what he wanted it to be? Would Bella be like Selina?

He shook himself. Why was he thinking like this? He didn't intend to marry, so the actions of a mythical wife could be of no concern to him. He must tear himself away and go to London. Dan would be there now. Then he frowned. He had committed himself to several engagements for the coming few days, and he might as well stay and attend them. Making his excuses and departing in haste might make people talk even more than they were already doing, and that might harm Bella. He could not do that to her, even if he had no intention of marrying her. He must casually announce his intention of leaving, and draw back from too much contact with her.

Bella was feeling guilty. She had been so preoccupied with her own affairs she had thought very little about the proposed house in Bristol. She borrowed Jane's coach, took Mary with her for the sake of propriety, and Jackson drove her to Bristol. When they reached the Tomkins's house she dismissed Mary and Jackson, telling him to rest the horses and Mary to amuse herself shopping, and call for her in three hours.

She was welcomed so enthusiastically that her guilt intensified. She'd let these people down.

'Of course not, my dear Miss Trahearne,' Mrs Tomkins assured her. 'We've only just found a suitable house. Would you care to inspect it?'

It was a tall house in a terrace near the docks.

'It needs some repairs,' Mr Tomkins said, 'but that will help us to purchase it at a good price.'

'I'll pay for the necessary repairs,' Bella assured them. 'Surely these are not major defects, more a general shabbiness, and we could install one of the new ranges in the kitchen, which would make life much easier for the children and the maids.'

'Oh, yes, there's nothing else too expensive for us to do,' Mr Tomkins hastened to reassure her. 'We have already found people to promise contributions for the maintenance of the children, and wages for the couple who will look after them. We can accommodate the first of the children in, let us say, a month from now.'

Bella nodded. 'So I will purchase the house, and pay for the essential repairs, and you will afterwards find the money to run it?'

'Of course; that is what Mr Jenkins told us was to be the arrangement.'

'I'll have Mr Jenkins draw up an agreement to that effect. Thank you, this seems eminently suitable.'

She drove back to Bath satisfied with her day. Her scheme for helping orphans by installing them in small, homelike houses, was looking both practical and worthwhile. Other people like the Tomkinses were eager to help, and if she supplied the initial capital to purchase suitable houses, there were local people who could do their bit in raising the money to run them.

On the way home, Mary had been very quiet, and Bella assumed she was tired. But when they reached the house Mary asked to speak with her.

'What is it? What's happened?' Bella asked, when they had reached her bedroom.

'Oh, Miss Bella, I saw those men again. One of them.'

'Which men?'

'Those who tried to – to make me go with them, when you threatened to shoot them,' Mary said, her voice shaking.

'In Bristol?'

'Yes, in the town.'

'Did he recognize you?'

'I – I think so. He leered at me in a nasty sort of way.'

'Did he speak?'

'He warned me to take care. He said there wouldn't always be someone to protect me.'

Bella tried to reassure her. 'He can't know you live in Bath. He won't find you here.'

'But he followed us to where Tom – I mean Jackson, had stabled the horses, and I saw him talking to the ostler as we left to meet you.'

'Had Jackson told him we came from Bath?'

'Yes, when we first got there. He knew the man, you see, and was telling him about his new job.'

'Well, you'll just have to take extra care, and not go anywhere lonely by yourself. They can hardly abduct you from the middle of Bath!'

'No, Miss Bella,' Mary said, but doubtfully.

Bella sighed. She supposed she would now have to order Jackson to accompany Mary on her errands into the town. She suspected they would neither of them object, and wondered whether she was assisting in a budding romance.

A select riding party gathered outside Lord Dorney's rooms in the Royal Crescent on the following day. His cousin Alexander was there on a showy black, in attendance as usual on the lovely Miss Hollings, mounted on a beautiful but frisky little roan mare. A young matron was introduced as her married sister, Lady Andrews, and an older man as Sir John Andrews. A recently married couple, Mr and Mrs Dudley, completed the party.

Soon they were riding up Lansdown Road, Lord Dorney on his magnificent grey hunter close beside Bella.

'Where are we going?' she asked.

'First to see the old battlefield, then eastwards across the hills to where my servants will meet us with food for an alfresco nuncheon. If everyone has the energy we can go a little further until we come to the Avon and return along the river-bank. Are you happy with your mount?'

Bella patted the neck of her chestnut gelding.

'He's not like my own beautiful Lady, but a good enough ride,' she replied.

'I hoped you might be taking us to visit Dorney Court,' Lady Andrews, who had been riding behind, interrupted.

'That's rather too far away for a single day,' Lord Dorney replied easily.

'Dear Felicity is so eager to see it,' her sister went on, edging her horse forward so that she rode on Lord Dorney's other side. 'Alexander has told her so much about it, you know.'

'It's not very splendid, just a couple of hundred years old, built in the local stone, and with what these days are considered small rooms,' he said dismissively. 'My brother built on an extra wing with a ballroom, but that was really for his wife. I cannot imagine what I shall use it for. I might even pull it down.'

'That would be a great pity. Does your brother's widow live there?'

'Selina lives in London, with a cousin,' he replied shortly.

He seemed unwilling to talk either of his home or his widowed sister-in-law, and Bella observed him curiously. She had heard the occasional comment about his family from people in Bath. Unusually reticent, she had not liked to question him herself. There was some mystery, she was sure, and it seemed connected with his brother's widow.

As Lord Dorney spurred forward to ride with the Dudleys, Lady Andrews moved closer to Bella.

'Such a pity Dorney Court is so far away, and no hostess there so that Felicity might visit for a while. But he seems to dislike it. She's naturally anxious to see the place, you know,' she confided. 'Alexander is such a pleasant boy, don't you think?'

'Is he? I mean, yes, of course, but I don't know him very well,' Bella answered, and contrived to drop back to ride with Jane.

'She's hinting her sister and Alexander are betrothed, or likely to be,' she told Jane. 'Clearly she sees Felicity as the future mistress of Dorney Court. I suppose Alexander's his heir?'

'So I believe. They are cousins.'

'But Lord Dorney isn't much older – it could be years before he dies and Alexander could inherit. And he might marry. Or Alexander die.'

Jane glanced back. 'Felicity would do better to set her cap at Lord Dorney if Dorney Court is her main objective. Though it would not serve, I'm sure. She's far too young for him, not at all the sort of girl he seems to admire.'

Bella nodded. 'But Lady Andrews said he, Lord Dorney, dislikes the place. I wonder why? Do you know what happened to Lord Dorney's brother? How did he die? Was he in the army?'

'No one ever says,' Jane replied slowly. 'It's odd, but they always change the subject.'

'And Lord Dorney seems ill at ease whenever he's mentioned, or his widow. I wonder what can have happened? I've no doubt Mrs Eversley knows.'

'Don't ask questions,' Jane warned.

'I'll ask Lord Dorney some time,' Bella promised, and laughed at the look of horror on Jane's face. 'Don't be concerned, not yet,' she added.

Her resolve was severely tried during the rest of that day. It was clear that Lady Andrews knew the story, for she took several opportunities to drop hints and what could have been construed as warnings in Bella's ear. They were mainly concerned with Lord Dorney's reluctance to marry, and Felicity's prospective future as chatelaine of Dorney Court.

'For Lord Dorney spends remarkably little time there,' she told Bella. 'Alexander hasn't more than a small house in Bath, and he has to let his mother and sisters live there. I suppose he could buy a house in London, but he'd need somewhere in the country too. I'm sure Lord Dorney would let him live there if he married. He never seems to live there himself. I understand he lives mainly in London now, or at one of the properties his mother left him. She was quite wealthy, you know. Has he told you whether he intends to remove to London?'

Bella tried not to reveal how shatteringly unwelcome this possibility was. She could not, in her current identity, follow him to London. Somehow the possibility that his stay in Bath was only a short one had never crossed her mind. Her plans would have to be changed if he left but, numb with shock, her brain refused to provide any solutions.

They halted at midday for the alfresco meal Lord Dorney had arranged. Afterwards they strolled about the clearing in the woods, admiring the primroses which covered the ground. Alexander and Felicity Hollings disappeared along a winding path, and Bella caught

Lady Andrews looking after them with a complacent smile on her face.

Lord Dorney guided Bella along another path, explaining that it led to a slight hill from which they could look over the surrounding countryside. Bella was inattentive, wondering whether she dare ask him if he meant to move to London, and castigating herself for such uncharacteristic timidity.

'Do you like this country as well as your native Lancashire?' he asked, tucking her hand under his arm.

'I like it very much, especially the hills,' Bella forced herself to answer enthusiastically, 'but I'll never completely desert Tra—' She stopped in confusion. She'd almost done it again.

'Your home?' he asked easily, and Bella nodded, thinking furiously.

'But presumably your father will always be living there?' he said. 'You'll be able to visit, when, that is, you have a home of your own. Do you have brothers or sisters?'

'Oh, no, there's only me.' What unexpected traps her deception led to, she thought with a rueful sigh.

She moved away, ostensibly to admire the view, and they soon turned to retrace their steps.

The rest of the party, with the exception of Alexander and Felicity, were preparing to set off. The young people came hurriedly into the clearing after Sir John had called loudly for them, Felicity flushed and with her hair ruffled. She allowed Alexander to throw her up into the saddle without a word, just a shy smile of thanks, and then moved to ride with her sister.

Bella was silent as they rode towards Bath in the early evening, and took little heed of the delightful countryside, fresh and green as spring advanced. Her mind was too full of questions. Had she given anything away with her unpremeditated references to Trahearne House? Had her brief explanation been sufficient? Why had Lord Dorney started that conversation? Had he been intending to say more? And, most important of all, did he intend to leave Bath?

Expecting the worst, she found herself devising wild schemes which she knew were impracticable, and was paying little attention to anything else as they rode towards the village of Colerne. When the commotion began she was totally unprepared.

They were passing a small farmhouse, Alexander and Felicity in the lead, when a pair of dogs, wild, mangy creatures, came tearing out from behind a barn and began barking furiously at the party.

Felicity screamed, jerked on the reins, and her mare bolted. She clung desperately to the pommel, and her startled companions saw with horror that she had dropped the reins, which were in danger of tangling with the mare's legs and bringing her down.

'Hold on!' Alexander yelled, but before he could bring his own restive horse under control Lord Dorney had passed him at a gallop, and was rapidly overhauling the runaway.

All would have been well if the mare had not put her foot in a rabbit hole. Lord Dorney was only a few yards behind when the mare stumbled, staggered, but could not recover her balance and fell heavily.

Fortunately the girl was thrown clear, but when the rest of the party arrived to find Lord Dorney bending over her, she was ominously still.

'Felicity! Oh, my God, is she dead?' Alexander exclaimed.

'Of course not!' Lord Dorney snapped. 'Stop panicking and see to the mare. Leave the girl to her sister,' he added, and Alexander backed away at the tone of command.

To their relief Felicity soon began to stir, weeping and complaining her head hurt. When her sister tried to help her into a sitting position the child, for she was little more, gave a moan of agony and swooned again. Lord Dorney frowned and looked at her more closely.

'Her arm may be broken. I think it's nothing worse. Alexander, go into the village and find a hurdle or a gate we can carry her on, and blankets. Sir John, will you ask at the inn who is the nearest doctor and ride for him?'

'Can I help?' A new voice broke in over the lamentations of Alexander and Lady Andrews, and Lord Dorney glanced up to find a lady, accompanied by a groom, approaching.

'I was riding the other way and saw what happened. Those wretched animals should be better controlled. But Wally here can ride for the doctor, and my house is just beyond those trees. She'll be more comfortable there than at the inn. If two of you come with me I can give you a hurdle, and I'll make a room ready.'

'Ma'am, my grateful thanks,' Lord Dorney smiled at her, but with a brisk nod she had turned and ridden swiftly away towards the trees. Alexander and Sir John had to mount hurriedly and set their horses to a gallop in order to follow.

By the time they returned, Felicity had recovered her wits and was being comforted by a rather tearful Lady Andrews. Bella and Jane had dismounted and were waiting at a little distance with Mrs Dudley, while Lord Dorney and Mr Dudley were leading the mare slowly up and down and examining her to make certain she had no injuries other than a few scratches.

'She isn't lame, fortunately,' Lord Dorney concluded, but Felicity was far too wrapped up in her own misery to be interested.

Matters were soon arranged, with their involuntary hostess, who introduced herself as Mrs Ford, in smooth control. Felicity was installed in a large pleasant bedroom at the back of the square, stone-built house. The hastily summoned doctor pronounced her to have a simple fracture which he soon set, and a few bruises which would fade within a day or so. Lady Andrews was invited to stay until her sister felt able to travel in a carriage.

'May I offer you some refreshment before you leave?' Mrs Ford asked the rest of the party, waiting in some embarrassment in her shabby but comfortable parlour.

Bella inspected her with interest, admiring her calm competence. She was in her mid-twenties, tall and slender. She had pale, almost luminous skin, russet hair and huge green eyes. The black habit she wore was old and darned, but it fitted so well that in it she appeared elegant as well as startlingly beautiful.

They accepted small saffron cakes and wine, but refused to impose so large a party on her for a more substantial meal.

'It's excessively kind of you, but we ought to return to Bath before it grows dark,' Lord Dorney said.

'I'll come tomorrow if I may and see how the child does?' Sir John said.

'Bring her mother, and if the child isn't well enough to return with you her mother could stay here too, I've far too many rooms for my own use.'

'Her mother is unfortunately dead, but if I may I'll bring my wife's maid, who can help with the nursing if she has to stay with you.'

So it was arranged and a rather silent, depleted party returned to Bath. Alexander had clearly wished to remain, but could find no excuse for so doing, merely making sure that the invitation to visit Felicity on the following day extended to him too.

Mrs Dudley had attached herself to Jane, and Lord Dorney was unusually silent as he rode with Mr Dudley at the head of the party. Bella brought up the rear with Alexander, who was full of recriminations against himself for not taking better care of Felicity, threats against farmers who allowed wild dogs to harass travellers, and speculations on how soon Felicity would be restored to full health.

Bella found him exceedingly tedious by the third repetition of his complaints and unanswerable questions. She wanted to discover from him whether his cousin had any intention of removing to London. It was not a question she could ask without an appropriate opportunity, but her attempts to direct the conversation in that way foundered on Alexander's self-absorption.

Chapter Six

—◦◉◦—

'SO PLEASE WILL you ask around for me?' she said to Jane, as they
sat at breakfast the next day.

Jane promised to do what she could, as discreetly as possible, and
Bella had to be content.

Felicity returned to Bath a few days later. Jane and Bella met Mrs
Ford, dressed this time in a stylish black pelisse, the same day while
she was shopping in Milsom Street. Mrs Ford waved in a friendly
fashion.

'I took the opportunity of driving in while bringing Miss Hollings
home, to obtain some necessities,' she explained.

'She is better?' Bella asked.

'Pale and wan is how I would describe her, especially when young
Alexander haunts the house,' Mrs Ford laughed. 'I shall not be sorry
to have my house to myself again, since I have much to do before I
go to London.'

'When do you go?' Jane asked.

'In two weeks. My mourning will be over then, and my sister has
invited me to stay in Mount Street for the rest of the Season. My
husband died last year,' she explained, seeing the puzzled expression
on Jane's face.

'Oh, I'm sorry,' Jane said.

'You need not be,' Mrs Ford said briskly. 'He was much older than
I am, and it was an arranged match when I was barely sixteen and
didn't have the wit to refuse. I wasn't unhappy,' she added quickly,
'nor did he treat me badly. I only began to realize afterwards that
there ought to be something better to life.'

She refused Jane's invitation to return to Henrietta Street for a nuncheon, saying she had too much to do before setting off for home, and they parted with hopes of meeting again when Jane herself moved to London.

'What a delightful person,' Jane commented. 'So sad to be widowed so early.'

'She didn't seem grief-stricken,' Bella commented. 'It was almost as though she couldn't wait to be rid of her blacks.'

'And they suit her so well, with her colouring. I suppose she's looking for a more agreeable marriage now. Come, we still have to choose those ribbons for your new ballgown.'

Soon they were deep in discussion of the relevant merits of different shades of pink. They forgot Mrs Ford, although the encounter had reminded Bella of her fears, never long dormant, that Lord Dorney might soon be going to London himself, and she urged Jane to redouble her efforts at discovering his intentions. He showed no signs of departing, however, and the next few days passed swiftly. The astonishment caused by his attentions to Bella changed to avid speculation on whether and when a betrothal would be announced. Sly hints were dropped, Mrs Eversley demanded outright to be told the truth, and Bella fumed and fretted inwardly as day after day went by. Did he intend to speak, and if so, when? For once in her life she found herself incapable of resolving her uncertainty by directly questioning someone. Even plain-speaking Rosabella Trahearne balked at the notion of asking a man if he meant to offer for her.

Lord Dorney was walking towards the Abbey early one morning, when his attention was drawn to a minor disturbance. A pair of schoolgirls, clutching each other's arms, stood watching a small, somewhat plump man dressed in breeches and a rather tight-fitting riding coat berating a lad who looked about ten years old. He held the child by the arm, and Lord Dorney was close enough to hear the words.

'How many times have I told 'ee what I'll do if 'ee ruins any more clothes? Well, go on, tell me!'

The lad's nankeen trousers were, Lord Dorney could see, muddy and torn at one knee. He was staring up into the man's face, and the resemblance between them was obvious, despite the man's heavy jowls and red cheeks. He was manfully trying to prevent tears from falling, but his lips were trembling.

'I dain't mean to, Pa! I tripped on summat. Please don't thrash me. It 'urts real bad!'

'I brings 'ee into Bath for a treat, and look how 'ee repays me. If 'ee 'adn't bin running wi'out lookin' where 'ee was going, 'ee wouldn't 'ave tripped. I'll teach 'ee!'

On the words he twisted the lad round with one hand and forced him to bend over, then lifted his other hand. Lord Dorney saw he carried a heavy cane. It came crashing down on the lad's posterior and the child let out a wail and began sobbing and wriggling in earnest.

As the cane was lifted again a small whirlwind rushed forward and without a great deal of surprise Lord Dorney saw Bella Collins grab the man's arm and try to prevent the second blow from landing.

'What the—? 'Ere, what do 'ee think 'ee's doing? Let go, ye blasted interferin' besom!'

'I'll let go if you stop beating him. How dare you, a great hulking brute of a man, use your strength on a child?'

'It be none o' your business what I do wi' me own lad. Look at the mess 'e's made of 'is new breeches. If you'm not careful I'll be thrashin' you next!'

Lord Dorney moved closer, but before he could reach them a small crowd of people coming from a service in the Abbey had begun to hover, wondering what the commotion was about, and the man began to bluster. One of the schoolgirls, glancing uneasily at the interested spectators, moved forward.

'Pa, let's go. Do come on, let's go home!'

He glanced round and his cheeks became even redder. 'See what ye've done,' he hissed at the lad, who was crouched in a miserable heap at his feet, sobbing and rubbing at his injured behind. 'Caused a blasted fuss, 'ee 'ave!'

Bella was delving into her reticule. She tugged out a purse and took some coins from it, which she handed to the older of the two girls.

'Here, make sure your brother gets some new breeches,' she said. 'Where do you live?'

'Brimmer's farm, miss, on the Bristol road,' she stammered, too overawed to ignore the note of authority in Bella's voice.

'Well, I'll come and see you one day, and I'll want to make certain your brother has his new breeches, and that the money hasn't been spent on drink,' she added, turning to the man.

Glaring at the spectators, he grabbed the lad by the arm, yanked him to his feet, and marched away. The two girls scurried after them, and the small crowd began to disperse. Opinion, as far as Lord Dorney could overhear, seemed equally divided into admiration for Bella's action, and disapproval of her interfering between a man and his son.

She herself turned away, and at that moment saw him. She blushed, and looked steadily into his face.

'Do you condemn me?' she asked bluntly, then sighed. 'I may have stopped that beating, but perhaps the poor lad will get an even bigger one when they're out of sight. I didn't think of that. I just had to do something to save the poor lad from being hurt. Oh, how I'd like to pay back vicious brutes like that in their own coin! Then they might not be tempted to use their strength against those weaker than themselves.'

As he prepared for the ball Lord Dorney wondered at his inability to leave Bath. Every day he told himself he must accept no more invitations, must reply to Dan's letter asking when he meant to be in London, and forget the girl who had taken such a hold on his imagination.

He was determined not to marry, after Robert's example. He had an heir, Alexander, who looked likely to provide him with another generation soon enough. If he married and had sons it would put Alexander's nose out of joint, but he gave his cousin credit for not being jealous in that event.

It all came back to Robert's disastrous marriage. Selina had indirectly caused Robert's death, and for that he could never forgive her. Yet she hadn't seemed to care, telling him that Robert was a fool, and she wished she had never married him. Almost immediately after his death she had departed to France, at last free of Napoleon's grip, with another lover. She had soon disposed of him, for now she was living openly back in London, with some Italian count she had met somewhere on the Continent.

He heard often about her doings from friends, though he'd never encountered her on his own visits to London. Ostracized by decent society, she flaunted herself in outrageous clothes. 'More like a cyprian, the necks cut so low they leave almost nothing to the imagination,' one had written after encountering her at Vauxhall.

He told himself firmly that not all girls were like Selina. She had used her fortune, and the huge settlement her father had insisted on, to do exactly as she pleased, knowing that Robert's gratitude for her money protected her from the normal restraints a husband might put on her activities. Girls more dependant on their husbands would not have that sort of choice. He sighed. He was not wealthy. He had Dorney Court and his title, but he would be struggling for years to bring the estate back to what it had once been. Could he ask any girl to share the sacrifices that would entail? There would be no lavish pin money, no gifts of jewels, few visits to London, and probably none of the advantages any girl would have a right to expect.

Bella Collins would not be mercenary enough to care, he told himself. She might even be a great support in his efforts around the estate. Briefly he smiled as he thought of her tackling some of his more difficult tenants, perhaps instructing them on how best to farm the land, or treat their children and animals. Did he have any right to ask a girl like Bella to share such a life? Yet could he be parted from her?

Bella was looking her best that evening. Her rose-coloured ballgown suited her dark looks better than the insipid pinks and blues most young girls favoured. Lord Dorney's marked attentions had, as usual, brought a sparkle to her eyes and a gentle curve to her lips which caused more than one gentleman to remark that he didn't know what it was, she wasn't beautiful, but the little Collins girl was a deuced attractive wench.

The occasion was a ball at the Upper Rooms. Lord Dorney escorted Bella and Jane to it in his own carriage, claimed her hand for the cotillion, afterwards leading her into the tea-room.

'You seem radiant tonight,' he murmured, as he settled her in a chair, then drew his own across to sit beside her. 'I find you more lovely every day.'

Bella's heart beat faster, but she made a huge effort to hide her agitation and chuckled. 'Stuff and nonsense, I'm not beautiful,' she declared. 'There's no need to flatter me, my lord.'

'I didn't say beautiful,' he replied. 'Lovely is even more enticing, for it encompasses character and behaviour. Beauty can be cold and unfeeling. You don't possess the classical beauty of form or features,' he went on, as though speaking to himself, 'though yours are well enough, not nearly so repellent as you seem to imagine—'

'I didn't say I was repellent!' Bella interrupted indignantly, and then giggled. 'You're roasting me.'

'You imply so often how disappointing you find your looks, I took it for granted that was how you regarded them,' he teased. 'I know you're not the sort of girl who wishes for constant praise, deploring her looks merely for the pleasure of being contradicted—'

'I should hope not, indeed!' Bella exclaimed, aghast. 'Is that how it seems?'

'Not to me,' he reassured her, but further private conversation was made impossible as Lady Andrews, towing behind her the tall, slender, and slightly embarrassed-looking man who was her husband, bore down on them.

'Dear Lord Dorney,' the lady greeted him effusively, while barely acknowledging Bella. 'Are you planning to accompany your cousin and Felicity tomorrow morning? She will take only gentle exercise, you know, since that terrible accident. A quiet drive in the company of people she trusts is ideal for her. Of course, she trusts your cousin, he's an excellent whip, as any pupil of yours must be, and naturally I shall ride with them.'

'I have other rather important business tomorrow,' Lord Dorney managed to say as she paused for breath.

'Oh, have you?' Lady Andrews said, with a suspicious glance at Bella, and proceeded to monopolize Lord Dorney's attention with a description of the concert she had attended the previous day, where the singers had all apparently been afflicted with an inability to sing in tune, and the instrumentalists had striven only to play louder than one another.

She talked until it was time for the next dance and Bella's partner, a pleasant young man who lived in a neighbouring house in Henrietta Street, came to claim her.

He entertained her with a description of how Rags, being exercised by Jackson, had eluded the groom and proceeded to make decidedly unwelcome overtures to a fat, pampered King Charles spaniel out for its mild constitutional.

'Unwelcome not to the spaniel, that is, but to the elderly maid who was trying to persuade it to move more than a few yards from its door,' he explained. 'Although I really believe if your man hadn't captured them, they'd have been off into the Gardens, and it's a moot point whether the spaniel or the maid would have had the first heart attack.'

Bella laughed. 'He's always been a plucky dog, but now he's well fed he's more than Jackson can cope with at times, always escaping from the kitchens or the stable. He really needs to be in the country. You don't know anyone who'd be willing to give him a good home, do you?' she asked, but without much hope. None of her acquaintances had volunteered to come to the rescue.

'Won't Dorney?' her companion asked. 'He's beso— I mean, he has a huge estate nearby, and would surely be willing to take one small dog.'

Bella changed the subject. She had not brought herself to plead Rags' cause with Lord Dorney, and she was at a loss to understand her reluctance to involve him. They chatted about other matters until the dance ended, and then Bella glanced over her shoulder, with an instinctive need to see where Lord Dorney was.

Instead she saw, standing close behind her, a slender exquisite of medium height, hair dark as her own, but with a pale, bony face and watery blue eyes.

He bowed as she caught his eye and moved forward, his hand outstretched.

'Well met, Miss—'

'Mr Salway! What a surprise. I'd no idea you were in Bath,' Bella gabbled, in a desperate attempt to prevent him from uttering her name.

Of all the people she'd met in Harrogate the despicable nephew of her former duenna was the worst. It was a monstrous piece of ill-fortune to encounter him here, for he knew not only her real name but the precise extent of her fortune. His aunt had been careful to ascertain that before taking on the task of chaperoning Bella.

Her partner, with a glance of curiosity at the newcomer, bowed himself away. Bella knew she had paled, then felt a rush of blood to her cheeks. Mr Salway took her arm and led her, unresisting, to a couple of empty chairs in a discreet alcove.

'My aunt still hasn't forgiven you for the despicable way you treated her, Miss Trahearne,' Mr Salway said quietly, but his eyes were cold, gleaming with malicious triumph. 'But forgive me, I'm at fault. I understand that for some odd reason you've changed your name?'

Bella seemed incapable of speech. She tore her gaze away from his icy stare, glanced with a shudder at his unexpectedly fleshy lips, which had more than once descended on hers when she'd been unable to avoid him swiftly enough, and down his slim figure. He was correctly attired in a well-fitting, dark-blue coat and black pantaloons, but they were adorned with an unusual and excessive amount of lace and fobs, and vulgar, ostentatiously large but probably fake diamond buttons.

'I don't intend to betray you, if you are sensible,' he said, and she looked up at him with mingled hope and astonishment, followed by swift suspicion. If he agreed to keep her secret he would demand an enormous payment, and from the way he was permitting his glance to rove slowly over her figure she suspected it would not be a mere financial bribe.

But she had to gain time to think. She swallowed hard, and nodded.

'Call on us tomorrow morning, early,' she suggested faintly. 'I – I would be grateful for an opportunity to explain what must seem decidedly odd to you.'

'Odd?' he mocked. 'Deuced smoky, if you ask me. Dorney won't be at all pleased, after what happened to his brother.'

'What do you mean?' Bella demanded, surprised, but he shook his head, smiled, and calmly took her dance card out of her hand.

'Well, you are popular, Miss Collins,' he sneered, and before she could protest calmly struck through the name written against the final dance and handed the card back to her.

'You can't!' Bella protested. The last dance had been promised to Lord Dorney. 'How can I possibly explain?'

'How can you possibly not?' he mocked. 'Tell him an old friend, a

71

very dear old friend, has unexpectedly just arrived in Bath. I'm sure he'll understand.'

'I won't!' she declared angrily, rising impetuously to her feet.

'You will, Miss Trahearne, indeed you will,' he said softly, rising with her.

He mockingly offered her his arm, but Bella swung away from him and walked rapidly towards the tea-room, where she hoped to find Jane.

She would escape, she vowed to herself. She would plead the headache and ask to be taken home. Then she straightened her back. No, she would not! She would not give that odious little man the satisfaction of knowing he'd driven her away. She'd ignore him.

She halted suddenly, oblivious of the strolling couple who almost collided with her, and deaf to their apologies as she stood still, her mind a turmoil of desperate plans.

She dared not ignore him. She was not by any means certain of Lord Dorney's intentions. She could not risk him discovering her deception until after he'd spoken, if indeed he was considering proposing to her, as the Bath gossips were predicting and expecting daily.

Firmly she suppressed the rising panic and forced herself to review the position. She loved Lord Dorney, although she had admitted this to no one and always brushed aside Jane's anxious queries with flippant remarks. She thought he loved her, but wondered forlornly whether this was hope rather than a reasonable expectation. If he did not, the deception she had practised, under-standable though she considered it to be, might give him a disgust of her. If he loved her he'd forgive her. But did he love her?

Slowly she resumed her progress towards the tea-room, unaware of the curious glances cast after her, noticing nothing until an avun-cular man, nearer her father's age than her own, touched her gently on the arm.

'Miss Collins, my dance, I believe?'

Somehow for the next hour she contrived to dance, talk about unimportant matters, and even to laugh. Beneath the surface calm her mind was wrestling with the problem, but without reaching any satisfactory conclusion. There was no opportunity to talk to Jane, and as the time for the last dance grew inexorably closer she sank into a lethargic acceptance. She would have to use the excuse Mr Salway had provided for her, and beg Lord Dorney to excuse her so that she could dance with the man she was beginning to hate.

'I've just met an old friend – acquaintance,' she amended quickly, suppressing the shudder all thought of a closer relationship with Mr Salway produced. 'He's from – from Yorkshire,' she explained halt-ingly when Lord Dorney came to claim her. 'He begged for this dance, so would you be kind enough to release me from my promise to you?'

'How can I refuse you anything?' he said gallantly. 'Much as I deplore this unknown rival I cannot deny you the opportunity of talking with an old friend.'

Bella gulped, smiled tremulously at him, and wished the floor would swallow her. It was too bad of that wretch to force her into such a horrible situation. Fleetingly the thought crossed her mind that it was her own doing she was masquerading under an assumed name, but she pushed it angrily aside. It had been a necessary decep-tion if she could ever hope to find a man who loved her and not her money.

She could say no more, however, for Mr Salway arrived beside her. Lord Dorney moved away, clearly not anxious to be introduced to the interloper, and Bella permitted her persecutor to lead her into the centre of the room.

'I propose to call on you in the morning,' Mr Salway announced as the musicians struck up.

Bella wanted to refuse, but she knew it would be to no avail. He could easily find her, and his enquiries might lead to unwelcome speculation.

Coldly she gave him their direction, and for the remainder of the dance they were silent. Bella had no wish to talk, for she was afraid if she did her anger would overwhelm her and betray her into an unseemly argument. Mr Salway seemed content to watch the other dancers. It occurred bleakly to Bella that Lord Dorney, if he were watching, could not help wondering why such declared old friends had so little to say to one another.

To Bella's relief Lord Dorney made no comments as they drove to Henrietta Street, and Jane was tired and wished to retire straight to bed. She went up to her own room and threw off her ballgown, then pulled on a wrapper and sat down by the window, looking out towards the hills where flambeaux lit up the buildings, and a full moon shone down on the elegant new crescents and squares which sprawled up the steep slopes.

Her brain seemed numb, apart from the bewildered repetition of questions. Why had Mr Salway come to Bath? What would Lord Dorney say when he discovered her masquerade? Did he love her? Would he make her an offer, or had she misunderstood his attentions? Would this revelation kill his love, if it existed? And, through it all, what could she do?

After several hours she rose, her limbs cold and stiff, and crept into bed, but sleep refused to come. It was almost dawn, and when the first faint gleams of sunlight crept through the window she gave up all attempts to sleep, threw off the tumbled bedclothes, and dressed hurriedly in an unfashionable but warm woollen gown.

She seized a shawl and ran down to the kitchen where Mrs Dawes was sitting with Lizzy, enjoying a pot of tea.

'Why, Miss Bella, is anything wrong?' Mrs Dawes asked anxiously.

'No, except that I couldn't sleep,' Bella replied. 'Where's Rags? I'll take him for a walk.'

'In the stables. Will you not have some tea first, and a few slices of bread and butter? Or I could make some chocolate,' Mrs Dawes offered, but Bella felt as though food and drink would choke her.

'No, thank you. I just want some fresh air,' she replied, and escaped through the door, making her way towards the stables where Rags was accommodated in an empty stall.

She decided to walk along the bank of the river, which would be deserted so early in the day, and had gone for almost a mile before she saw anyone else.

A horseman was coming towards her, ambling rather aimlessly, and with a sense of inevitability Bella recognized Lord Dorney. She felt a moment's panic, longing combined with apprehension. What could she say?

He recognized her at the same time and urged his horse into a trot until he reached her side. Dismounting, he tied the reins to the branch of an overhanging willow.

'Miss Collins, I'm surprised to see you so early in the morning,' he said, giving her a particularly sweet smile.

'I couldn't sleep,' she confessed. 'My bed became so uncomfortable it was easier to abandon it,' she added with a brave attempt at a laugh.

'Sleeplessness appears to be a common problem,' he said easily. 'I too was restless. Are you ready to go back now?'

Bella sighed. 'I ought to,' she admitted.

'Then I'll walk with you. I know Bath's considered a safe town, but I don't like the thought of your being alone.'

'Rags is excellent protection,' she avowed, but was inwardly warmed by this show of concern for her welfare.

They walked back with just a few remarks about things they saw, a clump of late violets, the first tentative cowslips, a scavenging squirrel, the burgeoning leaves on the trees, and the noisy birdsong. At the end of Henrietta Street, when Lord Dorney was preparing to leave Bella, he smiled down at her.

'May I call on you later in the morning?' he asked, and Bella looked up at him in some surprise.

He was being unusually formal. It had become his custom to call on them at least once a day, often to make arrangements for some entertainment he was escorting them to, or to suggest a ride or a drive. He did not as a rule ask for permission, and if they happened to be out when he called he would follow them to the Pump Room or Milsom Street.

'Of course,' she replied, forgetting in her astonishment that she was expecting a call from Mr Salway that morning, and with a brief smile of thanks he mounted his horse and rode towards the bridge.

Jane was eating breakfast when Bella found her.

'You're out early,' she commented. 'I haven't the energy. Tell me, Bella, who was that strange man you danced with last night? Lord Dorney looked black as thunder while you were dancing. Several people remarked on it.'

'Oh, I'd forgotten!' Bella exclaimed, realizing that Jane knew nothing of the problems besetting her. 'He's calling on me later. Oh, no, and I've said Lord Dorney may call too.'

'I don't understand,' Jane complained. 'Who is he, and why should

Lord Dorney need permission to call? He comes almost every day without asking. And why shouldn't they come at the same time?'

'He's Lady Salway's nephew, and he knew me in Harrogate,' Bella explained. 'He forced me to dance with him.'

Jane was gazing at her in dismay.

'Then he'll betray you? Why did I ever agree to this masquerade?'

'I won't allow him to ruin everything!' Bella declared vehemently. 'Jane, we must think of a way to stop him telling everyone.'

'Wait a moment. If Lord Dorney has made a point of formally asking whether he may call, he may be intending to speak. Could that be it?'

Bella stared at her, her mouth slightly open, a sudden wild surging hope showing in her eyes.

'Could it be?' she breathed. 'Oh, Jane, could that be the reason?'

'He may wish to speak to me first,' Jane mused. 'He may regard me as your guardian. But he'll certainly wish to meet your father. What have we said?' she asked, becoming agitated. 'How on earth are we going to explain it to Lord Dorney?'

Bella sighed. 'I don't know, but if he speaks first I know it will be all right. If he does love me for myself, it won't matter. Why should it? How could he possibly object to having a fortune as well as a wife, especially when he wasn't looking for one? A fortune, I mean,' she added distractedly.

'Would it be better to confess to Lord Dorney straight away?' Jane asked hesitantly.

'Not unless he offers!' Bella exclaimed. 'It would prevent him from offering, for he'd loathe to be thought a fortune hunter.'

'But what about this Mr Salway?'

'I must somehow contrive to keep him quiet for a few days. Even if it means appearing to agree to whatever he suggests.'

'I don't like it.'

'Nor do I, but what other course is open to us?'

They discussed the problem over and over, but could find no way round it. Bella at last went to change out of her old woollen gown. She put on a fresh muslin dress in a pretty shade of green, and took especial care brushing her hair, ready to entertain whichever visitor might come first.

She was descending the stairs when a sharp knock at the front door made her jump then run hastily past Lizzy as she came from the kitchen to answer it. She arrived breathlessly in the drawing-room with just sufficient time to seat herself on a small, brocade-covered sopha, before Lizzy announced the visitor.

Chapter Seven

———◦◦◦◦◦———

'M R SALWAY!' Bella gasped, the anxious hope dying from her eyes. She took a deep breath. If no miracle in the shape of Lord Dorney and his offer intervened she would have to use her own wits. 'Lizzy, pray tell Lady Hodder Mr Salway has arrived,' she ordered crisply.

'Yes, miss,' Lizzy said cheerfully. 'Would you like me to bring some wine?'

'Yes, please, but after you've informed Lady Hodder.'

'Good morning, Miss Trahearne, you look charming as usual,' he said smoothly, crossing the room to try and take her hand in his.

Bella glared at him as she moved behind a small table and evaded his outstretched hand. She caught Lizzy's surprised glance as the maid backed from the room and closed the door.

'What do you want?' Bella demanded bluntly.

'What have I ever wanted since first I set eyes on you?' he responded.

'Rather since your aunt told you the size of my fortune!' Bella retorted bitterly. 'You all but snubbed me at our first meeting. Though that was far preferable to your fawning attempts to ingratiate yourself later,' she added reflectively. 'Why are you in Bath? Did you somehow discover I was here?'

'Oh, no, I came here by chance, but now I've met you again I've not quite given up hope of persuading you to accept my suit,' he replied calmly, ignoring her strictures.

'I have nothing to say to you,' Bella said, but without much hope that he would accept this.

'However, I have things to say to you,' he replied with a smirk. 'But first, let me explain how I come to be here. After you left Harrogate I met a far more accommodating lady, a trifle older than you, to be sure, but still attractive. A widow, whose husband made a fortune running some deplorable manufactory in Birmingham, I understand. Since you declined to honour me with your hand I naturally turned to someone else. She wished to come to Bath and I offered to travel ahead and book rooms for her.'

'Then if you have such advantageous prospects why do you continue to persecute me?'

'In the first instance her income is unfortunately only a quarter the size of yours, my dear Bella. And in the second, to speak the truth, she's a little too old for my taste. Also I confess to a desire to make you eat your words. They were most hurtful, you know, almost contemptuous, when you spurned my very sincere offer.'

'You're contemptible!' Bella declared, 'and what you've just said abundantly confirms it. How can you treat anyone so badly, especially some poor deluded female who's depending on you?'

'I shall book her rooms, and I've promised nothing more,' he replied with a smile that set Bella's teeth on edge. 'Is it my fault if I renew acquaintanceship with a lady I'd once loved and thought lost to me? If I discover, to my joy, I was mistaken, and she favours me after all?'

'I do not favour you!' Bella said slowly through gritted teeth. 'Your first offer was unwelcome, and I have not changed my decision, and never will.'

'I accept the first, and it's unfortunate, I confess, but before you dismiss me entirely, remember that you've not yet heard my new proposition,' he reminded her.

'I don't need to. I'll not agree to any odious scheme of yours.'

'Why are you masquerading in Bath under a false name?' he asked, with a sudden change of subject that caused Bella to frown.

'That's my business,' she snapped.

'Also, surely, the business of any prospective husband,' he said quietly. 'I haven't been wasting my time since I arrived, my dear. It's common gossip that Lord Dorney is about to offer for you. What will he say when he discovers you've deceived him?'

'It's no deception.' Bella protested. 'At least, not in the way you mean. I'm not trying to gain anything by it which will be a disadvantage to anyone else. The opposite, rather!'

'You want to be valued for yourself alone,' he sneered. 'You despise men like myself who have inadequate means and take the only way open to us of improving the situation.'

'You have means enough to live better than most people, even if you're not wealthy,' Bella said heatedly. 'Why can you not make yourself content with that, or find a position with a salary, as your aunt did, instead of trying to marry an heiress you don't love?'

'Who says I don't love you?'

Bella snorted inelegantly. 'You wouldn't have given me a second glance if you hadn't discovered I'm rich!'

'Would you be content to exist in a couple of mediocre rooms, without a servant other than a drab, and no way of enjoying the finer things of life?'

'Yes, if I had to,' Bella answered. 'My father is far from rich, and I never expected to be.'

'But he has a house and an estate. He didn't lose it all as my father did by gambling.'

'I can hardly be expected to replace your father's lost estates,' Bella began indignantly, but he interrupted curtly.

'It is considered entirely acceptable, even estimable, for a girl to aim to wed a fortune,' he went on, disregarding her, 'yet a man must never be guilty of such despicable mercenary considerations!'

'With regard to what is acceptable, men have certain other advantages over mere females,' Bella commented drily. 'However, I'm growing bored, and I fail to see what all this has to do with your visit here.'

'I came to lay two alternatives at your feet,' he replied. 'Either you bestow your hand and fortune on me, or you make over to me half of your capital in exchange for my silence. I believe there are no tiresome restrictions on how you might dispose of your capital.'

Bella was staring at him in complete amazement.

'I don't believe it!' she whispered. 'It's monstrous. Half my fortune simply to buy your silence? It's incredible. As for the other, I'll never even consider marrying such a despicable little toad!'

He winced. 'I rather expected that would be your attitude,' he confessed. 'But you did hear correctly,' he assured her. 'Isn't it worth half your really rather disgustingly large fortune, which Lord Dorney knows nothing about and would despise if he did, to buy my discretion?'

'And afterwards you could marry your widow and take her money too!'

'And she would appreciate me,' he agreed. 'That course has its attractions, although her fortune is so much less than yours. Yet she is too malleable for my taste. I have a certain curiosity to see whether I could tame you. On the whole I prefer all your fortune, and you and your spirit with it.'

'Get out!' Bella almost screamed at him. 'Go away and never come here again! I wouldn't marry you if – if I were forced to the altar at gunpoint!'

He turned to walk towards the door.

'You're becoming hysterical, my dear. I'll return in a couple of hours for your answer. I trust you'll have seen reason by then.'

He opened the door to find Lizzy about to come in bearing a tray with a decanter and wine glasses.

'I'm sorry, miss, Mrs Dawes hurt herself and I had to help her,' Lizzy said breathlessly.

'No matter, I cannot stay,' Mr Salway replied, and with the briefest of bows towards Bella left the room and let himself out of the front door.

'Oh, dear, I'm sorry, miss, I hope the gentleman's not offended?' Lizzy asked anxiously.

Bella bit back her answer that she hoped he was, and reassured the flustered maid.

'Is Mrs Dawes badly hurt?' she demanded anxiously. 'What happened?'

'No, it's not bad. The pot slipped, and some hot water splashed over her arm,' Lizzy reported. 'Lady Hodder heard her cry out as she was coming here, and came down to the kitchen to see what was the matter. It were the shock most of all, and a bit of a scald. She's gone to have a lay down.'

'Take the wine away now, Lizzy,' Bella said, and as the maid left the room she dropped on to the sopha and stared blindly in front of her.

She was determined never to sink so low as to marry the despicable Mr Salway. And although her fortune was so large she was equally determined she would never submit to his blackmail and give him a penny, let alone half of it. She needed it for her orphans. Her one hope of getting out of the scrape she'd brought on herself was for Lord Dorney to arrive and make his offer within the next two hours, so that she could confess all and throw herself on his compassion. Then Mr Salway would present no threat.

She began to pace distractedly up and down the room, going to look out of the window every few minutes to see whether Lord Dorney was approaching. Her mood swung between hope, despair, fury and frustration. After what seemed hours Jane came in to find her with her nose pressed against the pane, staring blankly along the road.

'Bella, what in the world happened? What did he say?'

Bella pithily related the gist of the encounter.

'And I'm afraid Lizzy heard him call me Miss Trahearne,' she ended angrily. 'Did she say anything?'

'No, but she was big with some sort of news she wanted to tell Mrs Dawes. That must have been it.'

'Can we stop them gossiping?'

Jane shook her head. 'Better just ignore it, I think, and then they'll soon forget. At least there's no chance of them discovering the truth.'

'Jane, what shall I do? Lord Dorney hasn't come and he said he would.'

'But he didn't give a time, and it's still early.'

'Whatever happens I will not submit to that odious wretch's blackmail!'

'Then you must tell Lord Dorney the truth whether he offers or not. I'm sure he'll understand your reasons.'

Bella shook her head dolefully. 'I wish I could be as certain of that. And I can't speak unless he offers, it would look so coming of me!'

Jane finally went away to deal with various household duties, having insisted that Mrs Dawes rest after her accident. A few minutes later she put her head back into the room to say she was going shopping to fetch a few items Mrs Dawes wanted for dinner.

'She won't rest until she has them, and Lizzy is busy so I promised to go. I won't be long, and if Lord Dorney comes he can speak to you alone.'

Bella resumed her anxious pacing, not at all sure she wished to face Lord Dorney alone. Jane had not returned an hour later, however, when Lord Dorney's smart curricle drew up in front of the house. He sprang down, tossing the reins to the groom, and strode up the steps towards the front door.

Bella retreated further into the room as soon as she saw him and sank down on to the sopha. She didn't know which emotion was uppermost in her mind, relief that he had finally arrived, or apprehension about the confession she must make.

Lizzy once more showed a gentleman into the drawing-room and offered to fetch wine. This time Bella could not ask for Jane to be told, and she wondered if she imagined the sly look Lizzy cast at her.

'My lord,' she began, and then came to a halt, her mind a blank. It was as impossible as she had feared. How could she mention the subject of marriage unless he did first?

'My dear Miss Collins,' he replied. 'May I sit down?'

'Oh, yes, of course. I'm sorry,' Bella was confused, and when he took a seat beside her on the sopha it took all her resolution to remain there.

Seeking to put her at her ease, he chatted about the ball the previous evening, and seemed unconcerned at her monosyllabic responses. When Lizzy brought the wine he rose to pour two glasses and handed one to Bella.

'Your health and happiness,' he said, standing in front of her and raising his glass in a toast before drinking.

Bella tried to smile, gulped some of the wine, and developed a fit of coughing.

By the time he'd taken her glass, set it and his own down on a side table, patted her on the back, and handed her his handkerchief, Bella had recovered. She smiled at him through a screen of tears which the coughing had brought into her eyes, and he took her hand gently in his.

'My dear, when you look so vulnerable I cannot remain silent. I'd intended to visit your father, or at least speak first to Lady Hodder, who is in some way your guardian, but I understand she is out. I should properly beg her permission to approach you, but it's impossible to wait any longer! Bella, you are adorable!'

He sank on to one knee before her, but before she could reply there was a discreet knock on the door.

'C–come in,' Bella managed, as Lord Dorney, with a barely suppressed oath, rose to his feet and stepped across to the table where he had deposited their wineglasses.

'I beg pardon, miss, but the gentleman wouldn't take no—' Lizzy began, but was unable to continue.

She was pushed aside with scant ceremony and a red-faced, ruffled Mr Salway stormed into the room.

'Sir!' Lord Dorney protested coldly. 'How dare you burst into a lady's house in such a manner!'

'Lady?' Mr Salway sneered. 'Does a lady masquerade under an assumed name, hoping to entrap an honest man into marriage? After she's promised to someone else, but thinks she might better herself. It was fortunate I saw you, my lord, and could warn you in time. For shame, Bella, trying to escape from your promises to me like that!'

'Miss Collins, who is this fellow? Shall I throw him out?' asked Lord Dorney, grim faced and with hands clenched into fists.

'Miss Collins, that's a whisker!' Mr Salway laughed, but moved prudently away from Lord Dorney, who was the same height but of considerably heavier build, and moving now as though he was perfectly capable of carrying out his threat.

'Be silent!' Lord Dorney ordered, moving impetuously forwards.

'Ask her first whether Collins is her real name. Ask her whether she's truly Lord Hodder's cousin. Ask her whether she knew me in Harrogate!' Mr Salway gabbled. 'Very well indeed, she knew me,' he added with a smirk.

Lord Dorney glanced at Bella, and at the guilty expression on her expressive face began to frown.

'Is any of this true?' he demanded. 'Miss Collins – Bella, do you know this fellow?'

'Yes, unfortunately!' Bella found her voice.

'And is your name Collins?'

'No. My lord, I can explain—'

'Full of lies, she is. She was promised to me earlier in the year, and then decided I wouldn't do for her, she wanted a title,' Mr Salway went on. 'I came to Bath when I heard where she was, going under a false name, trying to buy a title with the fortune her uncle left her.'

'That's untrue!' Bella gasped. 'Yes, I knew you, and you offered for me, but I never promised anything. I told you to go away! And I don't want a title.'

'You'd best leave, sirrah!' Lord Dorney commanded, and moved towards Mr Salway in so determined a fashion that he cravenly edged out of the door and pushed past Lizzy, hovering avidly on the threshold, on his hasty retreat to the front door.

Lord Dorney watched him go, closed the door on the flustered maid, and came back towards Bella. He placed both hands on her shoulders and she shivered with a combination of despair and a wild, crazy impulse to throw herself into his arms and sob weakly on his chest. But Bella had never given way to tears and she wouldn't now, she vowed, however feeble her legs had become, and however tinglingly aware of him she felt.

'I think I deserve an explanation,' he said abruptly. 'Since you admit some of the fellow's accusations are true perhaps you'd better tell me the whole of it.'

Bella stared at him helplessly, overwhelmed with dismay at the cold, implacable expression in his eyes. She remained mute. What could she say?

'Let us start with your name,' he prompted impatiently, shaking her slightly. 'It is not Collins?'

Bella miserably shook her head. It was far, far worse than she had ever anticipated, for his eyes were like flints, cold and sharp in a grimly hard face which promised no mercy. Normally she cared nothing for the anger of others, but this was terribly, searingly different, and she was shattered at the realization of how much his anger distressed her.

'So what is it?'

'Trahearne,' Bella whispered.

'A normal enough name,' he commented icily. 'Why change it? What scandal attaches to it?'

'None at all!' Bella was stung into a reply, some of her customary animation returning.

'Is Lady Hodder any relation of yours?'

'She's my cousin, on my mother's side of the family,' she explained wearily, a great weight seeming to press down on her.

'You knew that fellow in Harrogate?'

'Yes.'

She seemed incapable of more than the minimum necessary replies, and tried to twist out of his grasp, but his hands merely tightened their grip. She turned away her face to hide the tears which threatened, despite her resolution, to disgrace her. Why did his nearness affect her so? He took her chin in one hand and turned her firmly to face him.

'Did he offer for you?'

'Several times.' With a tremendous effort she forced herself to answer calmly, thankful that her voice was steady, however the rest of her felt.

'And? He said you accepted him.'

'He lied.'

'Did he?' He stared down into her eyes and Bella, suddenly dizzy, swayed slightly and moved closer to him. 'You lied about your name, it seems. What was that about a fortune?' he demanded harshly. 'Was it true?'

'It's the whole wretched problem!' she cried in sudden fury, bringing her hands up between them and hammering with her fists at his chest. 'He offered for me, and so did others when they found out about the wretched money, but I always refused him as well as all of them!'

'You lied to me,' he repeated.

'No! Well, not really. What does a name matter?' she pleaded, gazing into his eyes so close to hers, willing him to understand. 'I'm me, Bella, how can it matter what else I'm called?'

'It matters to me. I admired you for many things, your compassion for creatures less fortunate, and your outspoken defence of them, but most of all I thought you were truthful. We were able to talk in a manner I've never achieved with any other woman. I imagined we could talk freely, openly, about anything, in the way friends can, but it wasn't so. It was based on a deception.'

'I couldn't tell you!' Bella exclaimed.

'You didn't trust me.'

'I didn't trust any man after the vultures of Harrogate!' Bella retorted bitterly.

'How fortunate I discovered it in time, madam. I was prepared to offer you my name and my hand and my love. You were the first girl I'd ever contemplated sharing my life with. But it was a sham, all based on dishonesty, a fraud! That is something I hate more than anything else; something I can never tolerate. Were you planning to find a husband when you came to Bath? How were you proposing to reveal the truth to him?'

'I don't know,' Bella replied tiredly. 'I hadn't thought so far ahead. I just wanted to be loved for myself, not my wretched fortune. I couldn't bear to marry anyone who knew of it, and thought if I used a different name I might find someone I could really trust, who loved me before he knew about the money.'

'You wanted to find trust without offering it in return? Somewhat naïve, was it not?'

'How could I ever know the truth of whether I was loved and not my money?'

'How does any man with a good income or a title know the same? Love must be built on mutual trust, Miss – Trahearne. My poor unfortunate brother discovered that, but I imagined I'd avoided his mistakes!'

'If you don't understand there's no more to say,' Bella managed, relapsing into her former state of lethargy.

'I understand only too well.'

His grasp tightened, his arms sliding round her back to pull her close towards him, imprisoning her within their circle.

As she glanced, startled, up at him, he bent his head towards her, his eyes dark and tortured just a few inches away from hers. She could feel his breath on her cheeks as he gave a faint groan, and suddenly his mouth covered hers.

His lips were hard and demanding, and Bella involuntarily opened her own in response to their message. How utterly different his kiss was to the slobbering wetness she had endured when unable to evade Mr Salway, she thought briefly.

Lord Dorney was firm, rough even, as he crushed her to him. She was overwhelmed, breathless, unable to think of anything except the exquisite bitter-sweet joy of being held in his embrace.

Without her noticing it her hands crept round him, and her lips grew soft. Briefly his own hard mouth relaxed, he responded with a gentler, softer caressing kiss, tracing the outline of her mouth with his tongue.

Then, so abruptly that Bella staggered and almost fell, he thrust her away from him.

'My apologies!' he jerked out harshly, turning away from the sight of Bella, her fingers unconsciously touching her bruised mouth.

'Richard? My lord!' she exclaimed, but he shook his head angrily and moved away across the room.

'I should not have done that. Perhaps I wouldn't if you had been the sort of girl I took you for,' he added bitterly. 'However, I'm thankful to have discovered the truth before it was too late. Pray give my regards to Lady Hodder. That is her name, I presume?'

'Of course it is.'

Bella was indignant, bemused, and utterly bereft at this sudden reversion into coldness and anger. For one blissful second she had hoped matters might after all have resolved themselves satisfactorily.

'Then I'll apologize once more and bid you farewell, Miss Trahearne. I shall be leaving Bath, and do not expect we'll meet again.'

She uttered a wordless cry, but he ignored her and was gone, closing the door behind him sharply. Bella pressed her eyes tightly shut, and to ward off the threatened tears began softly repeating over and over again all the unladylike expressions she had learned as a child from the stable lads.

Chapter Eight

———⚬◉⚬———

LORD DORNEY RETURNED to his lodgings and brusquely ordered his valet to pack.

'I'm leaving at once, I'll ride and will spend the night somewhere on the road,' he said. 'You can come tomorrow morning. Take it to Sir Daniel Scott's house.'

He changed into breeches and a caped riding coat. Having ruined the first two cravats he tried to tie he gave up and wrapped a loose neckerchief round his neck, tucking the ends into his shirt. He was furious, not so much with Bella, but with himself for having so far forgot his resolutions as to have been on the point of offering for her. And how he could have lost control of himself in such a deplorable fashion he did not in the least understand.

She was no lightskirt, whatever other faults he had now discovered. There had been no excuse for kissing her in such a manner. For kissing her at all. He tried to banish the recollection, but the memory of the sweetness of her mouth, the shy, tentative response to his assault, and this was the only word he could use for it, would not go away.

He tugged on his riding boots and, taking the saddle-bags his valet had packed and silently handed him, went down to the stables. Why had she lied? Her explanation of wanting to be loved for herself was nonsense. She was, if not in her first flush of youth, or conventionally beautiful, a pretty, vivacious woman, one many men would be only too happy to marry.

Her fortune, he recalled. She'd said she would be loved for that. Was it so large? But other heiresses had to endure such uncertainty, unless they married men who were equally rich. She could have trusted him. Then he cursed fluently under his breath. He couldn't marry an heiress. Not after Robert's experience. But what was he thinking? It was all over. He had no intention of offering for her now.

He rode out of Bath at a furious pace, until his anger cooled and he remembered to conserve his horse's strength. They had a long ride ahead of them.

'I won't stay in Bath,' Bella declared heatedly later that evening, as she and Jane sat at dinner.

'But I'm sure Lord Dorney won't tell anyone,' Jane pleaded. 'He'll not wish people to think he's been deceived.'

'I didn't deceive him! Not about anything really important,' Bella insisted.

'He thought so.'

'In any event I couldn't bear to stay here and have everyone speculating as to why he didn't offer after all, and left so hurriedly,' she said with a shudder. 'And how was I to know he'd be so stuffy about stupid matters? Besides, that wretch Salway will be bound to spread the news, so I'll be disgraced as well as humiliated.'

'Oh, not as bad as that, Bella!'

'If I'm not disgraced why did he reject me?'

Jane had no difficulty in identifying the 'he'. Bella had been white and trembling when she returned from her shopping expedition, but even during the vehement and occasionally incoherent telling of what had taken place not a single tear had fallen. The sudden crashing of her hopes had clearly affected her greatly, but Jane was secretly of the opinion that a hearty session of weeping would have been better than this brittle, dry-eyed anger.

'It must have been a shock to him. When he's had time to reflect he may realize he's been hasty.'

'I don't think he'd ever recall the words he spoke. He was too bitter. But Jane, I still don't understand what he meant about his brother. That's several times he's spoken of him in an odd way.'

'What do you mean? How odd?'

'As though his brother were disgraced, or – no, not that – rather as though he'd been let down, deceived or disappointed in some way.'

'Then he may be particularly sensitive to deception.'

'Oh, Jane, I wish I knew!'

'I'll go and call on Mrs Eversley tomorrow. She's bound to know and will delight in telling me.'

'While I pack.'

'Pack? You mean to leave Bath?'

'How could I possibly stay in Bath while that devil Salway is here? I'd want to murder him every time I set eyes on him, and one can't avoid people in Bath. Besides, you have to go to London soon.'

'Are you determined to go back home?'

'I'm not going home,' Bella announced. 'I'm going to London as well. I'll hire a house, and find a duenna. That – that obnoxious little beast shan't defeat me!'

'London? But – Bella, you can't! Everyone will know your name there, and all about your fortune,' Jane gabbled distractedly.

'So will everyone here by tomorrow. If I can no longer keep it a secret in Bath I may as well go to London. At least it will be livelier there!'

After some anxious discussion, during which Jane realized Bella was stretched taut with suppressed emotion, she suggested that Philip's godmother, Lady Fulwood, would be happy to have both of them staying with her.

'I've never met her, but Philip says she has a huge house and loves visitors. She always has friends and relatives staying with her. I'm sure she wouldn't object.'

'Jane, you're a dear. That would be ideal. Will you write to her at once?'

'Are you following Lord Dorney?' Jane asked apprehensively as she walked across to her small escritoire and pulled a sheet of paper towards her. 'Do you think that's wise?'

'I never want to see or speak to him again!' Bella announced bravely, but her lip trembled, and she had to blink rapidly.

'What about the fortune hunters?'

'I don't care a toss about fortune hunters! I don't intend to be taken in by them, either, if that's what you fear, Jane. I don't intend ever to marry and give a man power over me or my money. I shall either become an eccentric recluse, secretly devoted to good works, or live in London doing exactly as I wish, and Society can disapprove or not as it chooses. But you can wager it won't when it knows the size of my fortune,' she added cynically.

Bella retreated to her room and began to write letters herself. If she had rejected marriage, and she would marry no one but Lord Dorney, she would devote more of her time and fortune to her orphans. She wrote to George Jenkins, and after a moment's thought, to Mr Tomkins in Bristol, asking both if they had any contacts in London with people who might be suitable for running another house if she could find property there.

Lady Fulwood lived in Mount Street, so she asked them to direct any replies to her there. She apologized to the Tomkinses that she would be unable to visit them before she left Bath, but was sure they would understand and keep her informed of progress.

She ought also to write to her father. Her letters done, she went to the drawing-room to ask Jane if she wanted any help.

'It's all in hand, Bella. Forget about him. If he can't see you for what you are, he is not worth fretting about.'

Bella did not reply. She went to bed, but for most of the night she relived that kiss, trying to explore the new and strange sensations it had aroused in her. What blissful rapture had she lost by her mad masquerade?

Although Jane scrutinized her closely the next morning she could find no traces of weeping, just dark shadows under Bella's eyes which showed she had slept but little. After breakfast Jane set off to discover what she could from Mrs Eversley, while Bella announced to the astonished Mr and Mrs Dawes that they were leaving Bath in a few days.

'But we mean to give you what you would have earned if we'd stayed here the full two months as arranged,' she reassured them, 'as well as excellent references. Dawes, will you please ask Jackson to see about selling the horses? None of them are worth taking to London, I – we can buy better ones there. And return the carriage, we won't need it any more. Though if Jackson wants to come with us it would save our having to ask Lady Fulwood's coachman to drive us every-where.'

'Yes, miss. What about the dog?'

'Rags? Oh, dear, I'd forgotten him. Wouldn't you like to keep him?'

'No, miss,' Dawes said firmly. 'Besides, if we find other posts I wouldn't be allowed to take him there.'

Bella sighed. 'I suppose not. I'll have to take him with us. I'd be sorry to leave him, in a way, I've grown fond of him.'

'And he'd be lost without you, miss. Terrible fond of you, he is, always whining to come after you.'

Briskly Bella ordered trunks brought up, and while Susan was occupied in packing Jane's clothes Bella began on her own, with Mary's help.

'Miss Bella, I'm confused,' Mary said timidly. 'You're not Miss Collins, I heard.'

Briefly Bella explained, and Mary, to her relief, was both amused and sympathetic.

'Though if I had so much money I wouldn't want to be thought poor,' she said, folding Bella's new dresses with care.

The sight of the gown she'd worn during her first meeting with Lord Dorney almost broke her control. Mary had been unable to get rid of the blood from Rags, or the dirt where Bella had knelt on the ground, but Bella had refused to throw it away, saying blandly it would do for the garden when she went home to Lancashire. She crumpled it in her hands and buried her face in the muslin, and wondered briefly whether to abandon all her clothes again as she'd discarded those which reminded her of her unfortunate visit to Harrogate.

'I can't make a habit of that!' she gasped, half laughing, half sobbing, and thrust the garment roughly into a corner of the trunk. Hastily she tossed others after it, firmly suppressing the memories they evoked of driving with Lord Dorney, or dancing with Lord Dorney, or simply being worn when she had spoken to or merely seen Lord Dorney in the distance.

Jane returned after an hour, and Bella ran down to the drawing-room.

'Well,' she demanded. 'Did you discover anything?'

Jane was sitting at a small table, abstractedly smoothing the fingers of her gloves. She nodded, and gestured to Bella to sit down opposite her.

'It's bad,' she announced.

'Tell me!'

Jane took a deep breath. 'Lord Dorney's father gambled away most of his inheritance,' she began slowly. 'It seems he was a rogue, too, and weak, for he signed vowels which he'd no intention of redeeming and afterwards, if it was just his word against another man's, claimed they'd been forged. He was ostracized by decent folk, and retired to Dorney Court until he died five years ago.'

'No wonder Lord Dorney is so amazingly sensitive about deception,' Bella said softly.

'Yes. His brother, the new Lord Dorney, inherited estates which were badly encumbered, and thought he could redeem matters by marrying an heiress instead of retrenching, as his friends advised. He was charming and handsome and soon found one. They were wed a year after his father died. The debts were redeemed and the mortgages paid, and long-overdue repairs and other improvements made to Dorney Court. But Lady Dorney was a shrew and demanded the most unreasonable things, always pointing out it was her money which paid for them. The ballroom, for instance, which has been used once only since it was built, and is totally impracticable for a country house by no means large enough to accommodate all the guests who'd have to stay if they attended a ball.'

'Why did her husband allow it?'

'He was weak, too, and he loved her as well as needing her money which had saved his home. But she soon tired of country life and spent all her time in London, creating scandal with her wild behaviour. She was notorious for her indiscretions, and after a time was reputed to be living with a man who left his wife for her. This man was killed, shot in a duel, and Lord Dorney – her husband, not this one, of course, came home and killed himself.'

'Oh, no! How dreadful. Poor Lord Dorney.'

'It's worse. People at first naturally assumed he'd shot his wife's lover, then odd rumours started that it had been the present Lord Dorney who took his brother's place in the duel, because he is a much better shot. He's better at all sorts of sport, Mrs Eversley says. He's good with his fists, she said, and fences with the best. He can't afford to keep so many horses now, but he used to be one of the best riders to hounds, and drove with the Four Horse Club. He's supposed to have a fierce temper, and as a child and a young man often offended people by his outbursts.'

'He hasn't a dreadful temper!' Bella defended him, and then recalled the suppressed fury and passion in his kiss. It had been unexpected, he had seemed so calm beforehand.

'They say he's made a tremendous effort to suppress his instincts since then, and, of course, those who dislike him maintain it's because of guilt: either he doesn't want to add fuel to the rumours, or he thinks he caused his brother's death. Some even say he drove his brother into suicide to get the title.'

'What utter nonsense!'

'Perhaps. I cannot believe him so base. But you can understand why he dislikes heiresses and deception of any sort. He must have had a horrendous time with such a disreputable father and weak brother. Mrs Eversley says he's totally different, takes after his mother. She even hinted—' Jane stopped suddenly, and a slight blush suffused her cheeks.

'Hinted what? You can't stop there, Jane.'

'Well, it's probably utter nonsense,' Jane said in embarrassment, 'but rumour maintained his father was someone else, and Mrs Eversley claims he's so different from both his father and brother it's probably true!'

Bella laughed for the first time since Mr Salway had arrived in Bath.

'So I suppose he's defensive about that rumour too. I wish I'd known earlier, but it's all finished now. I have to forget him. When can we start for London?'

'Patience, Bella! There are matters to deal with here first.'

'Have you written to Lady Fulwood yet?'

'Yes, I sent it express and expect an answer in a day or so.'

Jane had had time to regret her impulsive suggestion, though she doubted whether Bella would have gone meekly home. She was becoming more and more apprehensive about Bella's intentions. She would have little hope of restraining the girl once they were in London, but if Bella had gone alone there would have been the most enormous scandal. At least she could prevent that by being with her.

Uncomfortable though it would be Jane considered it better for her to be on hand, when she might hope to talk sense into Bella and prevent the more outrageous actions if she could.

'You're a dear, helping me like this,' Bella said quietly, and Jane's feelings of irritation veered towards intense pity for her cousin's disillusionment.

It was late in the evening when Lord Dorney arrived at Sir Daniel's small town house. His friend greeted him without surprise.

'How fortunate you've come now,' he said. 'I'm off to Paris next week, and would have missed you.'

'For long? Is this a new appointment?' Lord Dorney asked. 'Shall I be in your way?'

'Of course not, you know you're always welcome. It's a short visit, no more than a week at most. And you must stay here while I'm gone.'

'I'm due to visit my godmother soon, but I came to London earlier than I'd planned. I intended at first to go to Dorney Court after I'd seen Alex, but I stayed in Bath instead. Dorney Court can do without me for a while. The builders there can get on with it by themselves. I – Dan, I need to talk.'

He saw the look of surprise on his friend's face and grinned ruefully. 'I've made a fool of myself. Despite not wanting to follow in Robert's footsteps I found myself considering marriage. I almost offered for someone. Found out in the nick of time she wasn't what I thought.'

Sir Daniel nodded. 'After all your protestations about not wanting to marry, she must have been exceptional.'

Lord Dorney nodded. 'Different, rather. You recall that incident in the inn yard, the chit who threatened those rogues with a pistol? Well, we met again in Bath.' He paused, recalling the various occasions when they had met. 'She was different,' he repeated.

'And?'

Lord Dorney shrugged. 'She wasn't the usual silly girl, concerned only with her clothes and flirtation. I thought she was open, honest. But she wasn't.'

'What did she do to offend?'

'She was using a false name.'

Sir Daniel raised his eyebrows. 'What the devil for?'

'To hide the fact that she was wealthy. Very wealthy. She had this notion of wanting to find a husband who loved her for herself, not her money.'

'Not an ignoble ambition.'

'But it meant she lied. And if she lies in one thing, how could I ever trust her? Have you heard of Nabob Trahearne, who died a year or so back?'

'Who hasn't? He's supposed to have come back from India with a shipload of jewels. One of the biggest fortunes ever made there. What has he to do with your girl?'

'She inherited it.'

'What?' Sir Daniel laughed and slapped his friend on the shoulder. 'And you object to that? Man, it would be the answer to all your problems. You could restore Dorney Court at once, and would have no need to sell your mother's houses. Has the sale of Fellside been completed yet? Did your cotton merchant or whoever it was increase his offer?'

'Not enough, but if he does offer what I am asking I will feel bound to sell. I won't go back on that, Dan.'

'No matter, there are other estates in the area if you want to buy one for the shooting. Or you could buy one in Scotland. That's becoming fashionable, I hear.'

'Dan, I don't wish for that, and how could I use my wife – my *possible* wife's money for such things? Have you forgotten what happened when Robert tried that? He thought marrying Selina would solve all his problems, but she made them worse. But why are we even talking of it? I won't follow in Robert's footsteps and marry for money, and then spend the rest of my life regretting it. It would be worse than parson's mousetrap; I'd be completely at her mercy, obligated to her for everything. I can't endure the thought of that.'

'Is your girl – what is her name?'

'Bella.'

'Well, is she like Selina? Would she flaunt her lovers?'

'How can I tell? How can anyone know such things in advance?'

'Some things have to be taken on trust. Do you love her?' he asked bluntly.

'I thought I did. Dan, I can't get her out of my mind! But it's hopeless. I made a mull of it, and in any event, I won't be castigated as a fortune-hunter! Robert had enough of that. It soured him.'

'Selina's activities did that, Richard.'

'Perhaps. I'm sorry, I've been so angry all the way from Bath, I had to tell someone, and who but my best friend? Now let's talk of other things. What's this mission to Paris?'

A few days later Jane and Bella were bowling out of Bath in a hired post chaise. They spent the night at The King's Head in Thatcham, near Newbury, Jane bluntly refusing to attempt the entire journey in one day.

'I've no wish to encounter footpads on Hounslow Heath, or arrive long after dark in Mount Street,' she insisted. 'One more day will make no difference.'

Bella, though thankful to see the last of Bath, and eager to reach London, was impatient, but had to agree, and it was mid-afternoon when the chaise came to a halt outside Lady Fulwood's tall narrow house in Mount Street.

To Jane's relief Lady Fulwood was at home, and received them with obvious enthusiasm. They were shown up into the drawing-room while her footman was ordered to take their trunks straight to the guest rooms.

Lady Fulwood was not so old as Bella had assumed from Jane's description. She was a thin, well-preserved lady in her mid-fifties, her neck somewhat scrawny, and her bony face lined, but from laughter rather than peevishness.

'My dear Jane, how lovely to see you! And your cousin, too. She'll be company for you until Philip arrives. I knew your father long ago, Bella, but I never met your mother.'

On the journey Bella had determined to have no more decep-tion. She was also concerned not to cause her hostess any difficulties should details of her Bath masquerade reach her from someone else, as was inevitable. Immediately they had washed away the dust of the journey and returned to the drawing-room she confessed.

Rather guiltily she told Lady Fulwood all about her visit to Harrogate, her detestation of the money-grubbing fortune hunters she'd encountered there, and her subsequent incognito visit to Bath.

Lady Fulwood startled her by the open enjoyment she evinced at the tale.

'Lord, how I'd have enjoyed doing that!' she exclaimed. 'But you gave it up. Why?'

Bella had omitted all mention of Lord Dorney, but now she explained how Mr Salway's reappearance had made it impossible to continue, and reconciled her to living as her wealthy self in London.

'You need not be concerned overmuch,' Lady Fulwood opined. 'I know every gazetted fortune hunter in the country, and can warn you long before you begin to feel a *tendre* for any of them.'

Bella refrained from announcing her intention of never marrying, suspecting it would lead to unproductive argument, and instead listened eagerly to the plans Lady Fulwood was rapidly evolving for introducing her visitors to the *ton*.

'What if anyone from Bath comes and recognizes us?' Jane asked.

'We laugh, admit it was a frolic, and tell them the reason,' Lady Fulwood replied robustly. 'It won't do any harm, in fact it might serve to warn the more obvious toadies away. Now, what good fortune I have no other guests here at the moment. My godson may arrive any day. His letter was vague, but his own house in Town is let for the Season and he indicated he might first spend a few days with a friend.'

'Will I be a nuisance, when your other guests arrive?' Bella asked diffidently.

'Of course not, child, I love having lots of people around me. Now we must concentrate on tonight. I've invitations to a ball, a rout, a musical evening and a soirée. Which would you prefer to attend first? I'd suggest the musicale, since we can slip away at the interval, there'll be more people there than at the soirée, which is rather select. Then we can go on to the rout and the ball if you're not too tired after your journey.'

'All of them?' Bella asked, astonished.

'Oh, yes, or we'd never be able to do much. Only the real friends of a hostess stay for the entire evening if there are other invitations.'

'But we have no invitations,' Jane objected faintly.

'No matter, everyone knows me, and would hardly refuse entry to my guests. For a start neither musicale nor the soirée will be well attended and they'll be grateful for more people. Then the rout will be such a squeeze they won't even notice you're there. And the ball is to launch a very lovely and moderately wealthy young lady, and though you're well enough, child, and will be better when my dress-maker has attended to it, you won't be considered a threat to her. I'll no doubt be able to introduce you to one of the patronesses of Almack's at the ball, and get vouchers for you both.'

Swept along by her enthusiasm they forgot the tedium of the journey, and after an early dinner set out for the round of entertainments.

Bella, at her hostess's insistence, submitted to the ministrations of Fanny, Lady Fulwood's elderly dresser. When she contemplated the finished result she had to confess that the new style of arranging her hair, and the faintest touch of rouge in her cheeks, somehow made an indefinable and attractive difference to her looks. Mary was competent at looking after her clothes, but she had less skill in dressing her hair. Bella determined that Fanny must teach her.

She wore a gown she'd had no opportunity of wearing in Bath. Lady Fulwood had inspected all her gowns and decreed she must make an initial impact. 'This is the one.'

It was too elaborate for ordinary balls and had been intended for a gala occasion. The underskirt was of her favourite deep shade of rose, topped with cleverly draped, shimmering gold gauze. The neckline was lower than she normally permitted herself to wear, and the enticing swell of her plump bosom was only partially concealed by swathes of the gauze. The skirt was edged with gold braid, and with it she wore the most fragile gold gloves, and carried a fan of delicate painted chicken skin.

'What jewels have you, child?' Lady Fulwood demanded when she came to inspect Bella.

'My uncle's jewels from India, but they are rather ornate. Otherwise I have only my mother's pearls,' Bella confessed.

'Eminently suitable for a young girl but hopeless with that dress. Will you wear diamonds? It isn't usual for a girl in her first season, but it's not your first season, and you're older than most of the chits and not the normal simpering miss.'

'I'd love to wear diamonds!' Bella declared, her eyes gleaming.

'Good, for I have just the thing. Fanny, fetch the old jewel case, the one I rarely use.'

When Fanny came back Lady Fulwood unlocked the wooden box and took out a large packet. She carefully unwrapped the silk outer covering and then layers and layers of tissue to reveal the most exquisite filigree gold necklace, with small, intricate and delicate clusters of diamonds representing flowers, some of them standing proud supported on almost invisible stems of gold.

'Oh, it's beautiful, but I daren't wear it!' Bella exclaimed, putting out a finger to touch the central large cluster gently.

'It belonged to my mother, and I've no use for such an ornament. It would look silly on my neck! Jane has plenty of her own, so I want you to borrow it, my dear. And don't worry your head about how fragile it looks, it isn't. Here, let me fasten it.'

So Bella wore the necklace, and knew it gave her an added glow of confidence. Every so often she would surreptitiously caress the central cluster of diamonds, as if it were a talisman. She could just glance down and see the stones gleaming in the lights of many candles, reflecting the gold and rose of her own gown and the many other colours of the gowns about her.

The musicale was as tedious as Lady Fulwood had predicted, and they were glad to leave early. The rout was far better attended, but the hostess had abandoned the receiving line before they arrived, and it was such a crush they never found her to announce their arrival or make their apologies on departure.

'She'll only be sure who was there when people send notes of thanks,' Lady Fulwood explained to her rather bemused companions as the carriage took them towards Grosvenor Square. 'It will be accounted a great success.'

A long line of carriages was queuing to deposit guests at the house where the ball was being held. Torches flamed, lighting up a large portion of the Square, and to either side of the awning groups of onlookers resisted all the attempts of two footmen to shoo them away.

Bella's shocked gaze roved over them. They were mostly wretchedly attired children strayed from the crowded tenements eastwards, nearer the old part of the City. She had never seen such abject poverty, even in the foul conditions of some Lancashire mill villages. And it was far too late for them to be out of their beds, she said indignantly.

Lady Fulwood shook her head. 'For many of them beds are unknown luxuries. They sleep in doorways and wherever else they can find shelter.'

The sight made her finger the necklace nervously. How could she justify wearing such finery and valuable jewels when these tiny children clearly hadn't enough to eat? She would start another of her houses somewhere near here, where there was country air and a few children at least could grow up in healthy surroundings.

It was half an hour before Lady Fulwood and her two young companions were being welcomed by their host and hostess, a stout couple who beamed jovially on their uninvited guests.

'You're most welcome, my dears. Your cousin's been a close friend for many years, and we've no shortage of men tonight,' Lady Trent announced proudly. 'Julia's already had more offers than we can count, despite having been in London for less than a month!' she added.

'Where is the child?'

'I sent her away to dance. No point in her standing here all night,' Sir George said heartily. 'Now you go away and find partners for yourselves, my dear young ladies. You should neither of you have difficulty in doing that.'

Lady Fulwood moved away, followed by Bella and Jane. The ballroom had been built out at the back of the house, and for this evening's ball it had been decorated with pale-green drapery, festooned with hundreds of yards of entwined branches of greenery and flowers. Huge tubs with full-grown trees and shrubs had been arranged artfully about the room to provide alcoves where the chaperons could sit and gossip, and an orchestra was playing on a dais at the far end. To one side open full-length windows led on to a narrow patio garden, lit with flambeaux, and opposite various anterooms had been set out with dozens of small tables as cardrooms and for refreshments.

Lady Fulwood progressed slowly along the perimeter of the room, stopping to introduce the girls to friends, and soon they each had several names written in their programmes. The cotillion which was just ending was followed by a waltz, and Jane was whisked away by a friend from the days before she'd married Philip.

Bella stood beside Lady Fulwood feeling rebellious. Whatever her thoughts about flouting the conventions of Society, she knew she dared not waltz until she'd been given express approval by the patronesses at Almack's. During her first season she had never been to that exclusive club, for her aunt did not have the sort of connections Lady Fulwood clearly did. She smiled wryly to herself. If she were never admitted into the highest ranks of Society in the first place she could hardly flout it as she half intended.

If Lady Fulwood was aware of Bella's feelings she ignored them, chatting to an elderly gentleman with a military bearing who was introduced to Bella as Major Wilkins. He knew her father, and demanded to be told in detail what Mr Trahearne had been doing in the last twenty years. Bella had little opportunity to watch the dancers as she responded, but just as the music came to an end with a gay flourish the major moved away and Bella turned to find herself looking straight into Lord Dorney's startled eyes.

She gulped, with a tremendous effort tore her gaze away, and with a further shock saw that he had his arm round the waist of the widow, Mrs Ford. That lady, last seen in mourning, was now dressed in a youthful blue gown, and looked scarcely more than twenty. She was smiling intimately up at him, unaware of Bella, and as Bella's eyes turned back towards Lord Dorney he swung his partner round and guided her across the floor to disappear into one of the refreshment rooms.

Chapter Nine

—◦◦◦—

DURING THE NEXT few dances for which, because they were not waltzes, Bella could accept invitations, she was thinking furiously. Mrs Ford was undeniably beautiful, and Lord Dorney might well be attracted to her. At the time of the accident to Felicity, when she had come to their rescue, she'd exhibited a calm efficiency which he would undoubtedly prefer to her own impetuous behaviour.

Then Bella recalled Mrs Ford's words when they'd met in Milsom Street. She had been going to stay with her sister in Mount Street. Lady Fulwood would be sure to know her. Even if Lord Dorney condemned her and Mrs Ford preferred to forget the acquaintance, she could hardly snub the guests of a neighbour.

How this could help Bella's own plans was unclear. She herself was unsure of what she intended. Half of her wanted to throw all caution to the winds and defy Society, but she also secretly hoped that Lord Dorney might, could she but explain to him, understand her actions and forgive her. Bella decided with characteristic optimism that it could do no harm if she were to meet Mrs Ford as soon as possible. When she escaped from her partner and went looking for the widow, however, Mrs Ford had vanished. So had Lord Dorney, and Bella went home in a state of suppressed fury tinged with anxiety that kept her awake for the remainder of the night.

There was no opportunity the following morning to talk to Jane, for Lady Fulwood swept them both off to Bond Street to replenish their wardrobes. After a nuncheon of fruit and ham the dressmaker came to begin work on the several ballgowns Lady Fulwood insisted were absolutely essential.

Fortunately that evening their hostess was engaged to dine and play cards with an old crony, and regretfully she decided she could not cancel this engagement.

'Have an early night, my dears. You look tired, Bella. You must be rested for tomorrow since I plan to take you to call on a few friends. In the evening we're going to the theatre, and afterwards to a reception.'

'Thank goodness for a moment to ourselves,' Bella exclaimed, as they left the dinner table and went up to the drawing-room.

'It has been rather strenuous,' Jane agreed with a laugh. 'Did you enjoy the ball?'

'Did you see Lord Dorney with Mrs Ford?' Bella demanded, ignoring the question.

'No! Where?'

'At the ball, dancing together. After he saw me they must have left. I couldn't find either of them later.'

'Why did you look for them?' Jane asked apprehensively.

'Why shouldn't I?'

'You must have had a reason. Bella, you can't go in pursuit of him, it isn't at all the thing!'

'I wasn't,' Bella began, and then she stopped. 'I don't know what I meant to do,' she confessed. 'It just seemed terribly important that I spoke to them. Do you recall Mrs Ford said she was staying in Mount Street?'

'With her sister? I'd forgotten.'

'Lady Fulwood will know them, doubtless. Jane, I must make him talk to me, and I can do it through them if he's friendly with Mrs Ford. If we meet there he can't possibly cut me. He'll have to speak!'

'He won't speak alone with you, and even if he did what good would it do to talk to him?' Jane asked. 'You couldn't give him any better explanation than you did in Bath. Forget him, Bella, and hope to find someone else.'

'I don't want anyone else,' Bella said obstinately. 'I'll make him listen! I'll force him to understand why I changed my name.'

She would not be moved from this stance despite all Jane's arguments, and her cousin was quite out of charity with her by the time the tea tray was brought.

'You're going to look foolish,' she warned. 'If you spend your time pursuing a man who doesn't want you not only will everyone gossip and laugh, you'll disgust any other men who might be interested in you.'

'I don't want any other men to be interested in me!' Bella declared heatedly. 'I won't marry anyone except Lord Dorney. I know he'd understand if only I could explain properly, now he's got over the shock, which I quite see must have been severe at first.'

As Bella began to repeat the same arguments, Jane, saying she was too weary to argue, left her and retired to bed. Bella sat on beside the drawing-room fire, wondering exactly what she was to do, and devising schemes for bringing herself and Lord Dorney together.

She knew only that her most fervent desire was to marry him. No other man would satisfy her. Not since she'd known him. If she couldn't have him she didn't care about her fortune, or the opinion of Society, or how she spent the rest of her life.

Would Lady Fulwood be sympathetic and, more important, helpful? If she confided in the older lady could she expect advice and assistance?

On the whole Bella decided she would be more likely to advise turning her attentions to other men. She wouldn't understand the total repugnance Bella felt at the very thought of marriage with anyone else.

Bella concluded she would have to be devious in using her hostess's numerous friends so as to contrive meetings with Lord Dorney. For a start she would announce she knew Mrs Ford, and hatch plans for furthering the acquaintance. She would have to confess her masquerade to that lady, but she would try and make a joke of it. If Lord Dorney had not told Mrs Ford about her there was the possibility she could induce Mrs Ford to look on it as a harmless prank, even to understand the reasons for it. After all, she had admitted her own marriage to a much older man had been one of convenience. Surely she would sympathize with Bella's repugnance at being sought for her money alone.

Satisfied with this hope Bella took herself to bed. In the morning she hovered on the landing when Fanny took in Lady Fulwood's breakfast tray and asked if she might speak with her.

'Come in, child,' Lady Fulwood called.

Bella blinked in surprise when she saw the bedroom. Lady Fulwood's enormous bed was draped with filmy gauze hangings, descending from a circular rail attached to the ceiling. It looked rather like a superior wigwam, pictures of which in one of her father's books had entranced Bella as a child. The notion made Bella choke back a snort of laughter. Lady Fulwood in no way resembled an Indian squaw.

She was propped up on a veritable mountain of pillows, their peach-coloured satin covers a delectable setting for her nightgown of deep green silk. She wore a nightcap of the same green silk, edged with Brussels lace, and a pile of unopened invitations was scattered over the peach satin sheets.

'Come and sit beside me.' Lady Fulwood gestured to a low chair near the bed. 'Are you rested? Have you had breakfast?'

Bella nodded. 'Yes, thank you. I came to ask you if you know a Mrs Ford, who is staying with her sister in Mount Street.'

'I don't recall the lady. What's her sister's name, child?'

'I don't know.'

'What does your Mrs Ford look like?'

'She's beautiful, about five and twenty, with russet hair and green eyes.'

'That sounds rather like Lady Belstead, she's got a flaming head of hair. They could be sisters.'

'You know her?' Bella breathed a sigh of relief.

'We've met, but she and Sir William are far younger than I am, and move in a different set. Do you want to meet this Mrs Ford? Is she a friend from Lancashire?'

Bella explained how they'd met, and although Lady Fulwood gave her a searching glance, she agreed to make an early opportunity of calling on Lady Belstead.

Satisfied, Bella asked permission to take Rags walking in the Park.

'Of course you may,' Lady Fulwood said. She'd been as welcoming to the dog as she had to Bella, stipulating only that he be confined to basement quarters. 'If Jane or one of the maids accompanies you it's quite permissible to walk there at any time. You ride, I suppose?'

'Yes, and I've been meaning to ask if I might buy a horse, and one for Jane too, and stable them somewhere nearby? And a pair of carriage horses. I mean to drive myself. Our groom Jackson will look after them.'

'My groom Masters will tell him where to go. I've a staid old hack, but I don't ride much these days. Keep him out of sentiment, I suppose. Masters hasn't enough to do with just old Sergeant and my carriage pair. You want to cut a dash. Have you driven a pair before?'

Bella shook her head. 'No, but surely driving a pair isn't so very difficult.'

'Masters could teach you to drive if you wish. I don't suppose your father did. He used to be a capital whip, but from what I remember of him he hadn't any patience with learners.'

'Papa?' Bella exclaimed in amazement at this new light shed on her scholarly father. 'He never drives himself now, but I drove a pony and trap at home.'

'Pity he couldn't have taught you, but perhaps you've inherited his skill.'

As she and Jane walked towards the Park, with Rags secured on a leash to which he took great exception, Bella's mind was busy with plans. If she rode or drove or walked the dog in the Park every day there must surely be opportunities for meeting Lord Dorney.

She was completely wrapped up in her scheming, paying no attention to Jane's desultory remarks about the unusually mild weather and the people and equipages they saw. They had scarcely entered the gates before Rags managed to wriggle out of his collar and dart off across the grass.

'Rags, come back!' Jane called, but the dog, revelling in his sudden freedom after days of being cooped up in carriages and kitchens, merely ran faster.

'Confound him!' Bella exclaimed. 'He really is a country dog. Oh, look, what's he doing?'

Rags was prancing at the heels of a magnificent black horse, which haughtily ignored the irritation, unlike the skittish grey mare beside him. This animal was doing its best to rear, and being thwarted in this endeavour only by the firm hand of the black horse's rider on the bridle.

'Rags!' Bella shouted, running across the grass towards her dog.

He turned towards her, his long tongue hanging out of his mouth as he panted with happiness. She went dangerously close to the restive mare in order to scoop Rags up into the safety of her arms, and only when she had him safe did she turn to apologize to the riders.

Lord Dorney was glaring down at her in fury.

'How dare you let that undisciplined mongrel loose amongst horses which aren't accustomed to having their heels snapped at!' he demanded.

As the familiar tones struck her ear Bella looked mutely up at him.

'Lord Dorney! I – I'm sorry. I didn't mean to let him loose. I don't want him trampled on!' she said in a stronger voice.

'It's Miss Collins, isn't it? I didn't know you'd left Bath,' said the rider of the grey, which had calmed down now Rags was under control.

'Everyone seems to have left Bath,' Bella said, suppressing a groan of dismay as she looked up into Lady Andrews' mocking face.

'It was fortunate I was riding Felicity's horse,' Lady Andrews went on. 'She's still unable to ride, but if she'd had another accident it would have been too bad! I think we'd best return to Hill Street,' she added, turning with a smile to Lord Dorney. 'The lawyers will be there soon, with the drafts of the settlements.'

'It was as though she was accusing me of causing the other accident!' Bella said angrily, as she turned on her heel and stalked off towards Jane, who had recognized the riders earlier and prudently remained at a distance.

They retreated from the scene, trying to lose themselves in the throng of pedestrians taking the air.

'He was furious, but at least he spoke to me,' Bella said in a small voice after a few moments of silence. 'And what settlements did she mean?'

'I can't imagine. But is his anger an improvement?' Jane asked. 'Bella, try to forget Lord Dorney.'

Bella shook her head, but for the next few days forbore to mention him, even when they caught a glimpse of him in the distance at one or other of the functions they attended.

'I need to go and see some people in Highgate,' Bella said to Jane one morning. 'I've just had a letter from Mr Jenkins that he's heard about a couple there who are looking after two orphaned children, and who he thinks would be suitable for another of my houses. He's written to tell them to expect me.'

'Let Jackson drive you. Lady Fulwood is happy to lend us her carriage if she doesn't want it herself. But please excuse me, I have so many letters to write.'

Bella set off an hour later, and they found the cottage where the Floods lived, in a small lane just off the main road into Highgate village.

Bella sat in the chaise looking at it. The small garden was neat, full of straight rows of newly planted vegetables and clumps of rhubarb and herbs. Two apple trees were in blossom, and primroses showed in the grass patch surrounding them. Chickens, confined within a run whose walls were made of plaited rushes, pecked busily, and Bella could hear the grunting of pigs from a sty out of sight beyond the cottage. A rope hung down from one sturdy branch, and a boy of Jed's age was attempting to climb it, watched by a small, plump woman who had paused from her digging.

Bella climbed down from the chaise. 'Please wait for me, Jackson.'

The woman had turned and, wiping her hands on the sacking apron round her waist, hurried to the gate in the fence surrounding the garden.

'Miss Trahearne, would it be?' she asked, and Bella detected the accent of Yorkshire in her voice.

'Yes. Mrs Flood, I think?'

'Come in, do. Mr Jenkins wrote you'd be along soon. Mr Flood's along at Widow Brent's, digging her garden for her, but Benny can fetch him in a trice.'

She turned and spoke to the lad, who looked curiously at Bella before running off down the lane. Then she ushered Bella into a small but pretty room at the front of the cottage.

'Is Benny your own?' Bella asked.

'No, we've none of our own. He's me sister's lad, and when she and her man died he was just a baby, so we took him in. What else could we do? But he's a good lad. Then we was asked to take in twins whose poor mother died giving birth. Her husband was killed, in the army, he was. It's better for them than they great orphanages. Good country air, too. We moved here after Mr Flood had his accident and couldn't work on the new docks no more. They're out somewhere gathering wood for the fires.'

Bella listed to the breathless recital. Mrs Flood was like one of the village women at home, full of talk whenever she had the opportunity.

'Mr Jenkins tells me you'd like to look after more children, but you haven't the room,' she managed to interrupt.

'Well, we've just the one bedroom, you see, and it wouldn't be right to crowd more of us into it. Not now they're growing. I know there's families where ten or more sleep in one room, but that wouldn't be giving the children a better chance. And we can't rightly afford it any road, we've only the few shillings Mr Flood can earn doing odd jobs. He's not strong enough since the accident to do a proper job. We grow most of our food, we manage fine, and we decided to help a few as much as we could.'

'But if you had more room, and a proper wage, you could look after more?'

'Mr Jenkins said you might help.'

'You rent this cottage?'

'Aye. How could we afford to buy it?'

'I see there's another next door. Is it the same landlord? Would he sell both to me? They're close together, you could build another room or two between and make one big house. Or would you prefer to have one of the new houses they're building, closer to London?'

Mr Flood, a large, red-faced man, had entered the room with Benny as she spoke.

'It'd be a pity to lose the garden, miss,' he said slowly. 'We get plenty of good food from it. And they new houses don't have much garden space.'

Bella introduced herself, and soon they were deep in discussion of possibilities. She found herself liking the Floods even more than she had the couples running her other houses, for their solid common sense and sheer goodness, and determined to help them as much as she could. This sort of work would, in part, make up to her for the loss of happiness and Lord Dorney, if she did not succeed in changing his mind.

In the few free hours between what to Jane seemed a constant round of shopping, morning calls, evening parties and sessions with the dressmaker, Bella found time to go with Jackson to inspect and buy a lively chestnut mare for herself and a grey gelding for Jane. She rose early and persuaded Jackson to give her driving lessons in the Park before many people were abroad.

'I drove a gig round the lanes at home in Lancashire,' she explained, 'but our pony was old and fat and couldn't have bolted if he'd wanted to. I imagine driving in all this traffic in the streets, and in the Park, is a little more difficult.'

'Yes, Miss Bella, it is,' Jackson said, and Bella ignored the grin he tried to hide.

To her delight she proved an apt pupil, and was eager to purchase an elegant curricle and a matched pair of black Welsh cobs to pull it. The horse she was using was sprightly, far more so than the pony she was used to, but she was ashamed to be seen in the carriage he pulled, which she considered to be no better than a country gig. She was highly indignant when Jackson, supported by Lady Fulwood's coachman, Masters, tried to deter her from buying a pair, for she had dreams of exciting awe and admiration as she handled them successfully.

Masters, as a result of a private consultation with Lady Fulwood, persuaded her she needed more practice first, and borrowed a frisky pair and a curricle from a friend, the groom of a noted whip presently out of town. After a lively and inconclusive tussle with them Bella conceded she would merely look foolish if she could not control a pair. Meekly she agreed she needed more experience before emulating the most famous whips of the day, promising herself that as soon as she felt confident she would acquire the showiest pair in London.

It was several days before Lady Fulwood found an opportunity of calling upon Lady Belstead, and to Bella's satisfaction no one else but Mrs Ford was present when the footman announced them. Soon she was able to move to sit beside Mrs Ford.

'I heard the story about your change of name in Bath, Miss Trahearne,' that lady said with a smile, her green eyes twinkling.

'Am I being very much condemned?' Bella asked frankly.

'By the older and staider people, perhaps,' Mrs Ford reported, 'but the younger ones on the whole think it a great lark, and rather admire you for it when they understand the reason.'

'Lord Dorney isn't old and staid, but he'll never forgive me,' Bella said gloomily.

'His background has made him peculiarly sensitive to deception,' Mrs Ford explained softly. 'Also, I'm afraid, wary of heiresses. You know his family's history, of course?'

'I do now, but at the time I couldn't understand.'

'He's a very different man from both his father and brother,' she said slowly.

Bella stole a glance at her. She was smiling reminiscently, her lips curving so deliciously that Bella's heart dropped. How could any man not immediately want to kiss them? She was beautiful, kind, and even being helpful to someone she might have regarded as a rival.

She pulled up her thoughts sharply. How could she possibly rival this lovely woman? Why Lord Dorney had singled her out in Bath remained a mystery. He might have been on the point of offering, but he couldn't have cared for her or he would not have turned away so easily.

At that moment more callers arrived, two men superficially so alike they had to be brothers. Both were fair haired, tall and slim, with light blue eyes and aquiline noses. They were in their early thirties, perhaps a year separating them, but the elder one's face was far more lined, and he walked with a slight limp. His eyes were keen, his glance piercing, while the younger, although smiling in a friendly fashion, had an abstracted, almost vacuous look on his face.

'Major Ross and Mr Frederick Ross,' the footman intoned.

Lady Belstead welcomed them warmly, and they were introduced. The major, who seemed to know Mrs Ford well, greeted her with a pleased smile and a query about her house. Mr Ross, after a vague, but somehow apprehensive smile at everyone else, promptly sat beside Bella and engaged her in a quiet conversation.

The major moved on and sat next to Jane, remarking he had met Philip several years ago.

'I came on his ship on my way home from the Peninsula, wounded, I'm afraid,' he added, indicating his leg. 'A good officer, the navy could do with more like him,' he opined. 'Is he coming on furlough soon?'

'I hope so; he is due for leave, but I'm not sure when,' Jane replied. 'He's been very busy taking troops out to India.'

Soon afterwards Lady Belstead demanded Jane's opinion of some swatches of material.

'I can't decide whether the colours shriek at my hair,' she said with a laugh. 'What do you think?'

The major turned to Bella, who had been quietly observing the newcomers, and asked how she was enjoying her visit to London. She found him a man of decided opinions, knowledgeable about the situation in India, which she would have expected in a military man, but also about political developments at home.

'You seem to know everyone,' she commented, after he had mentioned a recent conversation with several members of the government.

He shrugged. 'My family connections, of course, and then I make an effort to learn all the latest news whenever I'm in London. The normal gossip of London drawing-rooms bores me, I fear, although one has to meet people.'

'Is your brother in the army?' Bella asked, glancing across at Mr Ross, who had remained close to Mrs Ford, apparently absorbed in their conversation.

'Frederick?' The major gave a snort of derision. 'He thinks himself a poet, of all things. A second Byron. He says he's writing an epic in verse for the stage. An excuse for being lazy, I fear. I trust you won't encourage him as Mrs Ford does,' he added. 'I haven't been able to impress on her the folly of letting him imagine people take him seriously. His scribbling will never amount to more than a few vapid couplets and a sonnet or two.'

Lady Fulwood then rose to go and Bella, disappointed in her desire to meet Lord Dorney, came reluctantly to her feet.

'May I call on you? We could drive in the Park if your hostess permits,' the major suggested, bending low over Bella's hand, and she nodded permission.

'A conquest, my dear,' Lady Fulwood said drily as they walked the few yards to their own house. 'An old family, not a great deal of money, but enough to maintain two houses and permit Frederick to play at being a poet.'

'Isn't he any good? His brother was far from complimentary.'

'He published a slim volume last year which was well received, I believe, but I know nothing about poetry. I enjoy the theatre better than ballet, or the opera, I fear, and I like to read a good novel when I have leisure. But I rarely read poetry, unless it's something everyone enthuses about, like *Childe Harold*. One has to read that, of course.'

'I liked Lady Belstead,' Jane changed the subject. 'She asked me to call again to advise her on some dress patterns.'

'A compliment to your good taste, my dear. Is that chaise driving away from my house, do you think? It seems we've just missed a visitor.'

But when, instead of the butler, the footman opened the door to them and eyed them in some dismay until he recognized them, a scene of confusion met their eyes. In the narrow hall were two trunks, the maids were carrying some small items of luggage upstairs, and the butler was sharply directing a rather bemused boot boy to pick up the other end of a trunk and mind the table, or he'd find himself in trouble.

'Goodness, Simpkins, who's arrived with all this luggage?' Lady Fulwood demanded, but before the harassed butler could reply the visitor appeared from the morning-room at the back of the house, where he seemed to have taken refuge.

'It really isn't a great deal of luggage, Lady F,' he said with a laugh. 'You're not going to send me away, or deprive me of any of my very essential clothes, I trust? Not the action of the loving godmother I know you are!'

'Richard! Welcome, dear boy. I knew you were in town.'

'Yes, I spent a few days with Sir Daniel, but he's been sent on a mission to Paris.'

'You're here now. I must make you known to my other guests. Jane dear, my godson, Richard, Lord Dorney. I sent him to call on you the last time he was in Lancashire, Jane. I hope he obeyed me? Richard, Lady Hodder and Miss Trahearne.'

Bemused, Jane shook her head. 'I'm sorry. In Lancashire? When did you call on me?'

'Lady Hodder? Another change of name. But I understood you were Mrs Grant? I called when you were out, I'm afraid, and left the book.'

'I was. Mrs Grant, I mean. Philip had only inherited the title a few months before. I wondered who had left the book. Bates – that's my butler – had forgotten your name.'

'I probably forgot, and called you Grant,' said Lady Fulwood, laughing. 'I can't think of Philip with a title.'

'We met in Bath, not Lancashire, Lady F,' Lord Dorney said quietly, 'although I wasn't aware that Lady Hodder and Miss Trahearne were intending to visit you.'

He bowed briefly to Bella, standing rigidly beside her hostess, then smiled bleakly at Jane. She, looking up into the narrowed eyes, their expression hard, and shivered. How could Bella maintain she loved such a stern man?

For an endless moment Bella thought he was about to order the butler, halfway up the stairs by now and still admonishing the boot boy in frantic anguished undertones to be careful, to bring his luggage down again. Instead, after a searching gaze at Jane he shrugged slightly.

'It seems we are to be fellow guests,' he said calmly. 'I trust we can forget our differences and behave with circumspection.'

'Indeed,' Bella managed to reply. What did he expect? Her to fling herself into his arms with cries of rapture, or run screaming in terror from the house? She would show him! She'd be calm, dignified, and never mention Bath.

Chapter Ten

—❦—

LADY FULWOOD HAD planned to take Jane and Bella to the theatre that evening, which meant dining early. Lord Dorney begged her not to change her arrangements, saying he could perfectly well dine at his club.

Bella had no notion what the play was about, for she spent the entire evening speculating on how this latest turn of events could affect her. Would being in the same house as Lord Dorney help her own plans?

Waking early after a restless night she found herself the first to arrive in the breakfast-room. Abstractedly she helped herself to bacon and kidneys, then sat without eating, crumbling pellets of bread on her plate.

She jumped nervously when the door opened and Lord Dorney appeared. He bowed stiffly and, after a short pause during which she could see he was having an intense inward struggle, filled his plate and took a seat opposite Bella.

'I'm so sorry Rags upset the horses the other morning,' she said breathlessly, and he frowned, for the moment forgetting that episode. 'He wriggled out of his collar, you see,' she tried to explain.

'You've no business keeping an undisciplined dog in London,' Lord Dorney said sternly.

'I know, but no one else wanted him, and I could hardly turn him loose again in Bath!' Bella responded indignantly, her unwonted meekness rapidly retreating in the face of this lack of reason.

'You could have gone back to the country.'

'What? Why the devil should I?' she demanded, forgetting to use ladylike language in her fury. 'I have as much right here in London as you do, my lord!'

'Forgive me, I meant only that you could have taken him to your own home, since there must be people able to care for him. What you do otherwise is, of course, none of my business.'

Bella contemplated appealing to him then, but he looked so grim that, abandoning her by now cold breakfast, she cravenly escaped. As a result she fumed impotently until evening, when for once they had no engagements and were to dine at home.

She took especial care over her appearance as she dressed for dinner, choosing one of her new gowns in a particularly delicate shade of primrose, and driving Mary to distraction the number of times she changed her mind over details such as the slippers she wanted, or the style of her hair.

Conversation at dinner was rather strained. Lady Fulwood appeared to notice nothing amiss, but although Jane did her best to respond naturally, Lord Dorney's remarks were brief and Bella's virtually nonexistent.

'I saw your cousin Alexander's betrothal announced in *The Times* this morning,' Lady Fulwood said suddenly. 'Who is she? Has she any money?'

'A competence; it matches his own, which I always feel is the ideal situation,' he replied, with a glance at Bella. 'She lives in Bath. A mere chit, but of unexceptional family. She'll do for him, she has looks and is compliant, but without too many brains or opinions of her own. She's very young, but Alexander maintains he knows his mind and he's in no mood to delay. They plan to marry as soon as it can be arranged.'

For a while they discussed this, and then there was an awkward pause. Lady Fulwood broke it.

'I'm told Bella's shaping up admirably as a whip, in Masters' opinion. Why don't you drive out with her, Richard, and give her some instruction? You've always been one of the best whips in London.'

He looked aghast, but Lady Fulwood was looking at him expectantly. Making the best of it he turned to Bella and smiled stiffly.

'I should be delighted, Miss Trahearne.'

'Good, you can go tomorrow morning, both of you are early risers,' Lady Fulwood said complacently.

Bella bit back the excuses she'd been about to make. Here was a heaven-sent opportunity of having him to herself, in a situation where they could talk, she could explain her motives more clearly, and perhaps they might iron out the differences between them. Why, then, had she been about to tell him he wasn't obliged to carry out Lady Fulwood's imperious commands? Was she afraid of him?

She eyed him curiously as he turned to talk with his godmother, and tried to disentangle her confused emotions. Seeing him again had evoked all the longing she'd experienced in Bath. From the very first moment of their meeting she had known she loved him. It wasn't his looks, for although he was handsome she had met other men equally attractive in face and figure.

Her later knowledge of him, his kindness, their ability – once – to talk of anything they wished, might have explained a gradual falling in love. Those were characteristics not immediately apparent, yet she had known instantly he was the only man for her. When he had kissed her she had momentarily forgotten their disagreements and surrendered to a state of sheer bliss, natural and inevitable. Had he not felt the same? Why had he kissed her? Did men normally kiss women they were angry with?

She shook her head in bewilderment. She loved him, and if she were entirely truthful she was a little afraid too. She, Rosabella Trahearne, who had never before admitted to fear, was now experiencing it. Then a thought struck her: it was not fear of him, but fear of hurting him, fear *for* him, that produced in her this unaccustomed sensibility.

Lost in contemplation of this phenomenon, she did not at first respond when Lord Dorney spoke to her later in the drawing-room.

'I am promised to friends all day tomorrow, but on the following morning I am free. Shall I give you this driving lesson Lady Fulwood thinks I'm fit to administer?' he asked.

'Oh. Yes. That is, if you'd rather not ...' she stammered, and mentally kicked herself for her ineptitude. She didn't wish to give him an excuse to evade her, she'd already disposed of that impulse.

Fortunately he cut her short. 'I did agree,' he stated. 'Do you wish to drive the horse you're used to? It would be best, I think. Best also if we go early, before there are too many people about.'

'Don't you trust me not to upset you?' Bella demanded, stung out of her abashed mood. 'Or is it rather that you don't wish to be seen with me?'

He eyed her enigmatically, and she felt the colour rising in her cheeks.

'What possible reason could there be for that, my dear Miss Trahearne?'

She dropped her eyes, clenching her hands so that the knuckles grew white.

'You know perfectly well,' she muttered, so quietly that he had to bend forward to catch the whisper.

'Oh, you mean that unfortunate episode in Bath? But Miss Collins never was, and you are an entirely new creature, are you not, Miss Trahearne? How could our being seen together have any effect on either of us?'

Lord Dorney had already eaten when Bella came down two days later, and she was told he was in his room. She had dressed carefully in a wine-red pelisse and jaunty, military style hat for her driving lesson. She had a cravat frothing with lace about her neck, and after gulping a cup of chocolate and toying with a thin slice of bread and butter decided she could not eat anything. She wandered out into the hall and was pulling on serviceable leather gauntlets when he descended the stairs.

He smiled briefly and coldly at her. 'Shall we go? I see you're ready.'

Masters had brought the small carriage to the front door, and after Lord Dorney assisted Bella into it and leapt in after her, the groom handed the reins to him.

'Will you need me, my lord?'

'No, thank you. He doesn't look as though I'd be unable to control him.'

Bella stifled a giggle. She was having difficulty in preventing herself from trembling with nervousness.

'He's inclined to pull to the left,' Masters warned, as he stood away from the horse's head, and Lord Dorney nodded his thanks as he set off towards the Park.

For the next hour, as Lord Dorney instructed, demonstrated, criticized, and very occasionally praised Bella's handling of the ribbons, she had no leisure to think of anything but her driving. He was an excellent tutor, explaining what he wanted and why in clear, unambiguous terms, and when she failed to get it right the first time, analysing what had gone wrong. She almost always corrected her mistakes at the second attempt, and by the end of the hour felt as though she had made immense strides.

'I think that's enough for one day,' he said at length, when they had once again reached the far side of the Park. Bella turned impetuously towards him.

'Oh, but—' she began, and then paused.

'But what?'

He was smiling down at her in quite a friendly fashion, and Bella plucked up her courage.

'I hoped we could talk,' she said diffidently.

'Oh?' was the unpromising response, and he took the reins and turned the carriage to point towards home.

'I wanted to apologize. I didn't mean any serious deception,' she began. 'In Bath, I mean. It's just that I was so angry at being courted for my money rather than myself,' she finished with a rush.

'I understand how you felt, even if I disapprove of your actions,' he said, with a chill in his voice that made Bella shiver. 'I, too, must apologize for my intemperate response. Perhaps you've been told my family history?'

'Yes, and I do understand now why you felt as you did,' she said, a note of eagerness in her voice. 'Please, now we've both apologized, may we continue – friends?'

'It would be churlish not to behave as such, particularly since we are guests in the same house,' he replied after a brief pause. 'I believe we can do so amicably. Was it your fear, Miss Trahearne, that I would cut you and cause comment?'

'No it wasn't!' she burst out angrily. 'You know very well what I meant! I thought, in Bath, we truly cared for one another. I hoped that silly misunderstanding could be cleared up. I wanted—'

'Yes, Miss Trahearne, what was it you wanted of me?'

'To start again,' she managed. 'But matters are not the same as I thought they were.'

'Unfortunately things can never be the same between us after what has passed.'

Bella's patience, never strong, snapped.

'I thought you loved me!' she stormed. 'I know you were about to offer for me! Then because you discover the abominable fact that I have a larger fortune than you imagined, and because of the stupidity of people I've never even met, you turn against me! Is that just? Is it fair? Is it fair to me? I thought we could talk about anything!' she ended on a wail of distress, furiously blinking away the tears of anger.

'Do I understand you are offering for me?' he asked, in tones of such astonished disgust that Bella threw all caution and sense to the winds.

'I was,' she retorted, 'but I must have been mad! How could I ever have imagined I loved a stiff-necked, pompous bore like you! Pray give me the reins, sir. I won't drive a yard further with you.'

Rashly she snatched at the reins and he swung them away from her grasp. The horse, startled and unable to interpret this odd signal, and in addition made nervous by Bella's raised voice, took exception to what was going on and set off at an uncontrolled gallop.

'Sit back and hold on!' Lord Dorney commanded, and Bella was so aghast at what she'd done she obeyed speechlessly, clinging to the side of the seat as Lord Dorney calmly and quickly brought the animal under control.

The involuntary gallop had brought them close to the Stanhope Gate, and from there it was a short distance to Mount Street. Apart from the stifled, muttered apology Bella forced herself to give, they accomplished the drive in silence.

'Can you get down by yourself? I can't leave the horse, he's still excited. Pray give my apologies to Lady Fulwood,' Lord Dorney said to Bella as he drew up outside the house. 'I'll take the carriage round to the stables, and then I have other matters to attend to. Your servant, Miss Trahearne.'

*

'I'll show him! How dare he talk to me like that! I'll show him how little I care!' Bella was still fuming half an hour later as she strode up and down Jane's bedroom.

'Oh Bella, forget the wretched man!' Jane pleaded. 'It's hopeless to try and win him back, and from what you say now I don't think you really want to.'

'I hate him!' Bella declared. 'He was odious, he dressed me down as though I were some lowly servant taking liberties. I'll ignore him. I'll make him regret speaking to me like that! I – I – oh, Jane, what shall I do?'

'Find someone else,' Jane recommended.

'Yes, I'll do just that! I'll show him!'

Jane's apprehensions over this declaration were fully justified during the next few weeks. Bella was deaf to all her protests, and when Jane turned for help to Lady Fulwood, who had by now made her own deductions about the previous state of affairs between Bella and her godson, the only advice she received was an amused recommendation to leave well alone.

Lord Dorney spent little time in the house, for he had his own friends and social engagements, so they met more frequently at balls and other houses than in Mount Street. Bella found the situation intolerable, but could find no satisfactory way of changing it.

Fortunately for her standing with the *ton* she had already received vouchers for Almack's, and been granted permission by the patronesses to waltz. Otherwise, Jane knew, she would have flouted all convention by accepting invitations regardless.

Even so, her outrageously flirtatious behaviour raised many eyebrows, and drew to her many men, including some who were married, and others who were uninterested in marriage or her fortune, as well as dozens of impecunious suitors, young and old.

Bella seemed no longer to care whether she was courted for her money. Nor did she appear to notice the black looks cast at her by neglected wives, and debutantes whose prospective suitors appeared to be more interested in the latest heiress than in them, or hear the often deliberately loud comments about her fast behaviour.

She accepted all the homage offered, appeared to believe all the flattery, danced every dance and left twice as many would-be partners disappointed. During the daytime she drove or rode out with as many of her suitors as she possibly could, and seemed to have no time for rest or quiet reflection.

If Jane noticed that she was livelier and more intent on attracting attention when Lord Dorney was present, she kept the reflection to herself. Nor did she comment to Bella when, as occasionally happened, Lord Dorney asked Bella to dance. As a guest in the same house it would have been commented upon if he had not, she told herself, although she did not venture this opinion to Bella. It didn't mean he had changed his mind about the girl.

Bella had considered refusing to dance with him, but the old longing had been too fierce. She had even, on one occasion when he had arrived late at a ball, ruthlessly struck out from her programme the names of two of her promised partners and granted him the dances.

He rarely asked to waltz with her, and she was on the whole grateful. On those occasions his proximity, the clasp of his hand about her waist, and his lips so close to hers evoked a feeling of delirium so intense that she wondered how she had not swooned.

They talked of trivialities.

'You are well, I trust?'

'The rout last night was a squeeze, was it not?'

'Did you enjoy the opera?'

'I thought the soprano too weak.'

Eventually Bella plucked up the courage to mention her driving.

'I've been receiving instruction from several gentlemen,' she told him as they stood sipping lemonade at Almack's one evening, after he had danced with her. 'None has taught me so much as you did in just one lesson.'

'You are not, I trust, suggesting a repetition of that lesson? As I recall, you wished most vehemently never to drive with me again.'

Bella's face flamed. 'Do you have to remind me continually of every rash word or deed?' she demanded angrily.

'I apologize,' he said stiffly. 'I saw you driving most competently along Piccadilly this morning, and noted how much you've improved.'

'I didn't see you,' she was startled into saying.

'I was on my way to my club. I frequently spend part of the morning there.'

'Is that White's?' Bella asked eagerly. 'The one with the bow window.'

'Yes, it's a great attraction,' he replied, amused and speaking more naturally than for some time.

'I do so wish to see it, but Jane says I mustn't venture into St James's Street.'

'It isn't advisable.'

'Why not?'

'Ladies do not care to be seen in a quarter of the town almost exclusively occupied by men,' he said dismissively, and Bella glanced speculatively up at him through discreetly lowered eyelashes.

'Stuffy!' she remarked, and smiled at him sweetly as her next partner came to claim her and she was whisked away.

The next morning Bella summarily dismissed the swain who had hoped to ride out with her, giving the specious excuse that she had the headache. Half an hour later she surreptitiously left the house and went to the stables where she gave Masters orders to harness the carriage.

'Do you drive alone, Miss Trahearne?' he asked worriedly as he slowly complied. 'If so, I ought to come with you. Jackson's not here, he's taken one of the horses to be shod.'

'Lady Fulwood needs you to drive her to visit a friend,' she replied. 'You know I'm safe to drive on my own now.'

As soon as the carriage was ready she scrambled in, settled the skirts of her new, mannish driving coat which possessed several daring capes, and made certain her jaunty little hat, of the same olive green, and adorned with a perky feather, was securely attached to her curls.

Before Masters could argue further she gave her horse the office, and set off at a sedate pace towards the Park. Masters looked after her with a worried frown, but she had chosen her time well, for at that moment Lady Fulwood's footman appeared to say his mistress was ready, and would Masters bring the carriage round at once.

He could do nothing, and did not feel it his duty to inform Lady Fulwood of her young guest's behaviour. It was true she drove well, for she seemed to have inherited the skill of her father, but she was inexperienced. However, she could come to little harm in the Park. He dismissed her from his mind and concentrated on negotiating the crush as he drove towards the less fashionable part of the town where Lady Fulwood's old friend lived.

Bella, meanwhile, once out of Masters' sight, swung into a street leading towards Piccadilly.

The traffic was much heavier than she was accustomed to, and the horse was restive. Her nervousness was transmitted along the ribbons and caused him to break into a trot too fast for her comfort as she joined the flow of vehicles. By the time she had negotiated a dray, narrowly missing a stage coach travelling recklessly in the opposite direction, and squeezed with inches to spare between two high perch phaetons whose occupants, Corinthians of the highest order, had halted to engage in a conversation, she was beginning to wish she had never begun this expedition.

She made the turn into St James's Street without mishap, and breathed a sigh of relief to find it comparatively deserted. The horse had settled down and she brought it more under control, slowing down in order to stare about her.

So this was where all the gentlemen's clubs were, she thought, looking eagerly for the famous bow window.

She saw it at the very moment she heard someone calling her name, and with a startled jerk on the reins brought the carriage to a halt.

'Miss Trahearne, are you lost? You shouldn't be here, really you shouldn't!'

'Major Ross!' Bella exclaimed. 'Oh, I – that is—'

'Did the horse run away with you? He seems far too spirited for you to control. Would you allow me to drive you back home?'

'I can control him perfectly well, thank you!' Bella replied indignantly, and suddenly became aware of several men who had stopped and were observing her with considerable interest. She coloured, for in their eyes she read either a speculative interest or outright condemnation.

Tossing her head she made to move on, but, before she could, someone sprang into the seat beside her. Bella gasped in alarm, and then began to protest as the reins were taken ruthlessly out of her hands and the newcomer shook the horse into motion.

'Be silent! You may explain this deplorable behaviour when I've driven you home!' Lord Dorney snapped, and Bella, aware that most of the spectators had heard him, subsided against the seat and stared stonily ahead of her.

Lord Dorney walked swiftly through the august portals of Whites, ignoring the jocular comments of two of his friends about the correct way to treat disobedient chits, and made his way to the library, where he found Alexander slouching in a chair, his head in his hands.

'Alex, I'm sorry to be late. An unavoidable delay, I'm afraid.'

Alexander glanced up. 'So I heard. A pretty woman's always going to be an excuse. Sorry! I'm out of sorts, Richard.'

Lord Dorney sat beside him. 'What is it?' he asked.

'Felicity! She and Lady Andrews have come to London to choose her bride clothes, so I came up too. She's accused me of not trusting her. How can she? I only want to be near her.'

'Nerves, my dear fellow. She's very young, and almost all brides have occasional doubts.'

For a moment Alexander looked hopeful, then he shook his head. 'That doesn't explain why she's been riding in the Park very early for three days running with that fop, Frederick Ross.'

'Has she, by Jove?' Lord Dorney looked thoughtful. 'I don't know her very well, but is she the sort of girl to be flattered by poets swearing devotion to her eyebrows or similar nonsense?'

'I didn't think so. She's always seemed very sensible in Bath.'

'Is this her first visit to London? Surely, if she hadn't accepted you, this would have been her come out?'

Alexander looked startled. 'I hadn't thought of that. She's been out in Bath society for a year.'

'Then perhaps her head has been a little turned by all the attention. She's a very pretty girl.'

'That could be it.' Alexander was looking more cheerful.

'Give her time, and be patient,' Lord Dorney advised. 'Have you fixed a date for the wedding?'

'The end of July, we thought. We didn't see any point in waiting; we know our own minds. At least, I thought we did.'

'It's to be in Bath?'

'Yes. Most of our friends live there. Richard, will you support me? I'd rather have you than anyone else.'

'Of course I will. Now forget your poet and don't quarrel with Felicity, and all will be well.'

Chapter Eleven

---⁕---

'Miss Bella, they're too lively for you,' Jackson protested. 'Nonsense.' Bella patted the nose of the dappled grey Welsh cob as he looked out from the stable door. 'They're beautiful, perfectly matched, and I'm told they belonged to a man who was a capital whip.'

'Why has he sold them?'

'I believe he had a reverse at cards, and has gone abroad for a while.'

'They'll need expert handling if he was as good as you've heard.'

'Do you imply I can't? That I'm not expert enough?'

'No, no, Miss Bella—'

'I've driven myself for years in Lancashire. Just one pony, I'll admit, and driving in town traffic, or even a pair in the Park, needs extra skills, to be sure, but I've had lessons for weeks now. I've driven a few pairs, and I'm tired of always having to be escorted!'

'Yes, Miss Bella,' Jackson said, but in a tone that clearly implied he didn't agree.

'It's just that they haven't had much exercise the past few days. But if it makes you any easier, you shall drive out with me when the curricle arrives. I bought it yesterday and it should be here this morning.'

'Curricle? But – yes, miss,' Jackson said again.

Bella smiled to herself as she wandered back into the house and sat musing in her room. He'd clearly understood she meant it, and had given up protesting. After a few drives, she would be competent enough to cut a dash in the Park. So many men had offered to teach her, but she was bored with all of them.

Lord Dorney had not offered after their last encounter, when he'd driven her home from St James's Street. He spent most of his time with friends or at his clubs, and though she tried to be in the breakfast-room at the same time as he was, on most days he either rose very early, or came downstairs long after she felt unable to remain, toying with a roll, and the servants eyeing her with ill-concealed curiosity or amusement.

There was a limit to how much she could pursue him, she told herself, after enduring a sleepless night during which she had rejected several notions of how to attract his attention as either impracticable or just silly. So she would forget him. As she had no desire to marry any of her other suitors, who were all, she was convinced, as attracted to her fortune as her person, she would behave as she wished.

She scorned the conventions of Society, listened to Jane's advice politely, but ignored it. As Lady Fulwood's guest politeness dictated she must conform to her hostess's notion of proper behaviour, but that would soon end. She would rent for herself a house in London and move there as soon as possible. In fact she was already negotiating for a small one in Dover Street. If Jane refused to come with her, and since Philip was expected home at any time this was a real possibility, she would hire a companion. Even Bella recognized the impossibility of living totally on her own. She did not wish to be ostracized by all but the fastest set. And a compliant companion could write notes and run errands for her.

Bella shivered slightly. It wasn't what she really wanted, but she could not impose on Lady Fulwood if she did things that lady disapproved of. Jane, and Philip when he came, would soon be going home to Lancashire. What would Lord Dorney do? He seemed to lodge with friends when in London, but there would be a limit to how long he could do that. Would he go to Dorney Court when the Season ended? What would she do then?

There was a tap on the door and Mary appeared.

'Miss Bella, there's a visitor for you. Are you in?'

Bella looked up. 'Who is it?'

'He says he's your cousin, Mr Gareth Carey.'

*

'Dan, the whole situation is impossible!'

Sir Daniel looked at Lord Dorney with sympathy in his eyes. 'Only in your eyes, Richard. You're being too stubborn. You love the girl, so why don't you admit it?'

'I don't know what I feel for her! I thought I loved her, but when I discovered she'd lied to me, I began to question what I felt.'

'Shock, I imagine. Richard, no woman's perfect, and she lied, assumed a different name, for what seemed to her a very good reason. Can't you see it from her point of view? If you had a fortune, would you want to be pursued by girls and their mamas who were interested only in your money and not yourself?'

'Of course not, and I understand that.'

'It's rather different for a girl. A man with a fortune can choose the girl he wants to wed, and ask her. Girls have not the same freedom. They can't offer for the man they want.'

Lord Dorney laughed ruefully. 'But she did, in effect.'

'Then why the devil can't you see that she wants you, and accept? Give away all her money if that would make you feel better!'

'I think she might have something to say about that!'

'Well, arrange the settlements so that she has total control over the money. But consider, would you want her to live at Dorney Court in its present state, with workmen all over the place? Doing small jobs as and when you decide you can afford them? She could pay for your renovations and have the place fit for her within weeks, a month or so. You wouldn't need to let your London house, but if you did would you refuse to bring her to London because you couldn't afford a suitable house for the Season?'

Lord Dorney sighed. 'I'm too confused, and at the moment she's behaving in the most outrageous ways, encouraging all the fribbles in town to dangle after her. If she's not careful, the high sticklers will lose patience with her and she'll find herself excluded from all decent society. She'll become intimate with rogues like Lambert and Mrs Williams, people who aren't invited even to the biggest routs.'

'And you could prevent all this.'

'Could I? Dan, I need to get away, free of the risk of meeting her every time I step out of my room at Lady Fulwood's. I'm going to Leicestershire.'

'Not at this time of year, surely! What on earth would you do there? Hack about the country on your own, not knowing how you feel? That might, or more likely might not, resolve your doubts, but in the meantime, what will happen to her? I suspect, if you leave, and she doesn't have even a hope of seeing you, she'll do even more shocking things than driving down St James's Street!'

Lord Dorney clutched his already disarranged hair. 'Dan, you're my best friend, and usually I'd listen to your advice, but this time I simply don't know what to do!'

'Come back to stay with me. I'm fixed here for the next month or so, and then, you tell me, you'll have to go to Bath for young Alex's wedding. Lord, it doesn't seem long since he was a schoolboy, following you around at Dorney Court demanding to be allowed to shoot rabbits.'

'Gareth. I didn't know you were in town.'

Bella's tone was coldly polite. She had never liked her cousin, who was several years her senior, and had, as a boy, made her life a misery whenever he and his parents had visited Trahearne House. He either teased her, broke her toys, and, as he grew older and became a pupil at a minor public school, spoke to her in Latin and scoffed when she failed to understand him. His worst crime, one she still recalled with impotent fury, had been to throw a new and much-loved doll into the nearby river and crow with laughter as it was carried away, bouncing against rocks and finally disappearing into a muddy pool.

Growing up had not improved him, in her opinion. He was pompous and stuffy, convinced of his own superiority and free with unwanted advice to whoever he could persuade to listen to him.

He smiled with an irritating condescension. 'Neither did I know you were here until a fellow at the club mentioned the dashing Miss Trahearne and her exploits which were scandalizing the *ton*. You'll have to take care, Cousin, or the best drawing-rooms will be closed to you.'

Bella fumed. The fact that what he said was true didn't improve her temper. 'If I ever want your advice, I'll ask! But it's most unlikely. You're hardly a pattern card of propriety. Has Helen dropped her cub yet? How long have you been wed? Seven months, I think, and that was done in a very hasty and secretive manner. I believe she had a respectable portion, and you could get hold of it only by seducing the poor girl! Papa didn't even receive an invitation to the wedding.'

He winced, and she knew she had touched on a sore point. 'I'll thank you not to slander my wife! Helen preferred a quiet wedding.'

Did she, Bella wondered. Most girls wanted the full ceremonial and all the fuss that attended weddings.

Gareth's face was red and he paced angrily about the room. 'I'll have you know the child was premature, and if you imply differently you'll be sorry!'

'I doubt it. But don't worry, I've no interest in your morals. Other people can count too.'

He pursed his lips but clearly decided to ignore this. 'Premature,' he repeated. 'But he's strong. He'll survive. I have an heir, Bella. Which is more than you have, and more than you're likely to have the way you are behaving! No decent man would consider an alliance with you.'

'Not even with my grand fortune? You can't know how many offers I've had, both here and in Harrogate.' Bella grinned, recalling some of the latter. She had no intention of marrying any of them, but it did no harm to give Gareth a fright. She could get her own back for the many annoyances he'd caused her in the past. 'I may well surprise you and upset your hopes. I'd rather give all my fortune away than let you and your family get your hands on a penny of it! But that's enough. Why did you come to see me?'

'I thought it time to mend fences. I'll ignore what you've said today. I quite understand that you must be feeling out of sorts when Society is so critical of you. But with my help, if they see your family support you, your good name could be reinstated. We want you to come to the christening. To be a godmother to little Henry.'

Bella was speechless with astonished fury. To have Gareth, her despicable cousin, holding himself out as a means of restoring a good name she had not – yet – lost, was beyond enough. It certainly wasn't because he wanted to help her make a good match. Indeed, the longer she remained single the better he'd like it, for it increased his chances of inheriting Trahearne House.

'I'll send Henry a suitable christening gift,' she snapped. 'I've no doubt that was your main reason for seeking me out. You don't care a rap for my good name, just my money! And thank you for the honour of asking me to sponsor your son, but I'm afraid I have to refuse. I'm surprised you're not worried I'd either drop him or drown him in the font!'

Without waiting for his reply she swept from the room, saw Lady Fulwood's butler hovering, and briskly told him to show the visitor out, and if he called again to say she was not at home.

On the following day Bella went to visit the Floods in Highgate. Her attorney had managed to purchase their cottage and the one next to it, and she had arranged for a builder to draw up plans for joining the two.

Jackson drove her in the new curricle, allowing her to take the reins only when the road was quiet.

She was pleased she was able to control the greys, but admitted this was only possible in the best conditions. She'd had a struggle to prevent them from bolting when a stage-coach had passed them as they crossed the New Road.

They were approaching Highgate Hill when she saw Mrs Flood walking along, and Bella pulled up beside her.

Jackson took the reins as Bella jumped down.

'What have we here?' she asked, pointing to the bundle Mrs Flood carried.

'Oh, Miss Bella, I was going to be at home when you came, but I had this message, you see. It couldn't wait.'

She lifted the bundle and Bella saw it was a sleeping child, she guessed a year or so old, but with the wizened face of near starvation. 'Who is it?' she asked softly.

'Little Samuel. I used to be in service with his mother. She lived in Clerkenwell after she was wed, but her man died of the bloody flux, and she had to scrape a living taking in mending and washing. I had a message this morning to say she was knocked over by a brewer's dray a week ago, and died yesterday. There's no one to look after the little mite. She was from Yorkshire, like me, and has no family. I don't think he'd eaten since she was knocked down. She was taken to the hospital, and the neighbours didn't care, until one of them found he'd crawled out into the road and then collapsed, from hunger, I suppose.'

'Oh, the poor little baby. Here, give him to me while Jackson helps you into the curricle. We can all squeeze in for the last mile or so.'

The child, disturbed by being moved from Mrs Flood's arms, began to cry, a weak, exhausted wail. Bella lifted him higher in her arms and held him over her shoulder, patting him on the back and shushing him until Mrs Flood was settled and she could hand him back and clamber into the curricle herself.

'Quickly, Jackson, the sooner we can get him home and fed the better.'

Lord Dorney had thought hard and long about Sir Daniel's advice. He couldn't get the wretched girl out of his mind. Did that mean he really did love her? He'd thought he did in Bath. He'd put aside his resolve not to marry then, but he hadn't known she was wealthy. Ought he to set aside his scruples now and renew his offer? But would she have him after the way he'd treated her? She could have any one of a number of men, all of them, he was sure, fortune hunters. He'd be one too if he offered for her, and after his brother's experience he had no desire to have a wife who might wish to rule him because she had a fortune.

An insistent small voice urged him that Bella would not be like that. Yes, she was headstrong, but all he'd seen of her told him she had a warm heart. She cared for those less fortunate than herself, unlike Selina. She wouldn't try to hurt him if they disagreed. He grinned. He was sure there would be disagreements.

Unable to think clearly he decided to ride out, not in the Park where he would have to keep to a staid canter, but up on the hills somewhere, with the wind in his hair, where he could gallop away his odd humours. He'd go to Highgate, it was time he looked at the two houses his mother had left him there, and decide whether it was time to sell them. With the money he could hasten the work on Dorney Court. Suddenly he longed to be back in that familiar and much loved place, restored to what it had been before Selina ruined it.

He was approaching Highgate village when he pulled sharply on the reins and halted. Was he seeing things? What in the world was Bella doing here? At least she had her groom, Jackson, with her. He would not have been surprised to find her out on her own, trying to control her new pair, which Lady Fulwood had described to him in detail.

'She'll break her neck one day,' his godmother had predicted. 'Fortunately Masters and Jackson both keep a close watch on her and won't let her take out this new curricle on her own.'

He watched as Bella stood there while an older woman clambered up into the curricle. Then his eyes widened in astonishment. Was that a child Bella was holding? How in the world did she come to be here, in this unlikely small village, with a child?

He sat still and watched as Bella handed the child up to the other woman, then climbed into the curricle. Jackson drove away, and Lord Dorney resisted the impulse to follow. There was some mystery here, but it was not his affair.

It might be, if the child belonged to Bella.

The unwelcome thought made him jerk the reins, and for some moments all his attention had to be given to the horse. When he was once more in control he abandoned his ride to Highgate and turned back towards London. A sudden vision of Bella, as he'd first seen her in Lancashire when he was visiting Lady Hodder, getting out of a coach and helping a small child out, came to him. He did some swift calculations. That child had been about five years old. Bella was three and twenty. But surely, Lady Hodder would not have countenanced—

He forced his swirling thoughts into some kind of coherence. There was a mystery, but he must not jump to conclusions. She'd told him the child was one she'd rescued from working in the cotton mills. Surely she would not have pretended that if he had been her own?

Then he recalled her response when he'd kissed her. It had been shy, tentative, not the response of an experienced woman who had known lovers in the past. She could not have counterfeited that.

Did he want to discover the truth? One part of him said he had no further interest in Bella Trahearne, but deep down he knew he must find out, if only to satisfy himself that she could not be as depraved as it sometimes seemed.

The house was in an uproar when Bella reached Mount Street. From the trunks and other baggage in the hall Bella knew someone had arrived. When she went into the drawing-room she found Jane sitting on a sopha, and her husband with his arm round her.

'Philip! Oh, how good to see you!' Bella cried, and Philip stood up to kiss her heartily on the cheek.

'You too, Miss Mischief. How come you and my wife have been gallivanting in Bath? I've no doubt it was your suggestion.'

Bella glanced swiftly at Jane, who shook her head slightly.

'Well, yes,' she began, wondering how much it would be wise to tell him.

'Oh, we'll talk about that later,' Jane said hastily. 'I want to know all about your voyage, my love.'

'Uneventful,' Philip said with a laugh. 'I'm sure Bath has been far more exciting.'

'Bath? Exciting?' Lady Fulwood said, laughing. 'It is never exciting in Bath, and it was the end of the Season there, and many people had come back to London well before my dear Jane and Bella came to me. The house has been far livelier with them here.'

'How long a furlough do you have?' Bella changed the subject.

'Two months, and I mean to enjoy every minute.'

'I – I suppose you'll want to take Jane home to Lancashire,' Bella said, suddenly realizing the implications of Philip's arrival. Of course he would want to be in his own home, and have Jane to himself. What would she do? Could she stay on in London with Lady Fulwood, or should she move to the little house she was thinking of renting? If she did, she would need to find a companion as soon as possible. She would visit one of the agencies that provided such people on the following day.

'We'll stay here for a short while, as I haven't seen my dear godmama for a long time,' Philip said. 'Then I want to go home.'

'You are welcome to remain with me, Bella dear,' Lady Fulwood said. 'I enjoy your company, and taking a young gal to balls reminds me of the days my own daughters were young.'

'I'm grateful,' Bella said. She felt an enormous sense of relief. If Lord Dorney remained too, they would inevitably be thrown together more. She still had hopes of making him change his mind, but she knew she had more chance of success if they were living in the same house.

*

They were invited to a ball that evening, but Philip pleaded tiredness, and with a smile Lady Fulwood bade him and Jane to have an early night. Jane blushed, then laughed.

'Very well, ma'am.'

Bella wore a new gown, in a delicate shade of green with a silver gauze overskirt. One of her uncle's necklaces was of emeralds, and Bella, feeling rebellious, determined to wear that instead of the discreet pearls Lady Fulwood preferred. She was very rich, and everyone knew, so why should she pretend not to be?

The first dance ended, and she was standing at the side of the ballroom with her partner. Her card was filling up quickly when she saw Gareth approaching across the room. He reached her and stepped slightly to the side, revealing Mr Salway who had been behind him. Bella's partner, bowing himself away, did not see her sudden pleading glance, and politely removed himself.

'Dear Coz,' Gareth said, with what Bella could only describe as a smirk. 'How pleasant to see you here, and so well provided with jewels. Or are they glass? I understand the Indians can be very clever at imitating real gems.'

'You understand nothing,' Bella snapped. 'I would have thought you were needed at home, to support your wife, and your son and heir!'

'Oh, nursery doings bore me. I'd far rather be in town. I believe you met Mr Salway in Harrogate? He's been telling me all about your successes there.'

'Has he, indeed? And his failures, too, I suppose,' she said, trying to drag her hand away from Mr Salway's, but he had pretended to shake it and was holding her too tightly, and she was not prepared to indulge in a public trial of strength, for she would be sure to be worsted. 'Pray release me, sir!' she added.

Mr Salway smiled, and instead of letting go her hand, carried it up to his lips and planted a wet kiss on her wrist.

This time Bella succeeded in snatching away her hand, and rubbed it furiously against her skirt. She looked round for help, but no one she knew was near enough for her to attract their attention.

'May I crave a dance?' Mr Salway was asking.

'My card is full,' Bella began, but Gareth twitched it out of her hand and held it out to Mr Salway.

'You can have the supper waltz,' he said. 'Won't that be delightful for you, my dear Bella? I'll find a partner and join you both. We'll have a cozy little chat over the salmon mousse and the crab patties.'

Mr Salway was writing his name against two other dances, and with a flourish handed Bella her card. She snatched it, and tore it into tiny pieces.

'I don't dance with you, Mr Salway,' she said, loudly enough for a couple of passing gentlemen to hear. They turned, eyebrows raised, and stared. With relief Bella recognized Major Ross, and before Gareth could intervene she stepped forward and grasped the major's arm.

'Please sir, will you escort me to Lady Fulwood? The air just here is decidedly malodorous!'

'Are they annoying you?' the major asked, and both he and his companion turned to face the other men.

They both showed clenched fists, and Bella shrank from an even more dreadful confrontation. 'No more than usual. The larger one is, unfortunately, my cousin, but I wouldn't dream of presenting either of them to gentlemen. It would be an insult.'

They moved away, the major bending solicitously over Bella.

'You're trembling, my dear. Do you wish to go home? I could call for our carriage and escort you, if you'd permit.'

Bella shook her head. 'Thank you, but it's fury rather than fright. Oh, how could they!' She laughed. 'Now I shall have to obtain another dance card and try to remember who I've promised dances to.'

'I'll find one for you,' the major's friend offered. 'Ross, as a medical man, I recommend you take the lady to find a glass of wine.'

Bella saw no more of her cousin or Mr Salway that evening. She was aware of Major Ross hovering nearby, and was grateful. He was large, strong and determined. She hoped Mr Salway had taken fright.

Gareth, however, appeared in Mount Street the following morning, and she had no chance to deny him since Lady Fulwood was with her and bade the butler show him in before Bella could protest.

'I am delighted to meet Bella's cousin,' Lady Fulwood said,

gesturing him to a chair. 'I understand your wife has just presented you with a son, Mr Carey. My congratulations. You must be over-joyed.'

'We're delighted to have an heir,' Gareth replied. 'He's the only boy in the Trahearne family,' he added, with a significant glance at Bella.

'Not a true Trahearne,' Bella said swiftly. 'Your mother may be my father's sister, but you are a Carey, so is your son.'

After a few minutes of general conversation, during which Bella remained silent, Lady Fulwood rose.

'I have no doubt you wish to discuss family matters, so I will leave you for a while.'

'Your behaviour last night was deplorable!' Gareth burst out almost before the door was closed. 'I was ashamed to be related to you. How could you treat a friend of mine with such discourtesy?'

'I'm even more ashamed to have to own you as a connection! As for that creature Salway, I can't imagine even you would approve of a man who tries to seduce an heiress just to gain control of her fortune! Though perhaps you consider it normal, acceptable behaviour. Now please go, I have nothing to say to you.'

She turned towards the door, but Gareth was there before her, and he grasped her arms and forced her close to him.

'Don't be so hasty! I've a proposition to put to you.'

Before she could reply the door opened, and Lord Dorney entered the room. He stopped short, and coughed.

'I beg your pardon,' he said coldly and began to leave.

'No, don't go!' Bella cried, wrenching herself free. 'It's not what you think. This is my cousin, and I want him to go. I never want to see him again! Please, can you throw him out?'

Lord Dorney raised his eyebrows at her vehemence, but came slowly back into the room. 'Are you Miss Trahearne's cousin?' he asked.

Gareth laughed. 'Of course I am. But I'm afraid Bella's taken offence at my attempts to help her. She always was hot at hand when she was a child. Gareth Carey, sir, at your service.'

He held out his hand, but Lord Dorney simply bowed slightly. 'Sir.'

Bella edged nearer the door. 'Gareth, please go. And don't ever come here again. I'll send your son's christening gift direct to Helen. And if you try to encourage that odious wretch Salway to make up to me again I'll – I'll shoot him!'

Chapter Twelve

———◦◦◦———

'RICHARD, WHAT CAN I do?'
Lord Dorney looked sympathetically at his young cousin. 'At first I understand Felicity was all in favour of a wedding soon. Now you say she hesitates, and won't fix a date.'

'She's regretting it, I know!'

'I don't think so.' He sighed. At least Alex knew his mind, was certain he wanted to marry Felicity. He didn't have the searing doubts, the unwelcome desires that plagued himself.

Seeing Bella almost every day was proving to be agony. He'd been pursued by many girls, undeterred by his lack of fortune. And before Robert died, they hadn't cared for his lack of title and estate. Now he had acquired both it seemed sufficient for most. They were unaware of how encumbered the estate still was, the traces of Selina's rule he needed to sweep away before he could once more be comfortable in his childhood home. They assumed he had a position to give them and could afford to keep them as they wished to be kept.

Until now he had been touched by none of them. But Bella, from the start, had crept past his guard. Perhaps it was the astonishment he'd felt when he saw her threaten those men in the inn yard, something he'd never expected of a female. Or her fierce compassion and lack of hesitation defending a mongrel dog, or a lad being beaten by his father. He smiled. But then she'd been revealed as a rich woman playing at being poor. Oh, he could understand her motives, but the horror of himself being stigmatized as a fortune hunter, as well as the foolishness he felt at being misled, had made him reject her. Now there was the horrid possibility that she had a child, even children.

And Lady Hodder must know, since the first child he'd seen Bella with had been at her house. He'd belatedly understood that the dishevelled girl he'd seen descending from the chaise on that occasion had been Bella. The woman in Highgate had looked, to his eyes, the sort of clean, poor woman he and his brother had been farmed out to in the village for the first year or so of their lives. They had been excellent wet-nurses, and he'd retained considerable affection for his own Bessy, visiting her regularly and making sure she and her brood wanted for nothing.

Alex was speaking again and he dragged his attention back to his cousin's concerns.

'I think I should insist she names a day.'

Lord Dorney shook his head. 'Females can be remarkably stubborn. If you challenge her, she's likely to accept it and give back your ring. It would be better, bring her to her senses more quickly, if you retired to Bath, told her you had affairs to settle there, and would await her decision.'

Alexander looked appalled. 'And leave her to Frederick Ross?'

'I suspect, if he is like most aspiring poets, that she will soon tire of him and begin to feel the loss of your company.'

'But she drives or rides with him almost every day, and dances with him at every ball we go to. People are beginning to remark on the partiality she shows him. And Lady Andrews has turned me away from the house twice, saying Felicity was tired and resting. I'm sure it wasn't that: Ross was with her. And she keeps asking me what your intentions are. She's afraid you'll marry after all, and I won't be your heir if you get yourself a son!'

'Are you worried about that possibility?' he asked.

Alexander shook his head. 'Of course not! I'm not rich, I don't have a big estate like you do, but I can support a wife in reasonable comfort, and when Mama dies, I'll have more. Not that I want her to die. I'm not counting on that.'

'Leave Felicity for a while. It probably flatters her to know you are anxious. Go away, back to Bath,' he repeated.

He wished he could follow his own advice and take himself out of London and the disturbing company of Bella Trahearne.

'You think that would bring her to her senses?' Alexander asked doubtfully.

Lord Dorney shook his head. 'I can't say, but if it doesn't, you have to ask yourself if she is the right wife for you. I'm sorry, Alex, it's brutal, I know, but you need to start married life knowing who is the head of the family. If you permit her to rule you now, what will your life be like in a few years' time? Do you want to marry a girl who will turn out to be like your mother?'

Alexander looked appalled. 'Not Felicity! She couldn't!'

'She might, if you give way to her. Let her see you can't bear to be away from her. You need to keep the whip hand.'

Some time later Alexander reluctantly agreed that he would return to Bath. Lord Dorney wished he could follow his own advice, then consoled himself that the situation was entirely different. He and Bella were not promised to one another. Soon she would be returning to Lancashire with Lord and Lady Hodder. He would be free of her disturbing influence. He could forget her.

Hiding her trepidation, Bella ventured into the Park for the first time on her own, driving herself in her curricle. Jackson, on the recommendation of Lady Fulwood, had taken the horses out earlier that morning, so their first freshness had been worn off. She negotiated the streets without mishap, though she had almost clipped the wheels of a high perch phaeton when turning out of Mount Street. Ignoring the imprecations of its driver, she reached the Park and relaxed.

After a few hundred yards, during which she had nodded at several acquaintances, she saw Major Ross driving towards her. Mrs Ford was seated beside him, looking very fetching in a pale blue pelisse and a jaunty little hat of the same colour.

They halted as the vehicles drew level. Major Ross was driving a phaeton, not so tall as the one Bella had encountered earlier, but high enough to cause her to crane her neck as they exchanged greetings.

'I see you have dispensed with teachers and grooms,' Major Ross said.

'You are a credit to your teachers,' Mrs Ford added, with an arch glance at the major.

Bella was intrigued. They were much of an age, and she had first encountered the major at Mrs Ford's house. She had not noticed that he paid particular attention to her on public occasions, but in future she would be alert for it. How appropriate it would be if they made a match of it. And how convenient if it removed Mrs Ford as a potential rival for Lord Dorney's affections.

'Do you go to the Kellaway ball this evening?' the major asked. 'If so, I must beg the pleasure of a dance.'

'I believe Lady Fulwood intends to go,' Bella replied. 'Of course I will keep a dance for you, Major. I think I'd better move on now, the horses are becoming restive.'

For the rest of her three circuits of the Park half of her attention was directed to the prospect of an engagement between the major and the woman she sometimes thought of as her main rival for Lord Dorney's affections. Mrs Ford was older, more sensible, calmer and much more suitable to become his wife. She didn't believe his declaration that he would never marry. He would change his mind at some time. Mrs Ford was still young enough to give him several children. Surely he would in the end prefer a son of his own to inherit rather that Alexander?

Bella had met him again on several occasions here in London, and had no great opinion of Alexander, whom she thought rather young and unformed in character. She doubted whether Felicity was the right wife for him, thinking her a rather silly, flighty chit who was displaying her immaturity by her encouragement of Frederick Ross. Bella had overheard several of the more staid dowagers commenting unfavourably on Felicity's behaviour, and she herself found Frederick decidedly tedious with his self-absorption.

But then Bella had little time for poets. There had been a couple in Harrogate, younger sons of Yorkshire mill owners, indulged by their fond parents who had considered their outpourings on a par with those of Lord Byron, and were quite ready to declare that the latter's fame rested more on his position in the *ton* than any intrinsic merit in the verse. She found them dreamy, abstracted and impractical. Did Felicity really prefer him to Alexander? Was she merely flattered? There could be no other reason. She must know Alexander adored her, so she had no reason to try and make him jealous.

Bella thrust thoughts of both Mrs Ford and Felicity from her mind, and prepared herself somewhat nervously for her return to Mount Street.

*

Bella had much to consider that evening. Alexander looked moody and resentful, and after one of the waltzes Bella observed what looked like a tiff between him and Felicity, who positively flounced away from him and went straight to Frederick, smiling up at him with what Bella considered artificial brilliance.

Soon afterwards she saw Lord Dorney conversing with Alexander, and the younger man gave a shrug and in a little while left the ballroom.

Bella happened to be watching Felicity, who was dancing one of the country dances with Frederick. She missed her step, and turned as if to leave the set and follow Alexander. Then, at a word from one of the other ladies, turned back and continued dancing.

Intriguing, thought Bella. She looked around for the major and Mrs Ford, but neither were to be seen until after the supper interval, when Mrs Ford, looking paler than normal, came into the ballroom escorted by her sister's husband.

Then Bella stiffened. Gareth and Mr Salway strolled into the room. They grinned across at her, but to her relief made no attempt to approach her, and soon afterwards the major appeared to claim his dance with Bella. He seemed his normal self, but Bella detected signs of strain under his habitual calm, and when the dance ended he disappeared into one of the rooms set aside for cards. She saw no more of him, and soon afterwards Mrs Ford departed.

What could have happened? Had they quarrelled? But they were both older and much more calm than she knew herself to be. Older, staider people did not quarrel. At least, in Bella's experience they did not. But she could do nothing to solve the mystery, and soon her thoughts turned to her own problems. It could not be long before Jane and Philip went home, and then she would have to decide what she herself wanted to do. Should she give up all hope of attaching Lord Dorney, and go home with them? Or should she create scandal by staying here in London on her own?

A week later Jane announced they intended to set off for home the following day. 'Bella, will you come with us? It really would be best.'

Bella shook her head. 'I can't,' she said simply. 'I need to stay in London.'

'Bella, dear, you've had several weeks here, living in the same house as Lord Dorney, and he's as cold as ever. He won't change his mind. Why do you keep hoping? Wouldn't it be better to forget him?'

'How can I? He's the only man for me, and while I am in London there is still some hope he will forgive me and change his mind.'

Jane sighed. 'I don't believe he is the sort of man who ever changes his mind.'

'Then if he does not, I can concentrate on my homes. I heard from Mr Jenkins of another married couple living south of the river who might be suitable to run another one. I mean to go and see them tomorrow. When do you leave?'

'Tomorrow. Philip wants to be at home for as long as possible. He's never liked London, and to tell the truth, neither do I.'

Bella hugged her. 'You've been so good to me! Thank you!'

'I'm sorry it hasn't turned out as you wished. Come home soon, I'll miss you when Philip goes back on duty.'

The next morning Bella left early, driving with Jackson to visit a couple living in a village near Greenwich. She didn't like farewells, and told Jane she thought it was for the best if there were fewer people to see them off.

Jane sighed, and turned her attention to ordering all the luggage, hers and Philip's, into the carriage he'd hired to convey it all to Lancashire.

Lord Dorney appeared, dressed for driving, and paused to wish them farewell.

'Miss Trahearne does not go with you?' he asked stiffly.

'No, she stays here,' Jane replied. 'Susan, I want that box inside, please. I wish she would come with us, but she prefers to stay here, with her children.'

Lord Dorney gulped. Her children? How could she be so open about it? 'Yes. Pray, how many does she have?'

Jane glanced at him. 'I don't know. They seem to multiply every day, from what she says. At least three in Preston, and some in Bristol. There was another child in Highgate only the other day, and now there will be others in Greenwich. It's fortunate she has enough money to support them all.'

Lord Dorney turned away, his head reeling. It couldn't be what he'd thought! But what was it? How could he have misjudged her so? He walked away, his head spinning. He had to find out about this. Did Lady Fulwood know? He'd ask his godmother as soon as the house returned to normal.

Bella was driving her curricle in the Park, still rather tentatively, but pleased with the progress she had made with her pair, when Major Ross, walking along by himself, hailed her. She drew to a halt and invited him to join her, which he did with considerable alacrity.

'My dear Miss Trahearne, I'm so glad to see you. I trust those dreadful boors from the other night have caused no more trouble? I saw them at the ball again, and hoped they had learned their lesson.'

'They did not speak to me at the ball, but my cousin inflicted himself on me and Lady Fulwood a few days earlier. He was told in a way he could not mistake that he was unwelcome. I was so grateful for your support the other night.'

'My dear, I would wish to support you all the time. I am only too conscious of the disparity in our fortunes, and our ages, but believe me, I am no fortune hunter. I would wish you to control all your money as you do now.'

Bella looked at him in astonishment. She'd known the major liked her, and she liked his sturdy good sense, but she'd had no intimation that he had warmer feelings for her. She'd thought those were reserved for Mrs Ford. But something seemed to have gone wrong between them. From his hesitant words she deduced that he was, however ineptly, making her an offer.

'Major?' she asked.

'My dear, I'm making a terrible mull of it. I'm not used – of course I'm not! Miss Trahearne, Bella, if I may be so bold, I have come to esteem you above all other ladies of my acquaintance. I do not think you have a *tendre* for any other man, and so I am hoping you might be prepared to listen to me. I have a pleasant house in the country, near Cambridge, and a competence. I could afford to rent a house in the best part of town for the Season, and perhaps in Bath or Brighton for a few months each year. I have no previous attachments, nothing to be ashamed of in my past career. But it is time I settled down. I would, if you were so kind as to accept my suit, immediately sell out of the army, and devote myself to making your life as comfortable and pleasant as possible. In short, my dear, I lay myself at your feet.'

Bella suppressed an urge to laugh. She had read innumerable novels from the circulating libraries, but in none of them had proposals been made with such stiff formality. Perhaps, she thought, stifling a giggle, driving in a curricle with a lively pair to control did not make for ideal conditions when a prospective bridegroom could press his suit.

'Are you asking me to marry you, Major?' she managed.

'But of course! Bella, you cannot imagine I would be asking you for anything less?'

'Do you love me?' she asked bluntly.

'Naturally.' He sounded surprised. 'I would not have made my offer if I did not.'

Others would, and had, she thought. What about Mrs Ford, she longed to ask, but prudence kept her silent.

'Major, I am flattered, but I never imagined – that is, I thought we were friends, but I have never contemplated a closer relationship.'

'Of course, I have rather sprung it on you. Rushed my fences. Attacked without due preparation. Very bad tactics.'

She stifled another giggle. 'Forgive me, Major, but this is so sudden.' Lord, she thought, I sound like a bad actress in a third rate theatre. 'May – may I have time to consider?'

'My dear girl, you may have all the time in the world!' he exclaimed.

By which time we will all be dead, Bella thought.

'If only I can hope.'

Bella felt a twinge of remorse. She could never love the major. She liked him, respected him, and was utterly certain he would treat her well, but could she ever marry him? Ought she to allow him to hope? Could she ever forget Lord Dorney? Was there the slightest possibility that he might change his opinion of her, renew the offer he had so nearly made? That would be heaven, she considered. Could she be happy with anything so far inferior?

'I will give it serious consideration,' she promised. Perhaps this was all that was left for her.

'I will await your decision,' the major said happily. 'Now, perhaps, you had best set me down, or tongues will begin to wag.'

Bella ignored the music, which was rather inferior, she'd decided after the first few songs. Why had this woman gained a reputation as an accomplished entertainer? She had to think about the major's unexpected proposal. She liked him, but could she live with him? Could she endure the intimacies between husband and wife? She shivered.

'My dear, are you cold?' Lady Fulwood asked.

'No, ma'am.'

'Good, I find it rather hot and oppressive myself. Would you mind dreadfully if we left at the interval? I can't say I'm enjoying this.'

'Nor I. I'd be happy to go home.'

'We'll have some supper first. I can't deprive you of that, and they do serve superior champagne!'

When they went into the supper room Lady Fulwood was drawn aside by one of her cronies, and Bella joined Mrs Ford and her sister. She might have some opportunity of finding out what had gone wrong between her and the major. Had he, she suddenly wondered, been rejected by Mrs Ford and proposed to her in the hopes of restoring his self-esteem? Or perhaps to demonstrate that he was capable of attaching a younger and richer girl?

Somehow Bella did not think he was so shallow, but then, she told herself, she was beginning to believe she did not at all understand men. She could understand those like her cousin and Mr Salway, for their motives were clear and despicable. It was the good men, those with strong principles, who perplexed her. They seemed to have such odd notions of what was correct. They followed incomprehensible rules of conduct rather than doing what they might wish.

'When do you return to your home?' she asked Mrs Ford. 'The Season seems to be coming to an end, so many people are leaving to go to the seaside.'

'I don't plan to go just yet,' Mrs Ford replied. 'It's my first year in London for a long time, and I mean to make the most of it. What of yourself?'

'I've no firm plans,' Bella replied. 'I too, am enjoying it far too much to want to cut short my visit.'

Mrs Ford turned to reply to a question from another woman Bella did not know, and she was free to wonder whether Mrs Ford's continued presence would affect her in any way. Had she rejected the major? Did she have hopes of Lord Dorney? Could that be the reason she had, if indeed she had, rejected the major?

Her musings were cut short as a man she did not know approached her.

'Miss Trahearne? It is Miss Trahearne, isn't it?'

'Yes, I'm Bella Trahearne. What can I do for you?'

'Lady Fulwood sent me. She swooned, but she is now better. Her coach has been summoned, and she wishes to go home.'

Bella jumped to her feet. 'Pray excuse me,' she said to the others, who were exclaiming in dismay. Ignoring them she hurried with the man to the front hall, where Lady Fulwood was being assisted into her cloak.

'I shall be perfectly all right when I get into the open air,' she was saying. 'It was the heat, I'm afraid. Bella, there you are. Come, child, we'll go home and spend the evening quietly. Not a word to anyone about this,' she added after they had been helped into the carriage. 'I can't abide people fussing around me. Particularly not Richard. Promise you won't say anything to him?'

On the following day Lord Dorney found Lady Fulwood reclining on a sopha in the drawing-room, half asleep.

'Ma'am, are you unwell?' he demanded. He'd never before seen his godmother flag, even at the height of the Season.

'Tired, Richard.'

'It's not noon yet. You weren't out late last night. Have you seen a doctor?'

'I'm getting old, my dear boy. That's all.'

'It's been too much for you, having us all here, gallivanting around with Lady Hodder and Miss Trahearne. I'll remove myself at once, and I'm sure that when she realizes the situation, Miss Trahearne will go home.'

'Richard, no! I won't spoil the poor child's pleasure. There are plenty of my friends who will chaperon her to parties if I don't feel able to. Mrs Ford and her sister have offered more than once.'

'Why don't you go to Brighton for a while? The sea air would do you good. And if you insist on keeping Miss Trahearne by you, take her as well.'

And if she were out of his orbit, he might be able to forget her.

He went at once to see Sir Daniel, and within the day was moving his belongings to his friend's house. That evening he made sure he attended the same concert which Lady Fulwood and Bella intended to go to, and in the interval steered Bella into a discreet alcove.

'My godmother is unwell,' he said without preamble. 'I have moved to Sir Daniel's house, and I want her to go to Brighton for the benefit of the sea air. Can you persuade her that you would like to visit there too? She will not suggest it while she has you to consider.'

'What you mean is you'd prefer me to go home,' Bella said. 'I'm sorry she is ill.' She considered her promise to Lady Fulwood, but if Lord Dorney had discovered for himself that Lady Fulwood was ill, and it seemed as though this was more than an isolated swoon due to the heat, ought she not to tell him? 'She swooned the other night,' she told him. 'She made me promise not to tell anyone, so please don't betray me. I thought she looked tired the past few days, but she assured me she was just a little out of sorts, missing Jane. Don't concern yourself, I'll go as soon as I can make suitable arrangements.'

He breathed a sigh of relief. 'I knew you would be sensible, and thank you. She means a great deal to me, has done ever since my mother died. Is there any way I can assist you? You'll travel post, I assume? And your maid will no doubt go with you.'

'Please don't concern yourself with my arrangements. I think the concert is starting again. We had better go back to our seats.'

On the following morning Bella ordered Jackson to find and hire some stables for her horses. 'We will be moving from Lady Fulwood's in a few days,' she told him, 'and I cannot leave them for her man to look after. Indeed, as she is going to Brighton, she may well take Masters with her.'

She hired a hackney and went to see the agent letting the house in Dover Street. 'I mean to take it, and want to be able to move in within two days. Please make the necessary arrangements. I know the servants come with the house, but I will have my own maid, groom and a companion, so please ensure proper accommodation for them.'

Reassured that all would be done as she ordered, she then went to the registry to ask if they had a suitable person they could recommend as a companion. 'Not too old, but old enough to give me respectability,' she instructed.

'I have two or three ladies on the books who are available, and who might suit, Miss Trahearne,' the manageress said.

Bella looked at the details provided. 'Excellent. I would like to interview them tomorrow if possible. I would need them to come to me the following day if they can.'

'I'm sure that can be arranged, Miss Trahearne.'

Only then did Bella inform Lady Fulwood that she intended to leave in two days.

'Then you can be rid of me, and go to Brighton to recover your strength. I am so very grateful for all you have done, and would hate to feel you forced yourself to entertain me when you are unwell.'

'Do you go home, then?' Lady Fulwood asked. 'I have so enjoyed having you and dear Jane here, but I confess I am feeling old! I would never have asked you to go.'

'But you are relieved that I am going. Dear Lady Fulwood, we can be honest with one another. I've enjoyed being your guest immensely. It has been so unlike my previous Season in London, when I was too young and green to make the most of it. I was terrified of upsetting the dowagers, who all looked so disapproving if I so much as fluttered my fan inappropriately!'

Lady Fulwood chuckled. 'Somehow I can never imagine you afraid of anyone. Would you mind if we dined quietly tonight? Richard has gone already, and we have never had the opportunity to talk about these houses Jane tells me you are setting up. It's an excellent idea, and when I come back to London I shall ask my friends to contribute towards the maintenance, which I think is your plan, once you have purchased the properties?'

They spent a quiet evening, and Bella went to bed feeling guilty that she had allowed Lady Fulwood to believe she was going home. She had not told any untruths, she consoled herself, but she suspected Lady Fulwood would not have approved of the idea of a young unmarried lady setting up home on her own, however many respectable companions she had around her.

Chapter Thirteen

───◦◦◦◦───

THE FIRST TWO ladies Bella interviewed at the registry on the following morning were quite unsuitable. The first was in her sixties, complained of rheumatism, and said she preferred not to stay out late in the evening air. The second was the widow of a cler-gyman, and larded her comments with Biblical texts, complete with chapter and verse reference. Bella was not particularly religious, but she had as a child been made to learn her collects, and she spotted at least one incorrect reference. When she gently queried it, the widow gave her a lecture on the inadvisability of contradicting an older lady who had been brought up in a cathedral close, and had always lived in vicarages, and might be expected to know better than a young lady whose occupations were frivolous, and who appeared to cling to the fringes of the polite world.

Bella began to despair, but when the third lady was shown in her spirits lifted. Miss Perkins was, she said, in her late thirties, and still pretty in a delicate way. She was a younger daughter of a clergyman who had died when she was sixteen, and she had been a governess for years, but thought she needed to change her position.

'I find that after fifteen or more years I have less and less sympathy with childish minds,' she said, laughing. 'I'm not a natural teacher, and I have found it hard. Besides, I cannot offer Italian or painting in watercolours, nor the harp, so I am confined to very young children.'

Miss Perkins would have to do, and Bella suggested a month's employment.

'I realize such a short time might not appeal to you, but I may be returning home to Lancashire after that,' she explained, 'and would have no further need of your services.'

'Even a month without small children for ever clamouring at my heels would be a holiday!'

'I am moving into my house tomorrow. Are you free to come at once?'

'Yes. I have been staying with my sister, who is married to a clergyman residing in the City, and though they have made me most welcome they have very little room, and will be thankful to see me settled, if only for a short time.'

'Good. I will expect you in Dover Street tomorrow morning.'

Bella returned to Mount Street and told Lady Fulwood what she had done.

'My dear! You can't! I will delay going to Brighton, until I can find a respectable family for you to live with if you don't mean to leave London. Or you could come with me to Brighton, be my companion and write my notes and run errands for me.'

'Dear Lady Fulwood, I couldn't dream of delaying you. And I shall be perfectly well served. Miss Perkins is a very respectable lady.'

Eventually, after remarking that she didn't know what Richard would say, she accepted Bella's decision. Mary had been busy packing Bella's clothes, Jackson had already transferred the horses to their new stables, and all that remained was to send the luggage to Dover Street. Bella sighed with relief when she went to bed that night. All would be well. She was still in London, and so was Lord Dorney.

The servants at the new house welcomed Bella, smiling pleasantly at her. Mary reported that they had found her a small attic bedroom, so she did not have to share with the housemaid. Jackson, she added, had a small room behind the kitchen and was well pleased with the new stables. Even Rags was welcomed, the cook saying he would earn his keep by catching any rats that found their way into the small garden behind the house. They spent the rest of the day unpacking, helped by Miss Perkins, who had arrived soon after they did themselves. Dinner was excellent, well-cooked and presented, Miss Perkins had a fund of funny stories to relate about the children she had taught, and Bella went to bed congratulating herself on her new domestic arrangements.

On the following day she went to visit the Floods and see how the building to connect the two cottages was progressing. She stayed later than she had intended, the Floods made her so welcome, and arrived home only just in time to dress for the evening's entertainment, a visit to the theatre with Major Ross and two other young couples, both men army officers, and the sisters of one of them.

Bella had avoided thinking of the major's proposal, but he gave her such a pleading glance she promised herself she would reach a decision soon. The play was uninspiring, and Bella soon stopped paying it attention. Could she marry the major?

He was a pleasant companion, was not poor, and would permit her to use her own money as she wished. And he could give her children. But he lived near Cambridge, and she had heard that the country round about was exceedingly flat. She would have to convince him of the need for purchasing an estate in a hillier part of the country.

Her recent encounters with Gareth had made her even more determined that he would never get his hands on Trahearne House. Her father had spoken as though it was inevitable, especially since she had inherited her uncle's fortune, and had no need of the security it offered, while Gareth, the only Trahearne left, had very little. Bella would need to convince him that Gareth was undeserving. Apart from Gareth, Jane and Philip were her closest family, and if he remained convinced she did not need it she might persuade her father to leave it to them. But they were older than she was, and had no children, or even other close relatives to leave it to after them. Could she convince her father that it would be better to leave it to provide more houses for her orphans? Yet part of her was reluctant. It had been in her family for generations, and she wanted it to continue.

She could have her own children if she married Major Ross. He, she was convinced, was honest and did not want her for her money. Yet if she accepted him, she would renounce all hope of marrying for love. She liked, but did not love the major. Richard was the only man she could ever love. Cravenly, she needed more time, and when, as they walked behind the boxes in the interval and she had the opportunity of a private word with the major, she begged him to be patient.

'I will give you an answer soon,' she promised.

'If you are still considering it, I have not lost hope,' he replied gallantly. 'Will you drive with me in the morning?'

She agreed, and he pressed her hand warmly. 'I will call for you. Now, I think we had better go back to the others.'

Mary had been given the evening off, and the butler said Miss Perkins had retired early with a headache. Bella undressed herself, and noticed that some of her gowns looked creased. She frowned. Mary was normally very particular in the way she stored Bella's clothes, but perhaps they had become creased during the packing for the move, and Mary had not yet had time to deal with them. It had been a very busy few days for them all.

Her more valuable jewels were kept in a locked box hidden beneath a pile of shawls, but the less valuable Bella kept in one of the drawers of her dressing-table. She opened this now, too tired to bother with the box. She would replace the pearls she had worn this evening in the morning. Then she frowned. She was certain she had left the necklaces more tidily when she had taken out the garnet necklace she had worn earlier in the day. But she was tired, she was probably mistaken. She put away the pearls and made ready for bed, and was soon asleep.

Mary woke her the following morning, bringing her breakfast tray. Bella had decided that she would have enough of Miss Perkins during the rest of the day, she did not wish for her company at breakfast too.

As Bella poured the chocolate Mary began to tidy the room.

'Miss Bella, these gowns are creased. I pressed them before I put them away, and left out the one you said you were wearing last night. Did you change your mind?'

'I didn't touch them,' Bella said slowly. 'I noticed them when I came home last night. The jewels, too. Mary, get the other box and the key,' she added, and deposited her tray on the bedside table. She pulled on a wrapper as she got out of bed. 'Could any of the servants have been poking around?'

Mary did not reply. She brought the locked box to the bed, then found the key which Bella kept in a small hidden compartment of her writing desk. Silently Bella fitted the key and turned it. She lifted the lid and they both stared at the top tray which held rings, ear-rings and bracelets, diamonds, rubies, emeralds and a few lesser stones.

'The diamond rings!' Mary gasped. 'There were two almost the same! Now there's only one. The biggest stone is missing. Someone in the house is a thief!'

'Let's not panic. Lock the door, Mary, while we go through the box.'

She tipped out all the jewels on to the bed, and they laid them out. Mary knew them almost as well as her mistress, and together they replaced them in their usual positions in the box. The larger pieces, the ornate necklaces which were, some of them, worth thousands of pounds, were all there.

'Whoever it was probably thought they were paste!' Mary said angrily.

'Not surprising,' Bella said, and found her voice was trembling. 'They do look too good to be true. But let's go through the rest.'

They went through with the utmost care, and even looked under all the furniture, in case something had dropped unnoticed, although Mary swore the box had only been opened the previous evening when Bella had chosen the pearls to wear, and they had all been present then. At last Bella sat down on her dressing stool.

'Not just the ring, but a pair of pearl ear-rings,' she said slowly.

'And you had three pairs of those, different sizes. I suppose whoever it was thought you'd be less likely to miss them. What about the ones in the drawer?'

They locked the box, and Bella hung the key on a simple gold chain which, she said, she would keep on her person in future. Then they checked the other jewellery. That was all accounted for.

'They thought it was all in the locked box,' Mary said furiously. 'What will you do, Miss Bella? Can we search the house?'

Bella shook her head. 'It would take hours, and how could we explain it? No, first let's try to find out where everyone was last night. Go and ask Jackson to come up here, please. Try not to let the rest know I've asked for him, but if any of them ask, I want to consult him about some sort of problem with one of the horses. They won't know better; they won't have seen the horses.'

'To your bedroom?' Mary looked so scandalized that even in her concern Bella smiled.

'I'll dress first,' she said.

When Mary ushered Jackson into the room a few minutes later Bella was decently gowned in a simple morning dress, her hair tied back with a ribbon.

Swiftly she explained, and Jackson was all for searching the servants' rooms at once.

'Not yet, Jackson. Think. Could any of them have had time to come in here and search? It would have taken more than a few minutes to find the box and the key. You were in the house last night. I didn't need you to drive me as the major called for me. After I went out, what did everyone do?'

He frowned. 'After the dishes were washed, we all sat round playing cards until Cook made us all some tea. Then the women went up to bed, and the men played on for a bit. Now I think of it we were all together until you came home. I suppose one of the maids might have slipped in after they'd gone upstairs, but it wasn't ten minutes before you came in, and Mary was a minute or two after you. Where had you been?' he asked, suddenly turning to her.

'With Joan, at Mount Street. You know we got to be friends while we lived there. You're not accusing me, are you?'

''Course not. I just wondered whether you were out with Tom footman from there. He was sweet on you.'

Mary tossed her head. 'I wasn't. But Miss Bella, if it wasn't the servants, it must have been Miss Perkins. She was here on her own, in her room upstairs. No one would have heard her moving about.'

Lord Dorney met the major outside White's.

'How do you do, Major? I haven't seen Frederick around for some time.' And I hope he has lost interest in Felicity, he added to himself.

'Frederick? Oh, he's in the throes of some new piece of nonsense. He said he would be ready to read it out to us all at the soirée tonight. I hope Miss Trahearne is well enough to attend.'

'Is she unwell?'

He suppressed the flicker of concern he felt at the news.

'She was a little abstracted at the theatre last night, but this morning, when I called to drive out with her, she sent a message to say she was indisposed. I trust whatever ailed Lady Fulwood was not catching.'

'I think not. My godmother is getting old, though she normally refuses to admit it. She was tired, knocked up by all the activities she insists on undertaking. I just hope she is less energetic in Brighton.'

'How is your nephew? When is the wedding?'

'I don't know. Major, can I have a quiet word with you?'

They found a quiet corner in the library, and Lord Dorney began to explain.

'Alex is very unhappy at Felicity's behaviour,' he said. 'And I fear it is because of your brother, who is paying far too particular attentions to her. She's had her head turned, of course, but does Frederick have any serious intentions towards her?'

'My brother does not confide in me, any more than I in him,' the major said with a shrug. 'But I doubt if he has any wish to marry, especially a girl as young as Felicity. He's never shown the slightest inclination for the married state. I suspect it's because he knows no woman will be able to love him as much as he loves himself.'

Lord Dorney gave a crack of laughter that had an elderly military gentleman snoozing in an armchair nearby glaring at him and muttering about inconsiderate young pups.

'That's an honest assessment,' he said.

'I've no illusions about him. He'll leave me to carry on the family name, for he cares about that as little as he cares about the silly chits he plagues with his tedious verses.'

'Are you planning to marry?' Lord Dorney asked. 'If so, I must give you my good wishes.'

'Well, she hasn't said yes yet, but I have hopes.'

'May I guess? Mrs Ford?'

The major frowned. 'I somehow don't think Mrs Ford and I would suit,' he said curtly. 'Now pray forgive me, I must be on my way. I'll give Frederick a hint, but I can't promise my opinion will influence his behaviour. It never has yet.'

He departed, and Lord Dorney sat staring after him. He'd been expecting an announcement of betrothal between the major and Mrs Ford for weeks, and he was sure many other people had noticed the growing friendship between them. What had gone wrong? And if it wasn't Mrs Ford, who else had the major been interested in?

The answer hit him suddenly: Bella Trahearne. The major had been planning to drive with her that very morning, and now he had thought of it he recalled seeing them together at every ball or assembly. They'd been to the theatre together only the previous evening. He stood up abruptly and began to pace the room, to the renewed irritation of the military gentleman. Surely Bella would not want to be married to a dry old stick like Major Ross? He might be only a year or so older than he was himself, but he behaved as if he were twice as old. He'd never been known to kick up a lark, or indulge in racing his curricle for a wager. She'd be bored to tears within weeks. But through his own stubbornness he had lost her, and it was all his own fault.

Bella decided that Mary should search Miss Perkins's room while she kept the lady occupied in the drawing-room.

'Jackson, you can keep watch on the back stairs and make sure Mary is not interrupted by any of the maids. And Mary, if you find the jewels, call Jackson in before you touch them, so that he can vouch for where they were. Then fetch me.'

Mary helped her to dress in a plain grey walking dress, which Bella said made her feel like the headmistress of a very stern seminary for delinquent girls, and arranged her hair in as severe a style as she could. Then she went down to the drawing-room and sent the parlourmaid to ask Miss Perkins to join her.

Bella wondered if she imagined Miss Perkins's slight wariness when she entered the room, but the woman smiled, asked brightly how she had enjoyed the play, and sat down with a piece of embroidery. She decided to attack without any warning.

'Miss Perkins, I have discovered that some jewels of mine are missing. Do you know anything about them? You were in the house on your own last night and had every opportunity to search my bedroom.'

The woman paled and dropped her embroidery as she sprang to her feet.

'Oh, how dare you! I thought you were an honest woman, but I see I was mistaken. How could you accuse me of such a thing? Me, the daughter of a clergyman, who has been brought up to respect truth and honesty above all things!'

Bella remained seated and tried to speak calmly. 'The jewels were there when the box was brought to this house. Did you try on some of my gowns last night?' she asked, suddenly knowing why they had seemed creased. 'Perhaps you wanted to see how the jewels looked with them?'

'Oh, this is monstrous! I can't stay here to be so insulted! I'm going to pack my bags and leave at once. And you can be sure I will inform the registry of your accusation, and warn them not to send anyone else here. It is no doubt your maid who has stolen them. If indeed any have been stolen and you are not simply making this up!'

'Mary has been with me for some time, with ample opportunity for theft if she was so inclined. And she was out last night.'

'Then the other servants here. You don't know them. I think the parlourmaid has a very sly look about her.'

'They were all together last night. They had no opportunity.'

There was a knock at the door and Mary, followed by Jackson, came into the room. Silently Mary held out one hand, and Bella saw the missing jewels. Mary then held out her other hand in which were a couple of pairs of kid gloves and an ornate ivory fan.

'Those too?' Bella asked. 'Where were they?'

'The fan was in a drawer underneath some shifts, and the jewels in a hollowed-out Bible,' Mary said, her voice full of disgust.

Jackson held out the book and, as Bella made to take it, Miss Perkins lunged forward and attempted to seize it.

'That's mine! I use it to keep my own jewellery safe! How dare you search my belongings!'

Bella waved her to be silent. 'You clearly came prepared for anything you could find to steal. I wonder how many other of your employers you have robbed? Jackson, fetch the magistrate, please.'

Miss Perkins broke down then, throwing herself on the floor and grasping Bella's ankles, moaning and wailing. 'I've three children to provide for,' she sobbed. 'I'm a widow, and my husband left a mountain of debts. I'm trying to pay them off, to clear his name.'

'By risking your own? You go about it in an odd way,' Bella commented.

'Oh, please, what will become of my little ones if I'm hanged or transported?'

'Perhaps you should have thought of that first. Very well, pack your bags and leave this house within the hour. Mary, you and

Jackson go with her and make sure she doesn't have anything else which doesn't belong to her.'

Bella saw that neither Mary nor Jackson approved of her leniency, but if it were true that three children depended on the woman, she could not bear to be the cause of their losing their mother. She would do without a companion, she decided. Let the polite world condemn her, she cared nothing for their opinion.

On the following evening Bella went to a small concert at the home of a lady she had met only a week before. She knew several of the people there, but as soon as she walked into the room her attention was taken by the sight of Alexander Yates and Frederick Ross sitting either side of Felicity. Frederick was leaning back in his chair, his head flung back, and looking from half-closed eyes at Alexander, a smile playing over his lips. Felicity was clutching to her bosom a rolled sheet of paper, and casting worried glances from one man to the other. Alexander was talking urgently to her.

The trio of musicians began to tune their instruments, and Alexander, with a sigh of frustration, sat back and crossed his arms over his chest, closing his eyes and pursing his lips.

Felicity glanced at him, stretched out her hand as if to touch his arm, and then drew it back hurriedly as Frederick murmured something to her.

'Hush!' a woman sitting behind them said, just as the opening phrases of the music began.

Bella was sitting on a chair against one of the walls, and a moment after the music began a young man slid into the chair beside her, giving those round about an apologetic smile. When there was a break for refreshment he turned to Bella.

'My apologies for my late arrival, ma'am. I trust I did not disturb your concentration?'

Bella had found the musicians less than perfect, their playing somewhat uninspired, and she had detected several wrong notes. 'It was of no importance,' she replied.

He looked round. 'May I escort you into the supper room? That is, if you are not engaged with anyone else.'

None of the men Bella knew had approached her, all of them apparently with ladies, so she smiled at the young man and nodded.

'My name's Lambert, ma'am. William Lambert, at your service.'

'Bella Trahearne,' she responded, and they moved towards the aisle between the rows of chairs.

Opposite them she saw Alexander hold out his arm to Felicity. Frederick Ross on her other side did the same, and the girl blushed, looking from one to the other in dismay.

'Oh, please!'

Bella caught the whisper. Why does she not take both and make a joke of it, Bella thought, irritated with Felicity's gaucheness. But she could hardly leave them in such a state of indecision. They were almost the last to leave the room apart from the musicians, who were stowing their instruments, and Alexander was looking as though he'd like to murder the older man. She halted, murmuring an excuse to her escort.

'Felicity, why don't you join us? Alexander, Mr Ross, how good to see you. Do you know Mr Lambert?'

In a flurry of introductions she got them out of the room. Mr Lambert bustled away to find them a table, and Bella briskly sent off the other two men to fetch food and drink from the buffet.

'Where is your sister?' she asked. How did it happen that Felicity was here unchaperoned?

'She couldn't come. I came with Lady Shaw, but she developed a headache and she asked Alex to escort me home. She knew I was particularly anxious to hear the concert.'

Then she had as little discrimination in music as she did in men, Bella thought in disgust.

Should she say anything to Felicity? Yet what could she say apart from scold the girl about the way she was treating Alexander? She had no right to tell the child to behave herself, to stop being so taken in by a long-haired pseudo poet. Then she laughed softly. She had no idea whether Frederick's poetry was good or bad. Not all men who scribbled verse were bad poets.

'Something amuses you, Miss Trahearne?'

She looked at Mr Lambert and shook her head. 'I have a feeling we have met somewhere,' she said, wrinkling her brow. 'Your voice, there is something familiar about it.'

'Not my face or my figure?' he asked in mock dismay. 'I am sure I have not had the pleasure of meeting you. I could not have forgotten.'

Smooth, Bella thought, amused. She turned to direct the conversation with the others so that Alexander and Mr Ross did not come to blows, which, judging from Alexander's expression, was what he would dearly love.

At the end of the concert she bade farewell to the attentive Mr Lambert, and saw with relief that Lady Andrews' footman was waiting for Felicity. As she waited for Jackson and her own carriage, she watched Felicity being handed into hers, and Mr Ross walking away. Alexander stood watching him, then turned and strode off in the opposite direction. Bella breathed a sigh of relief. For the moment, there would be no bloodshed. And surely Alexander would cool down when he could think rationally.

'Lady Belstead and Mrs Ford,' the butler announced the following morning.

Bella had been writing letters, but she laid down her pen and went to welcome her visitors.

'Do come in. Will you take tea, or would something cold be more welcome? It's a very hot day.'

'Tea will be refreshing,' Lady Belstead replied, and until the tray had been brought and the tea made and poured, they spoke of trivialities.

Lady Belstead sipped the tea, and then put down the cup.

'My dear Miss Trahearne, I'm fully aware that you will consider I take an unwarranted liberty in speaking to you, but I have a great regard for Lady Fulwood, and I know she would be saying the same if she were here. It will not do.'

Bella looked at her in astonishment. 'What will not do?' she asked, her voice harsh. She had a suspicion of what was coming.

'Your living here alone. Young ladies of good family cannot set themselves up in their own houses, without an older lady to give them countenance. It looks most peculiar.'

'Lady Belstead, I appreciate your concern, but I did have a companion.'

'A hired woman you did not know, and for whom I doubt you had a character. And you dismissed her within a day or so when she stole from you. That will merely convince people that you did not properly consider what you were doing.'

'I'm not sure how my business comes to be common knowledge,' Bella said curtly, reining in her temper with an immense effort. How dare these women come and chastize her as though she were a schoolgirl? The fact that she had been taken in by Miss Perkins simply added to her sense of outrage.

Lady Belstead smiled, and shook her head. 'Not common knowledge, yet,' she said. 'But I can assure you it soon will be.'

'Your groom patronizes the same drinking tavern as my footman,' Mrs Ford said gently. 'Knowing you had been staying with Lady Fulwood, he was interested. He told my maid and she told me.'

'Servants' gossip! It's none of their business to criticize me,' Bella exclaimed. Nor is it yours, was the unspoken thought, and she knew the ladies had recognized it.

'I can understand your desire to remain in London for the rest of the Season,' Mrs Ford said. 'And you are an independent young lady who can afford to do whatever you wish. However, you will be ostracized by most people if you continue in this way.'

'Pray reconsider, and come to stay with us,' Lady Belstead added. 'We can put it about that your chaperon had to leave suddenly for family reasons, and you were unfortunately left unsupported. If you move to my house today or tomorrow your reputation will not suffer.'

'Thank you, Lady Belstead, for your kind offer, but I cannot put you to the trouble. I may be leaving London in a few days, and the upheaval of packing twice would be too great an inconvenience.'

And I will look after my own reputation, she thought silently. She knew that people of great wealth, as she was, could be forgiven much that would be condemned in lesser mortals. She would be the eccentric Miss Trahearne.

'You go to join Lady Fulwood in Brighton?' Lady Belstead asked, relief plain in her voice.

'Or perhaps to my home in Lancashire,' Bella said.

She had not before considered it, the words had come to her lips without thought, but suddenly she felt tired of struggling, convinced she had not the slightest chance of regaining Lord Dorney's regard, and also that she did not in the least wish to be married to Major Ross.

Chapter Fourteen

❦

IT HAD BEEN a late night. Some old army friends had come to London on leave, and Lord Dorney had been talking to them until after dawn. So why was someone hammering on the door knocker at this hour? He glanced at the clock on the mantelpiece and groaned. Not yet nine o'clock.

A few minutes later his valet came softly into the room.

'It's all right, I'm awake. Come in. Was that infernal racket anything to do with me?'

'Master Alexander, my lord,' the valet said apologetically. 'He says he must see you and won't stir from the house until he does.'

Lord Dorney groaned. 'Blast the boy! Show him up here, and bring us a pot of coffee. A large pot.'

When Alexander burst into the room a few minutes later Lord Dorney was attired in a red silk dressing-gown, lounging in a chair beside the unlit fire.

'Now what's amiss?' he demanded. 'What has happened to cause you to wake me up when I've had only a couple of hours' sleep?'

Alexander paced about the room. 'Felicity! She sent me a letter. I had it barely an hour ago. She's called off the wedding!'

Lord Dorney groaned and held his head in his hands. He'd half expected this, and had known his young cousin would be devastated, but he had no notion of how to deal with the distraught lad.

'Have you brought the letter?' he asked.

Alexander dragged a crumpled sheet of paper from his pocket. 'Here. Do you think she means it, Richard?'

Lord Dorney read it swiftly, noting that the ink was running where tears – he presumed they were tears – had splattered on to the paper. How remarkably childish and ill-spelt it was, he thought. But the emotions were clear, stark and unambiguous. Felicity felt that her actions were being criticized unfairly, and she would not care to think that Alex would so misjudge her during the rest of her life, if they were to be married, which she would much prefer not to be, on more mature reflection. She thanked Alex for his past kindnesses, and enclosed the betrothal ring he had given her. She hoped he would understand and agree that she could keep the other trifles he had given her, the little pearl fan and the gold neck chain. The fan in fact had been damaged. She remained his devoted servant.

He almost laughed. The chit needed some lessons on how to write such letters, if she were to make a habit of breaking off her engagements, but seeing Alexander's distraught face he kept such reflections to himself.

'Do you know what brought this on?' he asked.

'Two nights ago, that oaf Ross was ogling her and reading her some of his insipid verse. I objected. Yesterday I told her that when we were married I would make sure she never met him again.'

'Unwise, Alex. Never challenge a woman. They're impulsive creatures and may accept your challenge!'

'I mean to challenge Ross! Will you be my second?'

All trace of amusement vanished. 'Don't be a fool! What good would that do? It won't bring Felicity back, and whether you killed him or not you'd have to flee abroad. Go home, and wait. The girl will have to return to Bath soon, and you will have opportunities of meeting her there. You can try to mend fences.'

'But if in the meantime she becomes engaged to Ross, even married to him, it will be too late!'

'I doubt you need worry on that score. Ross is not the sort to want to marry a chit just out of the schoolroom, if he wants to marry at all. Go home, Alex, and if you can be reconciled in the future, you will have a better marriage for it.'

And who am I to be giving out advice on matrimonial matters, he asked himself wryly, when I am making such a mull of my own concerns?

Alexander argued while Lord Dorney dressed. He argued throughout a substantial breakfast. Lord Dorney was amused to see that his agony did not extend to depriving himself of the good things Sir Daniel's cook thought suitable for young men. He argued when Lord Dorney insisted on driving him in the Park to, as he explained, blow away the remaining cobwebs of sleep. And he was still arguing when Lord Dorney delivered him to the hotel where he was staying.

'Go home, Alex,' he said wearily. 'It's the end of June, everyone will be off to Brighton soon, and by the time you see Felicity again she will have had time for second thoughts.'

Later that same morning Major Ross called on Bella. She had been reviewing her clothes with Mary. After the visit of Lady Belstead and Mrs Ford she had seriously considered whether to abandon London. She was making no progress with Lord Dorney, but she did not want to crawl home to Lancashire and admit final defeat. If only she knew what his plans were. If he were proposing to go to Brighton, as half the *ton* seemed to be doing, she would go too. But if he planned to go to Dorney Court, there was no way she could follow him. How could she discover his intentions?

She welcomed the distraction and went down to the drawing-room.

'Major, how good of you to call.'

He accepted a glass of Madeira, but did not take the seat she indicated opposite the one she had sat on. Instead he walked to the window and looked out.

'It promises to be a hot day,' he said. 'The sun is very hot.'

'Indeed it is.'

'Still, it is June, and if we can't have decent weather in June when can we have it in England?'

'When indeed.'

'Do you intend to visit Brighton?' he asked, suddenly swinging round and raising his quizzing glass.

'I really have not decided.'

'You would be advised to. Go and stay with Lady Fulwood. She would welcome your company, I know.'

'Advised? Just what do you mean, Major?' Bella asked sharply.

'My dear, you have two choices if you are to rescue your reputation.'

'I beg your pardon!'

'Now, don't fly up into the boughs, like a green gal. You must know that this situation cannot continue. You are the talk of the clubs, and I have no desire to hear such speculative talk about the lady I intend to marry.'

'Just what do you mean, sir?'

He began to bluster. 'This way of living, without a chaperon! It's just not done, my dear Bella! Now you could go to Brighton as I suggest, or better still, you could give me the answer I've been waiting for, and agree to wed me. I will take you to stay with my sister in Norfolk until the wedding can be arranged. In either case you will be protected from unpleasant gossip.'

Norfolk was even flatter than Cambridge, Bella thought, and stifled a giggle.

'Major, you have paid me a great compliment, but I have, after giving it deep thought, decided that I cannot accept your proposal. If I ever marry, I want to love my husband, and though I have great admiration and regard for you, I fear I cannot feel for you such tender emotion.'

There, she thought, that was very well expressed. She was pleased with herself.

'What? But Bella, my dear, you can't mean that. You gave me to understand it was simply a matter of time!'

She shook her head. 'No, Major, I don't think so. I asked for time to consider, and you were good enough to grant it to me. I have considered, and I don't think we would suit. I'm truly sorry, and I am sure you will make some fortunate woman a very good husband, but that woman is not me.'

'Well, you are an ungrateful chit! I come here, at some risk to my own reputation, in order to save you from ruining yours, and this is how you treat me!'

Bella was suddenly furiously angry. 'Major, can you honestly say you love me?'

'Love? Love? Well, that goes without saying, surely, or I would not have offered for you.'

'If you loved me, you would be prepared to accept me as I am. Now forgive me, Major. I have letters to write.'

*

It was a glorious summer day, and as Jackson drove her to the al fresco rout in Richmond, to which she had received an invitation several weeks earlier, Bella continued to ponder her future. It was almost the end of the Season. The town was already thin of company. This rout was one of the last big occasions, and after it most of the guests would be departing for Brighton and other seaside resorts. Sea bathing had become fashionable, and Brighton was the most fashionable resort of all since the Prince Regent had built his summer Pavilion there. Would Lord Dorney go there?

She hoped she might see him this afternoon, and somehow discover his plans. Or she might ask Sir Daniel. Or Alexander. She was past caring whether they thought her interest odd.

They had arrived at the country mansion where the rout was being held. Bella descended from the curricle and joined the stream of guests approaching the fanciful rustic archway which had been erected across a path leading to the rear of the house, which sloped down to the river. The duchess, the hostess, was standing beneath it to greet them.

The couple in front of Bella moved forward, gave their cards to the footman who announced their names, and made their bow and curtsy. Bella waited, trying to see past the archway to the guests who had arrived. Was Lord Dorney here?

The previous couple moved on. The footman took Bella's card, glanced at it, and announced in ringing tones, 'Miss Rosabella Trahearne.'

Bella dropped into a curtsy, and almost fell over as the duchess spoke.

'Pray escort this person off the premises.'

'What?' Bella demanded, aghast. 'But – my invitation!'

'Escort this – creature – away. She is not welcome.'

Two other footmen, barely suppressing grins, came forward and grasped Bella's arms. They were not gentle. Stunned with disbelief that she had been so publicly snubbed, she allowed them to lead her back to the main entrance, past incoming guests, who eyed her with a mixture of curiosity and disgust.

Her cheeks flamed, and she felt unaccustomed tears flood her eyes. She flung up her head defiantly, blinked back the tears, and tried to shake off the hands of the footmen.

'Let go of me! I have no intention of remaining where I am treated so disgracefully.'

Alexander, in a plain riding coat and breeches, waited patiently on his horse in the street just above Frederick Ross's lodgings. He'd discovered from the poet's valet, with the help of a couple of gold coins, that he meant to ride out to visit a friend in the village of Kensington that afternoon. That suited Alexander very well. He would have to cross Knightsbridge, notorious for footpads.

After an hour, when Alexander had begun to wonder if the valet had misinformed him, Frederick Ross appeared, nattily attired in a many-caped riding coat despite the heat. He sported a spotted neckerchief, and a high-crowned hat.

Alexander followed him at a distance. There were few people about, for which he gave thanks. He wanted as few witnesses as possible.

Frederick rode well, which surprised Alexander. He had thought all poets would be effete, inadequate sportsmen. He had to urge his own mount on to keep up as Frederick set his horse to a canter.

They came to a spot Alexander had marked out, where there were trees to either side of the road, and even on such a bright day the sunlight rarely penetrated the gloom.

He pulled his neckerchief up over his mouth, and the brim of his hat down to hide his eyes. Then he urged his own horse into a gallop, came alongside the slower horse and grasped its reins, forcing it to turn aside along a narrow track through the trees.

Frederick, taken utterly by surprise, was slow to react, but he began to protest and struggle to regain the reins, tugging fruitlessly at them.

Alexander laughed, then remembered to disguise his voice. 'You'll not get away so easily, my fine poet! Get off, or I'll push you off,' he said as gruffly as he could manage.

'What the devil's the matter with you? If you want my purse, take it!'

'Poltroon!' Alexander was scornful of Frederick's craven attitude. He'd expected, and would have welcomed, more of a fight. He brought his own mount up close, bent to catch Frederick's foot, and heaved him out of the saddle. The horse, given a thwack on the rump, took off as Frederick picked himself up from the ground and began to brush leaves and leaf mould off his coat.

Then Frederick jumped in surprise as Alexander's whip descended on his legs. He tried desperately to escape, but, mounted as he was, Alexander had no difficulty in following him, and the whip crashed down remorselessly on every portion of his body.

'I'll teach you to seduce young ladies!' Alexander panted. 'Take that, you miserable creature! Can't you even try to fight back?'

Unable to flee, Frederick, weeping unrestrainedly by now and pleading, between the sobs, to be spared, suddenly dropped to the ground and curled up into a ball, his arms protecting his head.

Alexander looked down at him in disgust, then turned and rode away. That should teach the miserable creature a lesson. He was only sorry Felicity had not been present to witness her poet hero's craven behaviour.

'I won't endure it!' Bella raged, striding up and down her bedroom while Mary tried to gather up the discarded clothes. 'How dare that woman snub me so publicly? What right has she to dictate my conduct? Why should she decide I'm not fit to go to her wretched party just because I don't keep a tame duenna? I'll show her! I'll show them all!'

She spent a sleepless night, going over and over her humiliation, and wishing she had thought of the many cutting responses she could have made. She slept late, and when she rang for her breakfast Mary brought several notes which had been delivered.

'So I'm not beyond the pale to everyone,' Bella said, inspecting them. She drank some chocolate, and set aside the tray while she opened the notes. Then she flung the first one down in a renewed fury. 'Lady Belstead, to say she told me so! How dare she!'

Two of the others were notes excusing the writers from the small dinner party Bella had planned for the following week. One suddenly had to leave town earlier than expected. The other gave no excuse, simply finding it inconvenient to attend. Bella wondered bleakly whether she would be sitting down to table by herself.

She eyed the last in some trepidation. However angry she was, she realized she had overstepped the bounds of propriety, and one part of her regretted that. She would devote herself in future to her orphans, become more involved in the actual running of the houses, rather than just the financing of them. She did not know the writing, and sighed as she broke the seal and spread out the paper.

My dear Miss Trahearne, the letter began, *we have not met, as I have been kept out of town until this week by a relative's illness. However, I was once acquainted with your cousin, now Lady Hodder. I am sorry to have missed her visit to town, but hope you will give me the pleasure of your company at a small party next week. Yours very sincerely, Amelia Stockley.*

Bella smiled. Not everyone was going to cut her. Yet, she amended. Of course, when this Amelia Stockley knew what had happened, she might be as unwilling to pursue the acquaintance as Bella's other so-called friends. She could only wait and see. But she would not be driven away by the opinion of stuffy, hidebound duchesses!

Bella was shopping in Bond Street later that day when she saw Mrs Ford turning into the circulating library. Would that lady snub her? She would follow her and find out.

Inside the library she could not at first see Mrs Ford, then she spied her standing beside two unknown ladies. Bella moved forward when she caught the name Ross. She paused, and saw that Mrs Ford had turned away from the perusal of the books and was listening to the conversation.

'Badly beaten, he was. They say it was footpads. Disgusting, that such a thing could happen so close to the highway.'

'Knightsbridge was always a haunt of footpads.'

'It's not sure he'll save the sight of one eye. And the lacerations! They had to cut his coat away from him, it was stiff with blood.'

'Poor man! I wonder if his brother will be taking him home to recover, if he survives?'

Behind them Mrs Ford gave a muffled cry, and slid down to the floor.

The two women stepped back hastily, then one knelt down beside her. 'Poor lady, in a dead swoon, she is. Here, some water if you please!'

Bella knelt down and lifted Mrs Ford's head so that she could sip the water one of the attendants had brought. Her eyes fluttered open, and she gazed round at the concerned faces, then gave a sob. 'Peter! Oh, and I sent him away!'

Bella patted her hands. 'Don't worry, I'll see you get home. Do you have a carriage?'

Mrs Ford shook her head. 'I walked.'

'Please, can someone find a hackney? I know the lady and will see she gets home.'

Within minutes Mrs Ford had been lifted into a hackney and they were driven swiftly to Mount Street. Bella plied the knocker and soon Lady Belstead's footman was helping Bella carry Mrs Ford indoors.

Lady Belstead, hurriedly summoned, guided them into the room her husband used as a library, and Mrs Ford was gently deposited in a deep, comfortable chair, her feet raised on a footstool. She tried to protest that she was recovered, but she was pale and trembling. Lady Belstead poured out some brandy and forced her to sip it.

'My dear, this is so unlike you. What caused you to swoon? Bella, dear, how fortunate you were there and could bring her home. But what happened?'

Bella shook her head. 'I'm not sure. We were in the library, and two women began to talk about a man called Ross who had been badly hurt by footpads. Mrs Ford, did you suspect they meant the major?'

Mrs Ford nodded, and struggled to rise. 'It must have been. Oh, and I treated him so badly! I sent him away.'

Bella glanced at Lady Belstead in surprise. 'Sent him away?' she whispered.

Lady Belstead nodded. 'Eleanor, my dear, you should go to bed and try to rest. I'll send someone to the major's lodgings to discover what has happened, if anything. I'll come and tell you the moment I hear anything.'

She and the maid helped Mrs Ford up the stairs, and Bella, consumed with curiosity, and speculating wildly on what this could mean, stayed where she was.

Half an hour later Lady Belstead returned and sank down into a chair facing Bella.

'He offered for her,' she said without preamble. 'She felt it was too soon after her husband's death, and she did not think it kind to ask him to wait, so she sent him away.'

This was no time for dissembling, Bella decided. 'Does she love him?' she asked bluntly.

'Yes, and she's been so miserable since then. He took his dismissal like a gentleman, I suppose, and refrained from seeking her out. She is convinced he has found someone else, but she doesn't know who. If he's badly hurt, even if he dies, which from what you overheard is not impossible, she will go into a decline.'

'I'm sure she is stronger minded than that,' Bella said. Should she tell Lady Belstead that she had been the new object of the major's gallantry, and had refused him? She decided to wait until they knew the precise extent of his injuries.

They speculated, but knew nothing until, after ten minutes, Major Ross himself came hurriedly into the room.

'Lady Belstead, what's this I hear about Eleanor?'

At the same time Lady Belstead spoke. 'So you are not injured!'

'She swooned, but she will soon recover when she sees you are not hurt,' Bella said crisply. 'She heard you had been beaten almost to death.'

'I need to see her. No, they exaggerate. Frederick was beaten, and he has some nasty cuts, and a couple of black eyes, but he'll mend. Now can I see her?'

He didn't even notice that I was there, Bella thought in amusement, after Lady Belstead had conducted him upstairs. He would, it seemed, soon be consoled after her own rejection. And how immensely fortunate she had rejected him. What a coil it could have been.

Lady Belstead soon returned, smiling. 'I think that all's going to be well,' she said. 'The major is going to take Frederick home to Cambridge where he can rusticate until he has recovered his looks. Poets with black eyes do not elicit the required female adoration! But he won't remain there. We are going to Weymouth and he intends to accompany us.'

Alexander looked defiant. 'You're not my guardian, Richard. I'm of age, and I won't be dictated to by you! Nor am I responsible to you for my actions.'

'Did you attack Frederick Ross? People are saying it was you. You've been complaining about him for weeks. They know you blame him for your broken engagement. He may not have seen you, or recognized you at the time, but there will be plenty of people to suggest it was you. And Frederick can be vindictive. He may bring a case against you.'

'The man deserved to be horsewhipped. I'll congratulate the man who did it.'

'You, Alex.'

'No one can prove anything.'

Lord Dorney sighed. 'I strongly recommend that you leave town. Go home to Bath. Let people forget.'

'Run away from the insinuations, you mean?'

'Sometimes a retreat makes sense. Alex, if you stay, you'll be the object of sly hints, and one day you'll say something that will condemn you. You won't be able to resist. I'm going to Dorney Court next week. Come with me. Leave Felicity to ponder on the loss of both her swains. Then when you meet again in Bath she might be more amenable.'

An hour later he breathed a sigh of relief. He had worn Alexander down, and eventually his cousin had agreed to return to Bath and join him later at Dorney Court.

He had made up his mind to go home. Bella seemed intent on causing scandal, and he suspected he was part of the reason for her behaviour. He had wavered between trying to forget her, and abandoning his own doubts and asking her to marry him. Unable to decide, he hoped that a few months away from her might clear his mind. If he could not forget her, then he would seek her out once more. If in the meantime she became engaged to someone else he would have to accept that she was not sincere in her protestations of devotion to him. He would, as he had tried to persuade Alexander with regard to Felicity, be better off without such a wife.

He didn't believe himself.

Bella set off for the party at Amelia Stockley's house in high spirits. She enjoyed meeting new people, and she had a feeling she might find people there who would not condemn her.

The house, in Portman Square, was richly, even lavishly furnished.

A footman in a powdered wig and black satin knee breeches escorted her up to the drawing-room. As she approached Bella could hear the buzz of conversation, almost drowned by the plaintive wail of a violin. The footman, with great ceremony, announced her, and for a moment all conversation stopped as people turned to look at her.

Bella was no shy, retiring violet, but this concentrated stare caused her to blush faintly. She threw back her head, smiled, took a couple of steps into the room, and waited composedly for her hostess to greet her. As one lady detached herself from the throng, the conversations resumed.

Amelia Stockley was a ravishing blonde, tall and voluptuous. Her gown clung provocatively to her luscious curves, and the *décolletage* was, Bella considered, almost indecently revealing. She wore a flamboyant necklace of blood-red rubies, in a rather antique setting, and ruby ear-drops which must, Bella thought, stifling a giggle, have been painfully heavy.

'My dear Miss Trahearne! How good of you to come to my little party. I have so longed to meet you. Tell me, how is dear Jane? It's such a pity she went back to Lancashire before I returned to town.'

Bella considered this speech as Amelia took her round the room introducing her to the other guests, none of whom she had met before. She could not imagine Jane, with her fastidiousness, being friends with such a woman. But perhaps, if they had been intimate many years ago, Amelia might have changed. She looked around and recognized no one. She'd never met any of these people before, and from the somewhat raffish air of the men and almost indecent attire of the ladies, decided they were not members of the *ton*, or not of the higher echelons, in any event. She shrugged mentally. She herself was being condemned by the best society, so she would make do with these others.

The room had seemed crowded, but in fact there were only a dozen people there. Soon after Bella's arrival they sat down to listen to some music. The violinist who had been playing performed first, then a rather nervous young lady sang some sentimental songs. To Bella's relief that was all, and the company trooped down to a buffet supper laid out in the dining-room and a large, overheated and humid conservatory which opened from it.

The food was ample, and better than Bella had expected. Clearly Amelia paid her cook more than she did her musicians. The other guests were friendly, and from what they said were mostly minor country gentry. There was even a banker and his wife, a middle aged couple who entertained Bella with stories of the stratagems some of the less wealthy young men, anxious to cut a dash, used to avoid paying their bills or borrow from the bank. Champagne flowed, and after two glasses Bella decided she must not have any more. She was feeling the effects more quickly than usual, and did not want to disgrace herself.

'Come, we'll go back upstairs,' Amelia said. 'Bella – I may call you Bella, I hope – you'll enjoy a game of faro. Or would you prefer a hand of piquet?'

Bella was amused. None of her previous hostesses would have dreamt of entertaining their guests by setting up a faro table in their drawing-rooms. A room set aside for cards, for the older guests who did not wish to dance, perhaps, but she had never before seen the entire company playing faro. They did so with enthusiasm, and Bella gathered that it was a regular form of entertainment.

The stakes were high, and after an hour, when an end was called to the game, Bella was surprised to see that the cards seemed to favour her unduly, and the pile of money in front of her had grown considerably. Her initial stake must have multiplied by at least four times.

'You have good luck tonight,' a woman whose dress was almost as revealing as Amelia's, said to Bella. 'You will have to come again so that we can take our revenge!'

Bella smiled her acknowledgment, but she was embarrassed. She could have afforded to lose, and she wondered whether all of these people could? One of the young men, who had been signing vowels towards the end, was looking rather downcast.

But she had enjoyed the evening. It had been different from the usual entertainments. Some of the company had amused her, and all had made her welcome. When Amelia said they were organizing a party to ride out to Richmond Park a few days hence, she readily agreed to join them. It was some time since she had ridden anywhere except Hyde Park, and that was always rather staid. She would hope for a good gallop. It might take her mind off her problems.

Chapter Fifteen

⁓◦◦⁓

THE DAY OF the outing to Richmond came. As she was dressing, Mary showed her the trimming on her newest gown, the one she'd worn to Amelia's house.

'It's coming loose, Miss Bella. And you've lost weight since you had the fitting. Shall I take it back to the dressmaker this morning?'

'Yes, please, Mary. It only needs to be taken in a little. She doesn't need another fitting, and I don't want to have to endure standing still while she tries not to stick pins in me.'

'You'll want it when you go to Mrs Stockley's house next week.'

'Yes, if I go.'

Bella had thought about the card party a good deal, and decided that in some fashion her good luck in winning had been contrived. Several of the other guests had known each other well, she had soon realized. Had they been involved in some sort of conspiracy against her, a new and wealthy heiress? Had she unwittingly stumbled on some kind of gambling fraud?

Rich young men were often lured into gambling dens, she'd heard, and allowed to win at the outset. Then they lost heavily, and many had been ruined trying to win back their fortunes. Were rich young ladies also in such danger? She decided they were, particularly when they had no chaperon or parent to warn them of the perils of believing they were lucky and would in the end win back whatever they had lost. She was undecided whether to return and test her theory, or make some excuse for not going. She could afford some losses, and it would give her satisfaction to know her suspicions were accurate. Also, she might be misjudging Amelia Stockley. If the woman were honest, did Bella want to cut herself off from the only people in London who did not despise her?

She would decide after the outing today, when something might be discovered to prove her theory or not. She returned her attention to Mary.

'And I need another pair of white gloves. You know my size, and I can trust your taste. You can purchase some for me.'

'Yes, miss. Oh, Jackson wants to see you before you go out.'

'Send him to the dining-room. I'll be down in a few minutes.'

Jackson came to report that one of the Welsh cobs had a loose shoe. 'I can't understand it, Miss Bella,' he said. 'Their shoes were all replaced a week ago. I'll have to take him to get it done today. You'll be wanting to drive out tomorrow, I think.'

'Yes, get it done. Do you want to go to a different farrier? Do you think the other didn't do his work properly?'

'No, Miss Bella, we've used him since we came to London, and Masters has used him for years. Perhaps it was a faulty nail. It sometimes happens.'

At that moment Mrs Stockley and the rest of her party arrived, and Bella set off with them. The day was warm, the skies cloudless, and Bella thoroughly enjoyed the opportunity of a gallop. She thrust away all thoughts of Lord Dorney and the snubs she had received from many of the *ton*. Tomorrow would be time enough to decide what she meant to do.

Meanwhile she was alert for any indication that she was being set up as a dupe for plucking. When they stopped to eat a nuncheon at an inn near Richmond she commented on how much she had enjoyed the card party, and how amazed she was at winning.

'For I have played very little,' she said. 'I know very few games of chance.'

'You will soon learn,' Amelia said. 'Why, a year ago I knew scarcely anything about cards. Then William – a friend – taught me. Now it's one of my greatest pleasures to sit down to a game of faro or piquet.'

The others in the party, who had all been at Amelia's house that evening, were equally reassuring. Bella concluded they almost certainly intended to ensure that she did not win any more. Should she give them another opportunity to prove it, or be discreet and make excuses to refuse further invitations?

*

As they rode home Bella's thoughts returned to the houses she was setting up. She would go and see the Floods tomorrow. Her scheme for providing homes for orphans was a success. She'd had letters from both Preston and Bristol to report progress, and all seemed to be going well. Other people were coming forward with money for the running costs of the homes. One elderly gentleman had offered to buy a house himself and leave all his money towards the cost of more, on condition they were named after him. A reasonable enough request, Bella considered. She would begin to look round for more suitable properties.

In Piccadilly, as she parted from the rest of the party and turned into Dover Street she saw Jackson running towards her. He ran beside her, talking so rapidly and with intense excitement that she could not make out any words apart from 'Mary'.

'Mary? What's happened?'

She halted the mare and turned to look at the groom. He was white-faced, his hair rumpled, and his coat buttoned up incorrectly. She'd never seen him in such disarray before. Normally he was neatly dressed.

'Mary! She's been took! She never came back from that errand you sent her on this morning.'

'What? You mean she's had an accident? Is she hurt?'

He shook his head. 'That's what we thought when she didn't come back. I went to see if I could find her, but she'd left the dressmaker's hours before. Then a note was delivered.'

'A note?'

He seemed calmer now and was able to explain. 'Yes. For you. A lad brought it, said he'd been given a couple of pennies, from a gentleman who was just getting into a closed carriage, to deliver it.'

Bella's thoughts were whirling. 'A note? From Mary? Where is it?'

As she stared at Jackson she became aware of someone else standing beside her. She looked up and saw Lord Dorney.

'Jackson, take the mare round to the stables while I explain to Miss Trahearne.'

He gave Bella his hand and helped her dismount. Bewildered, trying to absorb the implications of what Jackson had said, and why

Lord Dorney should be here at her house, she permitted him to lead her indoors, where she found the rest of her servants hovering in the hallway.

Lord Dorney waved his hand and they vanished to the kitchen quarters. He led her to the drawing-room and made her sit down. In a daze, she removed her hat and riding gloves.

'Well? What's happened? Why are you here?'

'Jackson was already worried, and when the note came he guessed something was amiss. Apparently the farrier thought the horse's shoe had been loosened deliberately, and Jackson suspects it was done to get him out of the way. He didn't know how long you'd be away, so he came round to me. Sir Daniel's house where I am staying is just round the corner in Bruton Street. I opened the note and read it.'

About to protest he had no right to read her letters, she had second thoughts. In such a situation speed might be all important.

He handed her a sheet of paper, and after a startled look she read it. It was short and it made her go cold with a mixture of dread and fury.

You were not there with your little pistol this time. If you want to get your maid back unharmed, tell no one, do nothing, and wait for further instructions. But have plenty of money ready.

'She's been abducted! Poor Mary! What can we do?' Bella asked.

'What it says, wait. We can't have any notion of where they'll have taken her, or who they are, though it would seem it's the doing of at least one of those rogues you threatened at the inn near Bath.'

'How – oh, yes.' Bella was annoyed with herself. She ought to have understood that immediately. 'My wits have gone begging. But I can't just sit here doing nothing! Should we call in the Runners? Perhaps someone near the dressmaker's saw something?'

'Sir Daniel took his man and a couple of friends to make enquiries in the streets and houses near there. As for the Runners, not yet. The rogues may be watching this house.'

'Then they'll have seen you come here! And they warned me to tell no one. They'll guess I told you.'

'It's not so obvious. All they'll have seen is a gentleman caller. They won't know I've read the note, for you've been out all day and wouldn't have read it by the time you met me.'

'But you've stayed a long time. When did you get here?'

'I came back with Jackson to read the note, then went to ask Dan to help. I've been back here for less than an hour, waiting for you to return. There is nothing unusual in that. Nor will there be when Dan comes back here to let us know what, if anything, he has discovered.'

Despite her concern over Mary, and what she might be suffering at the hands of those villains, Bella could not help reflecting that her reputation, damaged as it now was, would be irretrievably ruined if Lord Dorney stayed for much longer, and if she were seen to be receiving other young gentlemen. She didn't care for that. She needed his support and calm good sense.

'Is there nothing else we can do?'

'We have to appear to do as they say. In truth, we cannot do any more until they get in touch again.'

'If only we knew something about them! Who they are.'

Lord Dorney was frowning. 'That confrontation at the inn. When those young men tried to persuade Mary into their carriage. That must be what they meant by the pistol. Unless you have been threatening others with it since then?'

'Of course I haven't!'

'Think back, carefully. Can you recall everything that was said?'

Bella forced her whirling thoughts into order. 'They said they'd take her to Bristol. They – they said she could sit on their laps, something about being a bit squashed.'

'Then you produced that pistol and threatened them. Or at least threatened a delicate part of their anatomy.' He grinned, and Bella went hot with embarrassment.

She was calmer now, thinking back with deep concentration. 'And they scoffed, said a woman couldn't shoot straight. Oh, if only they were here now, I'd show them!'

'Then,' Lord Dorney exclaimed, getting to his feet and striding about the room, 'then the mail coach moved out of the way, and someone in their chaise called out to leave her. Can you recall the exact words?'

Bella frowned in concentration. 'He said she wasn't worth the trouble. No, that's not exactly it.'

'He mentioned a name. Wait, I have it. It was Land – Lambert!'

'Lambert?' Bella beat her fist against her brow. 'Are you sure?'

'Yes, quite sure.'

'Then I've recently met him. I thought his voice was familiar, though I didn't recognize his face.'

Lord Dorney crossed the room and took her shoulders in his hands. 'Bella, in that case we have something to go on! He's been in town recently. Tell me all you can. Where did you meet? When? Did he say anything to indicate where he was staying? Anything!'

She tried to ignore the feelings that threatened to overwhelm her as he held her shoulders. 'It was at a small musical entertainment. Alexander was there, with Felicity, and he and Mr Ross were vying for her favours. I was more intrigued with watching them, than paying attention to him.'

'What did you both say?'

Bella concentrated. 'I asked if we'd met before, said I thought I'd recognized his voice. He made some joke about it not being his face or figure, appearing to be disappointed. But he did not appear to know me.'

'I suspect he did. You are not easy to forget, my dear. Especially in the situation when you worsted him.'

She leapt to her feet in excitement, forgetting that Lord Dorney still held her shoulders. 'I've just remembered. He introduced himself as William, William Lambert.'

Suddenly she was clasped in his arms as he slid them round her. 'Wonderful! What's the address of the house where you met him?'

Bella, rather breathless, told him. 'But you know what these occasions are, even the hostesses sometimes don't know who is there, if people bring friends and relatives who've just come to stay. Lady Fulwood took us to all her engagements the first day we arrived, and I knew no one.'

'Even so, someone will know him, and where he is staying.'

'It might not be him. It could be one of the others.'

'Don't be such a wet blanket,' he said, shaking her slightly. 'If we find Lambert we can find the others. They were friends of his.'

'Yes, of course. I can't think straight.' And that was less because of Mary's abduction than the fact she was held in Lord Dorney's arms.

'Bella, I must leave you now, go and find Dan, and we will start asking around, at the clubs and so on.' He held her away from him. 'Will you be all right on your own? Is there a woman friend I can ask to sit with you?'

Bella thought of the people who had snubbed her. Did she have any friends left? Did she count Amelia as a friend? She certainly could not trust her, she decided.

'I'd rather be on my own. Go quickly, try to discover what you can.'

'I'll come back here to let you know if we've had any success. Eat some dinner, try not to worry.'

With a swift kiss on her cheek he released her and was gone. Bella sank back into the chair and held her hand to her cheek. They would find Mary. She would be released. And Lord Dorney no longer seemed angry with her.

He started at White's, but no one there seemed to know Lambert. He wasn't a member, so Lord Dorney decided to try some of the other clubs. He was leaving when he almost bumped into Alexander.

'Richard! I've been looking all over for you.'

'I thought you were going back to Bath?' Lord Dorney spoke impatiently. He didn't have time for Alexander's problems.

'I – well, I thought about what you said, and I intend to forget Felicity. She is not worth my attention if she can behave in such a fashion, and it's as well I have discovered it before we were married. So there is no need for me to go home and wait for her to find out she is mistaken.'

'Well, no,' Lord Dorney replied, suppressing the glimmer of amusement at Alexander's air of noble renunciation.

'Besides, I could not bear to listen to my mother's complaints and questions. So I will stay here, until she has had time to forget it.'

Lord Dorney doubted whether Mrs Yates ever would, but he sympathized with Alexander's less noble desire to avoid the inevitable inquisition. 'Wise,' he commented. 'Now, Alex, pray excuse me, I have urgent business to attend to.'

'At this time of night? I was hoping we could dine together. I won't sleep, I need to make a night of it.'

'I'm sorry, Alex. Maybe in a few days, but I don't know where I'll be for a while.'

'Oh, are you leaving town?'

An idea struck him. Alexander could be useful. 'Do you really mean that? Making a night of it? Would you be prepared to go to Dan's house and wait for messages? Dan will be coming back there, but I need to be at Bella's, in case they contact her during the night.'

'Bella Trahearne's? Whatever for?'

Lord Dorney drew him to one side, where they could not be overheard, and briefly explained. 'If Dan comes home, tell him where I am and both of you come round.'

It was almost midnight when Lord Dorney returned. Jackson, who had been sitting in the hall, let him in. Bella had sent all the other servants to bed, saying they could do nothing at this late stage, but she might need them in the morning. She had seen no point in keeping them ignorant of what was happening. They had known something was wrong when Mary had not returned, and the behaviour of Jackson had alerted them to it's being some disaster. Bella had been touched at the concern they showed.

'We all liked Mary,' the cook had said when she came and tried to persuade Bella to eat some of the dinner she had prepared. 'She had no side on her, like some of the ladies'-maids we've had here. And Jackson's going demented. Sweet on her, he is.'

Which explained his frantic demeanour, Bella thought. Lord Dorney would find her, get her safely back, she was sure. And his refusal to go to bed with the others was explained. Poor man, he must be even more worried than she was. She trusted he wouldn't be impelled to do anything silly which might endanger Mary or hamper Lord Dorney's efforts to find her.

'Have you found him?' Bella demanded, as Lord Dorney came swiftly into the drawing-room. Jackson followed him and hovered beside the door. Bella hadn't the heart to send him away.

'We know where he had lodgings, Dan found out from a friend of his, but he left there this morning, saying he was going to Brighton. He had hired a coach, which his landlord thought odd in a single gentleman, but he explained he was escorting an elderly lady. Alex is riding down the post road, enquiring at all the inns.

We'll know in the morning if he went that way, but I think it's unlikely. He'd have said that to put us off the scent, should we suspect him.'

'Alex?'

'I found him at White's, waiting for me. We'd had a slight disagreement the last time we met, and he's eager to make it right. When I told him what had happened he wanted to help. As he vowed he would not be able to sleep sending him on a night ride to Brighton seemed the best way of occupying him while we reserve our strength for tomorrow.'

'I won't sleep.'

'My dear Bella, there's nothing you can do tonight. You've heard no more, I take it?'

She shook her head.

'It will take him a while to get to wherever he's going and then send his demand for money. That is what I anticipate. Tomorrow we will try to discover where he hired the coach, and where it was going.'

'I'll do that,' Jackson interrupted. 'I know most of the stablemen round here.'

'There are a good many, and he might have gone further afield, to the City, for instance, where he was not known.'

'I'll get a couple of friends to help. They're London born and bred and will know where best to ask.'

'Good. But try to sleep for a few hours. We'll do Mary no service if we are all too weary to stay awake.'

Jackson nodded, but with reluctance, and with a brief bob towards Bella left the room.

'Are you going back to Sir Daniel's?' Bella asked. She felt horribly alone.

'If you have a spare room, and are not worried about your repu-tation, can I stay here? I'd like to be on hand if a message is delivered, to question whoever brings it.'

'You can have the room Miss Perkins used. I had the bed made up in case I ever found anyone else I could trust.'

'What do you mean? I heard, as I imagine most of the *ton* did, that you had dispensed with her services, but no one seems to know why.'

Briefly Bella explained about the theft.

'You poor girl. She's the culprit, but it's your reputation that is being made to suffer.'

'My reputation is the last thing I care about!' Bella said with a grim smile. 'People cannot think anything worse of me than they already do.'

Bella tossed and turned and fell into an uneasy sleep just as daylight began to creep into the room. She was horrified to see it was almost ten in the morning when she awoke.

Hastily she dressed and went downstairs. Lord Dorney was eating breakfast, and he rose to pour her coffee, and filled a plate for her from the dishes on the sideboard.

'Come, eat some of this excellent ham your cook has prepared. And there are eggs too. Or do you prefer the devilled kidneys?'

'I can't eat. Is there any news?'

'You won't help Mary by starving yourself. Be a good girl, Bella.'

She shook her head, but sat down at the table and sipped the coffee. After a few moments the appetizing smell of the ham made her pick up her fork and take a small mouthful, then another.

'Is there any news?' she repeated.

'Not yet. Jackson went out early, but it will take time for him and his friends to visit every livery stable.'

'Alex?'

'I'm expecting him back soon. He's had time to ride all the way to Brighton and back.'

'I've been thinking. Amelia, the woman who organized the party to Richmond, mentioned a William.'

'It's a common enough name.'

'I know, but I'm wondering if I was enticed away deliberately.' She explained her suspicions about the card party. 'If Amelia knows Lambert they could have plotted this together. My dress was torn after I'd been to that card party. It could have been done deliberately there. The loose horseshoe could have been to get Jackson out of the way.'

'We're assuming a great deal.'

'Yes, but it's possible.'

An hour later Alexander arrived.

'There's no sign of them on the Brighton road,' he reported. 'Is there any coffee?' he added, yawning widely.

Bella rang the bell. 'Cook has been pressing coffee on us all morning,' she said. 'She'll provide you with some breakfast too.'

'Good. Thank you, Bella. I didn't stop to eat.'

'So that was an attempt to throw us off the scent. Well done, Alex. Now when you've eaten go to Dan's house, and snatch some sleep,' Lord Dorney told him.

'I'm not tired. I want to see this through.'

'Even an hour will help. I can't have anyone delaying us through tiredness, so if you want to come with us do as I say!'

Alexander protested, but when he yawned again gave in and departed.

It was two hours after midday before Jackson returned. Bella and Lord Dorney sat in the drawing-room, both looking through the window, concealed from the view of anyone watching the house by carefully positioned curtains. They were too worried to make conversation. They both jumped to their feet when Jackson was seen walking rapidly towards the house.

'You have news?' Lord Dorney asked the moment he entered the room.

'They went east,' Jackson reported. 'The coach and driver had been engaged only as far as Upminster. He said Lambert said his sister was unwell, and they would stay at the inn there for her to rest. He, Lambert, carried her inside, saying she was unable to walk, but the coachman said she was all wrapped up in a cloak even though it's so hot. She looked as though she'd swooned. Just let me get my hands on that damned devil! Beg pardon, Miss Bella.'

'Damned is right, Jackson! How did he induce her to go with him in the first place?' Bella asked. 'Mary's a sensible girl.'

'Some lying trick, no doubt,' Lord Dorney suggested. 'It's possible he was watching this house, saw you leave, and then Mary go off on her own. He could have followed her. Perhaps he told her you had been involved in an accident and needed her. If she didn't recognize him, and I doubt she recalls much detail about what happened at that inn, she'd have been too frightened at the time. She'd have gone in a hackney, and he could have taken her somewhere while he organized the coach.'

'Just let me get my hands on him!'

'You'll have your chance, Jackson. Was he alone? None of his friends with him?' Lord Dorney asked.

'Yes, he was alone until Upminster, unless he had plans to meet someone there.'

'Unlikely, I think. It seems to have been a spur of the moment action, he took his chance when it offered, though I imagine he had it all planned and only waited for his opportunity.'

'He'll have to hire another carriage there, unless he's close enough to his home to have one sent,' Bella said. 'We can find out more there when we follow him.'

'Dan and Alex and I will follow,' Lord Dorney said. 'Jackson, you too. I'll go round to Sir Daniel's house and tell them to get our horses ready. Take the best horse you have, and I'll meet you there '

'Before you do that, Jackson,' Bella interrupted, 'fetch me another pair of your breeches and a jacket of some sort. You're not much taller than I am. And find a good horse and a saddle for me. I'm sure the stables will have something suitable.'

Lord Dorney stared at her. 'Bella, don't be stupid. You can't mean to create another scandal by riding through London in men's clothes!'

That 'another' hurt, but Bella was insistent. 'I've ridden astride since I was a child, at home.'

'He'll be sending a message soon. You need to be here to receive it, so that we can know his plans.'

She was exasperated. 'And what good would it be if I did receive it? There would be no way I could tell you if you are somewhere in the wilds of Essex! Would you prefer that I am left alone to deal with him? To be abducted as well, no doubt, if I don't do as he says?'

Lord Dorney frowned. 'You need do nothing except stay safely indoors. If he is here he can't be harming Mary.'

'I doubt he'll come himself.'

'He still won't harm her until he hears from you.'

'And if I'm not to be found he'll have to wait. That gives us more time to find her. Leave Sir Daniel's groom here in case a message does come. He can ride after us if it does, on the chance of finding us. I'm coming with you. And if you try to stop me I'll follow.'

'Heaven preserve me from stubborn women!' He glared at her.

'But pack a gown. And a long cloak. It may be necessary for you to change into petticoats, so be prepared.'

Bella chuckled. 'I won't delay you, don't fear. But you're delaying us if you want to argue with me.'

Chapter Sixteen

⁓◦◦⁓

A S THEY RODE, Lord Dorney told Bella what they had, between
them, discovered.

She had bundled her hair into a net, pulled a cap Jackson had
provided over it, and with his breeches and jacket, and a shirt he had
also offered her, looked a passable boy.

'Lambert is heavily in debt. He has been gambling on the cards,
horses, anything, it seems, where he is likely to lose badly. He inherited a moderate fortune but was soon going to the moneylenders. He
has a small estate in Essex, near the coast, about another fifteen miles
past Upminster.'

'Is that where he's taking Mary?'

'It might be, but he has servants there, and he may not be able to
trust them to keep quiet if he tries to keep Mary captive. And I
cannot imagine she would agree to stay otherwise.'

'She certainly would not! Mary is no coward, to be constrained by
threats.'

'Then he will be keeping her prisoner somewhere else. A cottage,
a barn, or even a boat as he's near the sea. There are lots of creeks
along the river where a boat could be hidden. When we are closer to
his house we can begin making enquiries, ask about possible hide-
outs. You and Jackson must stay out of sight. I mean it,' he added as
Bella began to protest. 'He knows both of you, but I doubt he knows
Dan or myself. Or Alex. Even if he has been watching you, none of
us has been seen with you recently.'

Bella, frustrated, had to admit the sense of this. 'But I won't be
kept out of any confrontation! Mary will need me.'

Lord Dorney laughed. 'Perhaps. But don't you think Jackson will be able to give her better consolation?'

'But if he's hurt her?'

'Bella, when she's free, and Lambert captured or fled, you can go to her. I don't want to risk anyone being hurt.'

She fumed, but nodded.

They had ridden about fifteen miles out of London when dusk began to fall.

'We won't achieve anything by riding further tonight. We'll stay the night at Upminster, where the coach left them, and we'll have opportunities there to ask questions,' Lord Dorney decided.

Bella agreed. Eager as she was to carry on, she knew it made sense to make enquiries at the last place where they'd been seen.

'Jackson, you can ask amongst the ostlers, find out what sort of carriage Lambert hired and if possible where he was going,' Lord Dorney went on.

It was almost as though he were organizing a military campaign, Bella thought.

'Right, sir, and I'll find out, don't you worry!' Jackson replied, his expression grim.

'Good man. Dan and Alex can mingle in the tap room and try to find out what they can there. Bella, you won't be able to pretend to be a boy close to others, so you can wear that cloak until you are safely inside the private parlour I'll hire for you. When you look respectable again you can gossip with the maid.'

Bella nodded. She would have objected to the word gossip, if she hadn't been so concerned for Mary. This was the second night that villain had imprisoned her, and she must be so frightened, terrified of what he intended for her.

'I have an acquaintance in the town, I'll visit her and discover what I can about Lambert,' Lord Dorney said.

Bella frowned. A woman? Then she told herself not to be selfish. She ought not to be considering her own situation with regard to Lord Dorney while Mary was being held prisoner. But she could not banish her thoughts, especially after she had been conducted to the private parlour, with a bedroom off it. She changed into a somewhat creased gown that had been hastily stuffed inside her saddle-bag, and was left to eat the solitary supper Lord Dorney had ordered to be sent up to her.

He had been supportive. He had held her closely. He had called her his dear. And now he was going to see a woman he knew. What woman? Bella's imagination conjured up a young, beautiful female. He had paid no special attention to any of the debutantes in London. Was that because he was in love with someone? At times she had thought he was turning his attention to Mrs Ford, after he had rejected her, but that was not the case. Was there an unknown women he admired? How convenient that they had stopped in the town where she lived, so that he could visit her.

She tried to still her confused ponderings. He had not planned this journey. It made sense to ask at this inn. And when the maid came to clear away her supper she had her own part to play.

'A friend of mine came this way yesterday,' Bella said, smiling at the young girl. 'She was unwell, and I'm on my way to her now. Did you see her?'

'Oh, yes, miss. Though I didn't see her properly.'

'What do you mean?' Surely, Bella thought, Lambert could not have covered Mary's face with a mask and a gag? That would have made people ask questions.

The maid explained. 'She was all wrapped up in a cloak, and her brother carried her in and said she was cold, but needed to rest for an hour.'

'Did you help her undress?' Bella asked, but without much hope of it. Lambert would have thought it too dangerous to allow anyone near Mary.

The maid shook her head. 'They had this very same room, but he said she didn't need me, she'd lie on the bed in the room next door. He had some food sent up, but none of us saw her.'

She must have been unconscious. Bella wished she had Lambert with her now. She wouldn't hesitate to use her pistol. Had he drugged her? Or even hit her on the head?

She forced herself to appear calm. 'And when they left? Did you not see her then?'

'Well, no, miss. I'd been to fetch the dishes, see, and was down in the kitchens. But Billy, one of the ostlers, said she was all wobbly on her feet, and had to be lifted into the chaise.'

'Chaise? Not the one they arrived in?'

'I wouldn't know, miss.'

That was all Bella could discover.

'She must have been drugged all the time,' Bella said indignantly later that night when they all sat round the parlour table comparing notes. 'She'd not have gone willingly with him otherwise, when there were people around who might have helped her.'

'I'm afraid so. What did you find out, Jackson?'

'Well, my lord, it was a post chaise he hired. But they were took to a private house, not an inn.'

'You have the direction?'

'The postilion didn't know who lived there, but he said he could find it again. I took the liberty of asking him if he'd guide us there tomorrow.'

'Capital! Dan?'

Sir Daniel shook his head. 'Lambert didn't go into the tap room. He stayed upstairs, had food taken up, and asked that everyone be kept out of the way while he carried his sister down, when they left. Said she was uncomfortable if people watched her while she was so ill and incapacitated.'

'He must have drugged her. I'll kill him!' Jackson snarled.

'Not before he's led us to Mary. I found out he has only a small manor house, and all the farms are let, so it's not likely she's concealed on any of them. He's not a good landlord, not liked by his tenants, so they would be unlikely to help him. He has a boat, but I wasn't able to discover where. Someone on his estate will be able to tell us, though. I suggest we make straight for there in the morning, if Mary isn't at the place the ostler takes us to.'

'He might be staying in his own house,' Sir Daniel said.

'He might, but I doubt he'd take Mary there. He wouldn't be able to trust the servants, particularly if he's late with their wages. However, you and Alex can go and make enquiries there. Now it's time for bed.'

'I'll be back to the stables, my lord. It's comfortable enough up in the loft, and I'd rather keep an eye on the horses.'

Sir Daniel and Alex went too, though Alex cast a speculative eye at Bella as he left. She felt her face grow warm. He would have known of the gossip in Bath, the expectation that Lord Dorney had been about to offer for her. And he'd have seen the coldness which had existed between them in London.

She slipped into the bedroom where her breeches had been hidden in the saddle-bags. With them was a purse. She took it out, went back to the parlour, and handed it to Lord Dorney. He frowned, and looked a question.

'Money, to pay for our expenses,' she explained.

'I don't need your money!'

His voice was cold, and he turned away abruptly.

'Mary is my maid, so I should be responsible for whatever it costs us to find her. She's not your responsibility, nor that of Sir Daniel and Alex. I'm grateful for your help, but I can't permit you to bear the cost.'

'Don't behave like a miserable tally clerk.'

Bella felt as though she had been slapped. How dare he throw such a wounding accusation at her! It was clear he considered her to be beneath him, unfit to be his wife. No wonder he had so swiftly recanted from his intended proposal when he found a reason to do so. He must have been regretting it even after the hints he had given.

'Then I'll say goodnight, my lord,' Bella snapped, and marched towards the adjoining bedroom.

'Good night. I'll sleep in here, so you needn't worry that Lambert might discover you.'

She turned and looked at him. She'd somehow assumed he had taken a room for himself. She didn't know whether to be pleased at this evidence of his care for her, or furious at his implied assumption that she might be afraid and in need of protection. Why did the wretched man make things so difficult? Sometimes she thought they were almost back to the friendly relationship they'd had in Bath, before he'd discovered about her fortune, then he would do something or utter some remark which clearly showed he had not altered his opinion of her.

She forced herself to swallow an indignant retort, and spoke calmly. 'I'm not worried by that poltroon! But where will you sleep? There isn't even a sopha.'

'I've slept on far harder floors on campaign.'

Bella could see there was no reasonable alternative. She could scarcely offer to share her bed, even if he'd accept the offer. She bade him a cold goodnight, swept through to the adjoining bedroom, shut the door and stood considering. Then she stripped one of the blankets from the bed, dragged off the bolster, and marched back into the parlour with them.

'At least have these,' she said curtly, and turned to go.

He had removed his riding coat and shirt, and was standing just in breeches. The muscles of his arms and back rippled, but as he turned towards her Bella saw an ugly scar running from one shoulder down across his chest and ending near his lower ribs.

She gasped. 'What happened?' she demanded, and stepped towards him.

'A stray bullet. At Waterloo,' he said, unconcerned. 'The fellow was flat on his back and he fired as I rode past.'

'Does it hurt?' Bella was only a step away from him, and she stretched out her hand and gently touched the scar.

Was it her imagination that his breathing quickened? He stepped back, out of her reach, and turned away.

'Go to bed, Bella. We have to be away early in the morning.'

Bella retreated to bed, and eventually fell into a restless sleep. Her dreams were all of battlefields, and once she woke up crying, to find Lord Dorney holding her hand and trying to calm her.

'What is it?' he asked softly. 'You were crying out in your sleep. Don't fret, we'll find Mary, and Lambert won't have harmed her.'

Bella clung tightly to his hand as she slowly regained her senses. 'I—'

How could she tell him that it had not been Mary and her plight which caused her dreams? That she had been imagining dreadful horrors, battlefield skirmishes such as those she'd read about in the news-sheets, and his own near encounter with death? Over and over she'd seen some French soldier, probably dying himself, but with just enough strength to fire his pistol at an enemy, in the hope of taking one more with him to whatever eternity awaited.

'I – I know,' she managed. 'I'm sorry if I disturbed you.'

'Old soldiers sleep lightly,' he said, releasing her hand.

Bella restrained the impulse to cling to him. 'You're not old,' she said, sleepy again.

'Old enough,' he replied. 'Will you be all right now?'

She nodded, and turned over in bed, sinking almost immediately into sleep. Was it her imagination, she wondered as she lost consciousness, that he dropped a light kiss on her brow?

They rode swiftly eastwards on the following morning. Bella was back in her boy's clothing, after a restless night when she had dreamed Lord Dorney had come to her, held her hand and kissed her. Of course he hadn't, she told herself firmly. He had seemed more friendly this morning, after the coldness of the previous evening, and he was putting himself out by searching for Mary, but that didn't mean his feelings towards her had changed. He'd merely wanted to keep her spirits up. He'd called her his dear, she argued. But that was merely the sort of patronizing address older people used towards those they considered were being nuisances. As for his help, he was the sort of man who would want to put right any injustices. It didn't indicate any warmer feelings towards herself. The situation had not changed. Indeed, it had probably been made worse by her outrageous conduct of the previous few weeks, when she had scorned the opinions of society and gone out of her way to antagonize them.

She forced herself to push these musings to the back of her mind, and try to plan for any eventualities that lay ahead. It was Mary who mattered. Their first task was to find and rescue her. If they could apprehend Lambert too, and charge him with abduction and blackmail and extortion, she would not hesitate. Bella was uncertain of the legal charges they might bring, but she determined that nothing would stop her from making him pay, and heavily, for what he had done.

The postilion from the inn led them to a small villa surrounded by an overgrown garden and orchard. No one was at home, not even servants, and Lord Dorney, dismissing the postilion with a large tip, and a recommendation that he told no one of their movements, turned to his companions.

'There's the village inn, and the neighbours,' he said. 'Jackson, go to the inn and try to find out who lives here and where they are. Dan, you and Alex can ask the neighbours. Say you're looking for someone else and must have mistaken the direction. They'll tell you who lives here, maybe even where they are to be found. Bella, you and I will go and ask the vicar. But you must remain silent. If he invites me inside, you'll stay outside to care for the horses. You look like a groom,' he added.

'Rendezvous?' Sir Dan asked briefly.

He was a man of few words, Bella decided. At least he was friendly towards her, hadn't been shocked by her boy's apparel, and didn't talk down to her as a mere woman.

'A mile outside the village, on the road eastwards. The chances are it will be on our way. And Lambert's house is a few miles further on. We'll try there next.'

Bella, fuming inwardly, did as she was bid and waited some distance from the rectory. She knew he was right, and close to she could not be taken for a boy, but the need to be inactive while others made all the enquiries, made her impatient.

Lord Dorney merely nodded as he returned half an hour later, took the reins of his horse and mounted. He set off without waiting for her, and she scrambled up into the saddle, her temper barely under control, and followed.

The others were all waiting for them, sitting in the shade of a huge beech tree. Lord Dorney dismounted, hitched the reins over a low branch, and sat down with them. Bella followed suit.

'The house belongs to a young fellow who sounds like Lambert's twin,' Sir Daniel began. 'Benjamin Hill, by name. He's the son of a master bootmaker, trying to be a gentleman. Apparently he's run through the small fortune his parents left him, and is waiting, impatiently, for an elderly aunt to die and leave him her money. He's rarely at home, takes no interest in the place, neglects repairs, and forgets to pay the caretaker and his wife, who are his only servants. But during the past week he's been kicking his heels here, drinking at the inn every night until he's barely able to stagger home to bed.'

'He's been put to bed by one of the ostlers more than once,' Jackson added. 'Can't think why the fellow bothered, unless he managed to pick his pockets on the way.'

'More or less what the rector told me. Hill and Lambert were at school together, and do little but gamble, drink and wench. Most of the people round here will have nothing to do with them, and several shopkeepers have refused to extend any more credit. Is it known where he is?'

Jackson nodded. 'He and Lambert went off in his old chaise, towards Leigh, with just a pair pulling it. They'll have Mary with them. The man I spoke to said the chaise was ancient, hadn't been out on the roads for years, and the horses were more used to pulling a hay wain than a coach. Hill was driving, which he thought made it certain the coach would overturn if it met a deep rut or some other obstacle. He didn't think either the carriage or the horses would survive more than a dozen or so miles.'

'Leigh is near Lambert's house. It's less than twenty miles from here. Perhaps they won't have reached there. In which case they might have some difficulty concealing Mary. But we're on the right track. Let's follow.'

They mounted and set off. Bella fretted that they were not making plans for how to rescue Mary, but Lord Dorney and Sir Daniel both said they would have to wait and see what the situation was when they found her. Jackson rode in grim silence, but Bella could see his lips moving, and she suspected he was cursing Lambert and rehearsing what he would like to do with the man. She had a few ideas about that herself.

They had gone about ten miles when Alexander's horse cast a shoe.

'Leave me. There was a smithy a mile or so back. I'll catch up with you later,' he said.

'If we have time we'll leave a message at the nearest inn,' Lord Dorney suggested. 'If there's nothing you'll have to wait there until one of us can come and meet you.'

An hour later they drew rein at the small lodge which, they had been informed in the village, marked the main entrance to Lambert's small manor house. Walls, overgrown with moss, stretched in either direction. The driveway curved round, lined with ancient oaks, and hiding the house from view. It looked almost as unkempt as Hill's house, and presumably Lambert spent nothing on any but essential upkeep.

There was no sign of life in the lodge, and the gates, with lank grass growing around them, had clearly not been closed for a long time. They rode inside and Lord Dorney led the way behind a thicket of overgrown bushes.

'We'll wait here, out of sight. Dan, he won't know you. Can you go and ask if he's at home?'

'And presumably be a friend of his father's, just home from soldiering, come to pay his respects?' Sir Daniel asked with a grin.

Lord Dorney grinned back. 'You'll know what to say. If he's not, find out whether he has other property nearby.'

'Aye, aye, Captain.'

'It's not a game!' Bella burst out, as Sir Daniel rode off along the drive. 'You two treat it as though it's some form of sport, while poor Mary may be undergoing all sorts of ill treatment, as well as being frightened out of her wits!'

Lord Dorney sighed. 'Bella, would it help Mary if we spent the time wailing and gnashing our teeth? I am as determined to find Mary as you are, and to hunt this man down and punish him. But the punishment will be through the law, not by a pistol. And if you have any intention of shooting him, forget it now! You would be at fault.'

She ground her teeth in frustration, but the sensible side of her had to admit he was right. She could not shoot the man down even though she considered him no better than vermin. Unless in self-defence, she decided, and smiled grimly.

'Can't we be doing something? Asking round the village to see if Lambert has some place where he could hide Mary?'

'We could, but that might possibly alert him to our presence. I'd prefer to act more silently if possible, take him by surprise. First we need to know if he is at home, or has been here. If he isn't here, and Dan doesn't glean anything, we'll begin to ask.'

Bella subsided. When Sir Daniel came trotting down the driveway towards them, she urged her horse forwards to meet him. He was shaking his head.

At that moment a shot rang out, and Sir Daniel clapped his hand to his shoulder and toppled slowly from his horse.

Chapter Seventeen

─◦⊙◦─

As Bella and Lord Dorney dismounted and ran to Sir Daniel, Jackson urged his horse out of the thicket and pointed it in the direction from which the shot had come. Bella had a fleeting impression of him passing them, but her main attention was on the wounded man.

He had fallen on to his back, and lay frighteningly still. His horse had bolted through the gates and vanished. Blood was oozing from the wound in his left shoulder.

Lord Dorney was kneeling beside his friend. He pulled a small knife out of his pocket and began gently cutting away the sleeve of Sir Daniel's riding coat.

'Untie my cravat, and let me have your shirt,' he said calmly. 'If we can pack it well enough we can stop the bleeding.'

Bella fumbled to untie the muslin cravat, and then slipped out of her own coat and dragged off the shirt she was wearing. A cool breeze played on her skin, and she flushed as she realized her nakedness. Pulling on the jacket, she tore the shirt into large pieces and began to fold them.

Lord Dorney had cut away the coat to reveal the wound. 'It's just a flesh wound, it hasn't hit the bone, and the bullet isn't lodged,' he said as he took the folded pieces of material and pressed them against the wound. 'It passed right through. He must have hit his head when he fell. Now, can you hold this firm while I bind the cravat round it?'

Before they had finished Sir Daniel began to groan and try to sit up. Lord Dorney gently held him down.

'Steady, Dan. It's only a flesh wound. How's your head? There's a huge bump coming up where you hit the ground.'

Sir Daniel's eyes were glazed, he groaned and subsided on to the ground. He looked ready to pass out again at any moment.

Lord Dorney glanced up. 'Get my horse, Bella. We must get him to the inn where he can be properly examined. He's a big man, but between us we can lift him up.'

'Who was it? Did you see?' Bella asked as she went to the horses.

'No, but Jackson's ridden after him. I hope the man manages to keep out of trouble.'

'I hope, if it's Lambert, Jackson catches him and thrashes him till he squeals!'

It was difficult, for Sir Daniel was both tall and heavy, a dead weight and unable to help them. They were anxious not to dislodge the makeshift bandage, but they eventually hoisted him into the saddle. He slumped forwards so that Bella was afraid he would fall off again.

'Now your horse. Can you ride alongside and try to hold him steady? I'll walk on the other side and do the same. We'd best make for the inn.'

They walked slowly out through the gates and turned towards the small village. A couple of children playing in the road in front of the first cottages stared, thumbs in mouths, at the little procession, then with shrieks of excitement turned and rushed inside.

'The whole village will know before we even reach the inn,' Lord Dorney said with resignation. 'I'd have preferred a less dramatic arrival!'

'Lambert will hear about it. But if he shot Sir Daniel, he'll know in any event. And we'll lose the advantage of surprise.'

'If Lambert knows we are here delay won't matter so much. We simply change our tactics.'

'Perhaps he'll move Mary from where he's keeping her,' Bella said. 'If only we knew where that was.'

'He won't have many places where he can keep her hidden.'

She had to be patient. Much as she wanted to find Mary, she accepted she could not do it on her own. She needed Lord Dorney, even more now Sir Daniel was injured, unconscious and unable to tell them what he had discovered at the manor.

*

As they approached the tiny inn, little more than a tavern, a man appeared in the doorway. Lord Dorney hailed him.

'Come and help us lift our friend down,' he said, and the man slowly moved forwards, chewing a piece of straw.

'What's the matter wi' fellow? If it's cholera he'll not set foot in 'ere.'

'He's been shot, and was knocked unconscious when he fell from his horse. Help us, there's a good man, he's heavy.'

Bella steadied the horses as Lord Dorney and the innkeeper lifted Sir Daniel down and began to carry him towards the inn.

'There's only tap room table,' the innkeeper warned. 'Two ladies are in the only bedroom.'

'I doubt we could carry him upstairs without disturbing the bandage. Is there a doctor nearby?'

'Ten miles or more, and by this time he's most like under the table, too drunk to see straight.'

'Then we'll have to manage as best we can. Bell, take the horses round to the stables,' he added.

Bell? Confused, Bella wondered if this abbreviation of her name was a form of familiarity, even endearment, then, as she caught the innkeeper eyeing her bare neck, revealed by her lack of a shirt, she realized he was preserving her identity, as if Bell was her surname.

She turned away to hide a grin, and tried to make sure her jacket was fully fastened as she led the horses to the back of the inn. There was no one in sight, and no other horses in the stable. There was plenty of straw, though, the stable looked used. She tied them up, found a couple of hay nets and hung these up for them to nibble at, unsaddled them and rubbed them down with wisps of straw. Then she filled two buckets from the well, picked up the saddle-bags and was able to go into the inn.

Had Sir Daniel recovered his senses? Had he been able to tell what he'd discovered at the manor? Would they soon be able to resume the search for Mary? And where was Jackson?

Until now she had only had time for fleeting concern about the groom. Had he hoped, unarmed, to catch the gunman? Why should anyone want to shoot them, unless it were Lambert? He didn't know any of them apart from herself, and she thought her male disguise would have fooled him, at least at a distance. He probably knew Jackson, she realized, if he'd been watching the house in Dover Street.

Sir Daniel, lying on the trestle table in the dimly lit tap room, was still unconscious. As Bella's eyes adjusted to the gloom she saw a thin, elderly woman hovering round, holding a cushion clutched to her bosom. Lord Dorney glanced up from where he was cutting away the remains of Sir Daniel's riding coat.

'Bell, lift his head so that the cushion can be put there. Gently, now.'

She nodded and did as she was told. She dared not speak, her voice would betray her. The woman fetched a bowl of water and an old sheet which Lord Dorney handed to Bella.

'Tear it up.'

He undid the makeshift bandage, took the first rag and began to clean the wound. The bleeding was less now, and when the woman came in again with a salve she said was her own recipe, with comfrey and witch hazel for healing and garlic to keep the wound clean. Lord Dorney spread some on a clean rag and laid it against the wound, bandaging it up more tightly.

Sir Daniel was stirring. He opened his eyes, groaned, and tried to touch his shoulder with the other hand. 'What—?'

'You're all right, Dan. It was probably poachers; you were shot,' Lord Dorney said. 'Lie still, or you might roll off the table! You'll be able to sit in a chair soon. Landlord, could you find some food for us? And some ale?'

When the innkeeper and the woman departed, Bella was able to speak. She had been fretting to know what he had discovered.

'Is Lambert at home? Has he any other places to hide Mary?' she demanded.

'Lambert?' Sir Daniel replied, looking puzzled. 'Richard, it's you. Mary? Who are they?'

'Oh no, he's lost his wits! That bump on the head.' Bella almost wept with frustration.

'Just his memory. We'll just have to find out elsewhere. The innkeeper will know.'

'He's not exactly welcoming,' Bella muttered.

'If he thinks we're friends of Lambert, and Lambert has a bad reputation here, is that surprising? When we've had some food we'll ask him.'

The woman came back in then, struggling to control a large sack filled with straw.

'I've two o' these. When my man comes back ye can lift yer friend on to 'em, so 'e'll not roll off table.'

'Thank you,' Lord Dorney said gravely, and went to help her lay it out in a corner. When the second had been brought in, and a sheet spread over them, the innkeeper returned, and the two men, with Bella steadying Sir Daniel's head, lifted him on to the makeshift bed.

The woman smiled, and went to fetch a tray, laden with plates of ham, loaves of bread, and a sirloin of beef. She placed the food on the table, and Bella realized with some amusement that she had been less concerned with Sir Daniel's comfort than her own need for a table on which to set the food.

The innkeeper brought in jugs of ale and two tankards. 'Yon fellow won't want any food yet,' he said. 'Best if he can sleep.'

He was turning to leave when footsteps could be heard approaching. The door opened, and Alexander walked in.

'What the devil?' Alexander demanded, looking at Sir Daniel lying on the pallet.

'Alex, glad you caught us up. Bell, go and take his horse to the stables. And find yourself another shirt. Alex, go and get your own gear.'

Bella was about to demand how he expected her to find a shirt out in the stables when she recalled her new role. She was dressed in groom's clothing, she had to play her part. Alexander was looking puzzled, about to burst into speech, so Bella jerked her head and marched out of the room. Meekly he followed.

She didn't speak until they had reached the privacy of the stable, and found Alexander's horse tied to a ring outside. Then, as they worked together, she swiftly explained what had happened.

Alexander frowned. 'So we're no further on.' He opened one of his own saddle-bags. 'Here, you're more my size than Richard's. You'd best have my spare shirt. I wondered why I got sent out here as well. It must have been so that I could sacrifice my shirt.'

'I don't have a spare shirt, only a gown,' Bella said, laughing. 'And if they think I'm a groom it would hardly be fitting for him to let them see him give me his!'

'What do we do now?'

'How can I guess what's in your cousin's head? I don't think he trusts the innkeeper, but we'll have to ask someone about possible hiding places. The entire village will know we have been to call on Lambert. So will he if it was him that shot Sir Daniel.'

'I'll go back in and you can change,' Alexander said. 'I think I saw some food, and I'm devilish peckish.'

Swiftly Bella put on the new shirt, and was just shrugging the jacket back on when Jackson's head appeared round the door.

'Miss Bella, I think I've found her!'

'Jackson! Thank goodness you're all right.'

'I'm fit, miss.'

'Why did you ride off like that?'

'I saw the flash as he fired, but he was well away by the time I got round those bushes. His horse was fleeter than mine, but I managed to follow for a while. It wouldn't have made sense to drag his lordship away from Sir Daniel. Was he badly hurt?'

'Just a flesh wound, but he fell and hurt his head. He can't recall anything of what he learned at the house.'

'So he's out of it.'

'Alexander is here. Who was it you were chasing? Did you discover it?'

'I've never seen Lambert, but who else would shoot at us? Who else has cause?'

Lambert might know they were in the area, if it had been he who shot at them, and Bella could find no other explanation.

'I wonder if he was at the house when Sir Daniel called? How else could he have known about us? So what happened?'

'He made for a creek. His land goes right down to the sea, I think. It's marshy round about, lots of little streams, but this one was wide, big enough for small boats. Anyways, I lost sight of him, so I scouted around for a bit. The creek got much wider, and there was a sort of boathouse, he'd tied his horse up outside it. There was another horse too.'

'Were they the two who'd pulled the coach? From what we heard, they didn't sound like fleet ones.'

'No. I reckon those are in the stables at the manor. The coach, too. These were high-bred nags. Lambert probably keeps them here for when he's at home.'

'Mary might be inside the boathouse.'

'I don't think so. There was a boat, looked like a little yacht, moored a few yards out. A little rowing boat was tied up to it, so I guess he'd gone aboard. Two of them, there were, standing on the deck. It must be Lambert and the other one.'

'He didn't see you?'

'No, I'd left the horse way back. I was on foot, hidden by some sort of reeds. Miss Bella, they must have her there! I was tempted to try and tackle them, but they've got a pistol, and there were two of them. I'd never be able to get near!'

Bella was thinking rapidly. 'What we need is some sort of diversion, to draw them away from the boat. Before they take her away. They could sail her somewhere else, and we'd lose them again.'

'We've got to hurry, miss.'

'You'll stay here and care for Dan. There's three of us; we can overpower Lambert and his friend. But when Dan recovers his senses he'll need to know what's happening.'

'We can leave a note. I'm coming with you! Mary is my maid, my responsibility.'

Lord Dorney sighed. 'Bella, you're wasting time. I don't want you hurt, nor do I want to be distracted by having to guard you.'

With that he turned away and went out of the inn. Alexander, with a sympathetic glance at Bella, followed. Jackson was already in the stables, saddling the horses.

Was it male arrogance that assumed a woman could not take care of herself? Or did he, a small hopeful voice within her said, really care for her, if he didn't want her to be hurt?

She watched from the small window as they rode past, going back the way they'd come, away from the manor.

Whatever Lord Dorney meant, she was not staying here, meekly playing nursemaid. Then she swung round, hearing a rustle of straw. Sir Daniel was stirring. He'd probably recover his senses soon.

She was wondering whether she dared ask for paper and a pen, to leave him a note, whether the risk of betraying her sex was worth it, when Sir Daniel spoke.

'Miss Bella? Where's everyone else? And what happened?'

'Oh, you're better. Do you remember going to Lambert's house?'

'Is that where it was? But my shoulder's bound up.'

'You were shot. Don't you remember? As you rode back down the drive. And you fell off the horse, that's when you hurt your head. It was Lambert, we assume. But it's not serious, Lord Dorney said, just a flesh wound.'

'Serious or not, it's damnably sore. I don't remember a thing about being shot. Where are we? This looks like an inn. And where is everyone?'

'It's the village inn. They couldn't carry you upstairs, and some ladies have the only bedroom. Jackson chased the man who shot you, and found a boat moored in a creek. Mary is probably on it. He's taken the others there. Do you remember what happened at the house?'

Sir Daniel frowned. 'They were a surly couple, and they seemed upset. They said I'd just missed Lambert, he'd been to the house demanding food. When I asked if he was expected back soon they muttered something about they hoped not. It would seem he's provisioning the boat, and means to stay there. Oh, and they said he'd taken a fowling piece and a rifle, as though he meant to shoot duck.'

Bella went cold. 'So he'll have more than a pistol! And they won't know. I'll have to go after them. You'll be all right here, the landlord's wife seems kind enough. Friendlier than he is, I think. I must go.'

He began to speak, but she shook her head and ran to the stables. Her fingers seemed numb as she struggled with the bridle, but eventually she fastened all the buckles. Then she heaved on the saddle, led the horse out into the yard, and used the mounting block to scramble into it.

She set off after the others at a gallop. They had ten minutes' start on her, but she might be able to catch them up before they reached the boat. They'd be going cautiously, anxious not to announce their presence.

It was so overgrown with straggling bushes she almost missed it.

A small track left the main road half a mile out of the village and, as Bella paused to try and decide whether they might have gone that way, she was certain she could smell the salty tang of the sea. She looked more closely at the ground. It was soft, and there were several imprints of horses' hoofs. She pushed her way through the bushes and followed.

Lord Dorney held up his hand. 'I think we'll leave the horses here. There's less cover ahead. How far is it now, Jackson?'

'Half a mile, I'd guess. Less as the crow flies, but there's some deep streams in between, too deep to wade and too wide to jump. We have to go round 'em, where we can cross.'

They dismounted and tied the horses so that they could graze.

'You know the way, Jackson. Let's go. As soon as we see the boat we'll decide what to do. No talking, the sound will carry over water.'

They went in single file, Lord Dorney bringing up the rear. The ground was criss-crossed with small streams, and more than once they had to retrace their steps when they came to places which were too wet and marshy to pass over. The only cover was the reeds, growing in clumps. They could hear the sound of waves as they broke against the shore, and this sound gradually got louder. Suddenly Jackson halted and lay down amongst the reeds. The others followed suit.

Lord Dorney edged his way forward until he was beside Jackson. He could see the yacht, no more than fifty yards ahead of them. There was no sign of life aboard her. Jackson pointed to his left, and there was the boathouse. Only one horse was tethered there. Then he pointed to where a small rowing boat could be seen, partly hidden amongst the reeds.

'One of them's left,' Lord Dorney whispered into Jackson's ear. 'We need to bring the other on deck.'

He went cold with fear. It was quite possible Lambert had seen and recognized Bella if he had been lying in wait while Dan went to the house. Her disguise was not difficult to see through close by. He wouldn't have risked shooting her, for she had the money he wanted. He could have shot Dan to prevent them from knowing he was nearby. Had he now gone in search of her? If so, what did he intend? To trick her on to the boat, or bring her by force to join Mary?

Speculation was pointless. Their first task was to disarm whoever was left on the boat, and rescue Mary. Then he could deal with any threat to Bella.

He beckoned to Alexander to crawl alongside. 'Listen carefully,' he breathed, so softly they both craned nearer to hear him. 'Alex, you move back until you can see anyone approaching the boathouse. Hoot like an owl if anyone comes. Jackson, get behind the boathouse, ready to let the horse go. Drive it away, but stay behind the boathouse. We don't want him to shoot at you. Wait until I've swum out beyond the boat. I should be able to get aboard without him hearing me, so when he comes on deck I'll get him. Alex, you stay here in case the other one comes back, while Jackson rows the boat out for us to take Mary off.'

He shrugged out of his coat and dragged off his boots. Nodding to the others he waited while Alexander wriggled backwards until he was hidden amongst the reeds, and Jackson crawled towards the boathouse. When they were both in position he crawled to a spot where he could slip into the water out of sight of the boat. Marking its position, he took a deep breath and dived beneath the water. He thought he could swim the distance under water. He'd often swum as far in the lake at Dorney Court. But he had to go slowly, make certain there were no splashes to alert Lambert or his friend, whichever one of them was on the boat.

Bella came upon the tethered horses and dismounted. She saw that the trees ended within yards, and assumed the men had gone forward on foot. She would do the same. Taking her small pistol from her pocket, she went forward cautiously, dropping to a crouch as the cover became sparser.

Then she came to a deep, wide stream, and almost wept in frustration as she had to follow the bank until it was narrow enough for her to jump across. When this delay had occurred for the fourth time she vowed she would wade through the next stream, even if the water came up to her neck. The delay was too long; she'd never catch the others and be able to warn them about the guns Lambert had with him.

Finally she came to an open patch of ground, and could see the boat. It was riding gently on the waves, twenty yards or more away from the bank. No one was visible on the deck. It was small, but there appeared to be a cabin, for she could see something which looked like a raised roof at one end. She looked around, hoping to see the men, wondering where they were, desperate to pass on her message. She frowned. There was only one horse by the building she assumed was the boathouse. Had one of them ridden away, or was the other tethered out of sight?

As she watched the horse neighed loudly, reared, and turned to race away. Bella glanced back at the boat and saw a man emerge on to the deck. Even from this distance she was sure it was Lambert. He held a rifle and pointed it towards the shore. Then her eyes widened, for someone was scrambling out of the water on to the deck. She gasped with fear. It was Lord Dorney, and Lambert had heard him. He swung round, pointing the rifle and, without thought Bella aimed her pistol and fired.

Chapter Eighteen

---•◦◉◦•---

LORD DORNEY SURFACED just beyond the yacht and took a deep breath. He was beside the anchor chain, and as he reached out to grasp it the wind veered and swung the yacht towards him. A loose rope, which had, he presumed, tethered the rowing boat, swung free a few yards towards the stern. As he let go of it, the anchor chain rasped against the hull, and he heard footsteps on the deck approaching the side. He cursed his inability to see what was happening above his head, and dived back under the water.

Cautiously he swam towards the stern, where he would be shielded by the small cabin. Once more he surfaced, clinging to the outward sloping boards. He shook his head to clear the water from his ears, and tried to distinguish sounds from above. Footsteps again, and then the slam of either a door or hatch. He couldn't tell which, but he had to take a chance.

He approached the dangling rope, pulled it cautiously, and breathed a sigh of relief when it became taut. Stealthily he began to draw himself up, hand over hand.

The wind was increasing, and the yacht swung round again, so that now he was visible from the shore. He was almost at the top of the rope when once more he heard footsteps approaching. He was not near enough to the rail to clamber over before the man approaching would see him, and if he dived back into the water the splash would reveal his position. Climbing upwards and taking Lambert, if it were he, by surprise, was the only option.

His head was just level with the rail when a startled voice spoke.

'Who the devil are you, and what do you think you're doing, trying to board a private boat?'

It was Lambert. He had seen him only once, at the inn near Bath, but there could be no mistake. The man was dressed in breeches and a shirt, a neckerchief tucked into it.

'William Lambert? I wanted to talk with you,' Lord Dorney replied, continuing his ascent. He had one leg over the rail when Lambert moved a few steps back and reached to the bench behind him. He swung round, a rifle in his hands.

'I've nothing to say to you. Go, before I send you to the bottom plugged full of holes.'

He raised the rifle and pointed it at Lord Dorney. Before he could dive back into the water a shot rang out and Lambert, clutching his right arm, dropped the rifle and staggered to the side of the boat. Lord Dorney swiftly climbed on to the deck, picked up the rifle and pointed it at Lambert.

He glanced round, wondering where his salvation had come from, inwardly praying that whoever had shot Lambert was a friend and not some madman who would shoot at anything, or Lambert's friend Hill who might have shot Lambert by mistake. As far as he knew Jackson had no pistol, and from his knowledge of Alexander's ability he didn't think his cousin could have shot so accurately by design.

Neither of them was visible, so he wasted no more time. Keeping below the rails just in case the marksman was Lambert's friend, he wrenched the neckerchief from Lambert's neck, and ordered him to turn round and put his arms behind his back.

'My arm! It's bleeding! I can't,' the man groaned, clutching at his injured right arm and trying to roll up his sleeve to see what the damage was.

Lord Dorney prodded him in the side with the rifle. 'The sooner you comply the sooner I'll do something about it. It doesn't look more than a scratch.'

Grumbling and wincing, all defiance gone, Lambert did as he was told. When Lord Dorney had tied his wrists together, he looked round for something to use to secure his legs, and with an inward grin hauled up the dangling rope and used that. If by chance his friend Benjamin Hill returned, he would be unable to board.

'Where's the girl?'

A faint spark of resistance flared. 'What girl?'

'Don't be foolish. The maid, Mary. We know you have her. Do you want me to shoot you too?'

Lambert shuddered. 'We haven't touched her! She's in the cabin.'

Lord Dorney went to the doorway and looked in. Mary lay on a bunk, her ankles tied together and her hands bound behind her. He stepped inside, and taking a knife which lay on the small table, cut the bonds.

She struggled to suppress sobs. 'Oh, my lord, I'm so thankful to see you, I've been so frightened.' She sat up, rubbing her wrists. 'Miss Bella hasn't given them money, has she? If she has, because I was so careless, and believed him, I'll never forgive myself!'

'No money has been paid. You'll be off this boat soon,' he promised.

'How did you find me? Is Miss Bella all right?'

'Yes. She's waiting at the inn with Sir Daniel. My cousin and Jackson are with me, keeping watch. I'll signal to them all's well and they'll be here in a moment. Now I'd best be making sure Lambert isn't up to mischief.'

He took the rope which had bound Mary and used it to tie Lambert's feet.

'Where is your friend?' he asked.

Lambert continued to moan. 'I'm bleeding to death. You've as good as killed me!'

Lord Dorney looked contemptuously at him. 'Your friend, Mr Hill? Where has he gone?'

'To – to fetch some wine from the house,' Lambert gabbled, all defiance gone. 'I couldn't carry that as well as the food. My arm! I need a doctor.'

'You'll get one, as well as a constable.'

'I haven't done anything! It was a jape, that's all. She wasn't hurt. It wasn't my idea.'

Hearing the sound of voices Lord Dorney spared a look towards the shore. He blinked, then grinned. He might have known. There were three figures emerging from the reeds. Lord Dorney raised his voice. 'Jackson, Alex, come aboard. And bring Miss Trahearne too.'

'I'm bleeding!' Lambert whined. 'Aren't you going to do anything?'

'Why should I care if you bleed to death? You were prepared to shoot me, no doubt to kill me, without a second thought.'

He watched Alex help Bella into the small rowing boat. Jackson scrambled in after them and took the oars. It was a tight squeeze for three, and the boat rode so low in the water that the occasional wave went over the sides. The distance was short, though, and soon Bella was being helped on to the deck. Alex and Jackson followed, the latter glancing down at Lambert and clenching his fists.

'Mary?' Bella demanded. 'Is she here? Is she harmed?'

'I'm here, Miss Bella,' Mary said from the cabin doorway, and began to sob. Before Bella could move, Jackson pushed past her and drew Mary into his arms.

'You're safe now, my lass. We'll look after you. There's nothing to worry about now. Did they hurt you?'

She shook her head. 'They drugged me, kept me tied up, and gagged me when there were other people around, but that's all.'

'How did they get you?'

Mary shook her head. 'I was stupid. He spoke to me when I came away from the dressmaker's. Said Miss Bella had been thrown from her horse on the way to Richmond, and they thought she might have broken her neck. He said he'd take me to her, but when I got into the hackney he went the other way. Oh, Miss Bella, I'm so sorry!'

'You're not to blame. But it proves Amelia Stockley was part of the plot!' Bella interrupted. 'How else would he know I'd gone to Richmond?'

'He could have heard from one of the others in the party,' Lord Dorney said.

'It wasn't my plan,' Lambert said. 'Amelia thought of it.'

'And no doubt you wanted to share in the money you'd extort from Miss Trahearne, as well as have your revenge for the manner in which she bested you the first time you met.'

'I say it wasn't my plot!'

'If I have my way he'll hang for this!' Jackson said.

'The first thing to do is get everyone away from here,' Lord Dorney said. 'Alex, I suppose we'd better bind this fellow's wound. Was it you who shot him?' he suddenly demanded of Bella.

She nodded. 'He was going to shoot you. I told you I would,' she said, suddenly turning to Lambert. 'You didn't believe a woman could shoot straight when we met before. Now you know better. Be grateful it's only your arm!'

He just groaned.

'I'll get something from the cabin,' Alex said. 'No doubt they have some spare shirts or cravats there.'

Five minutes later Alex and Jackson lifted Lambert down into the boat. His arm had been bandaged, but his feet and hands were still tied together.

'He looks in no shape to run away, miserable poltroon,' Alexander commented. 'He only fights defenceless females.'

'Not all are defenceless,' Lord Dorney said, glancing at Bella. 'Alex, you can go for our horses. Jackson, come back for Mary, and the two of you can take her and Lambert to the village and find the constable. One of you bring the horses back for us.'

'What about Hill?' Alex asked. 'He might come back.'

'Somehow I doubt he'll want to attack us. We have several weapons, it seems. I expect Mr Hill will be making his way back home as fast as he can, if he has a horse!'

When they were alone Bella looked at Lord Dorney and her heart began to beat faster. He was wet through, his shirt clinging to his body and revealing taut muscles and broad shoulders.

He seemed to read her thoughts, and grinned. 'We appear to be using up an uncommon number of shirts between us. Forgive me for a moment and I'll see if our friends have another supply. Can you do sentry duty in case I'm wrong, and Mr Hill does come back? Shoot at him, by all means, if he tries to damage the rowing boat. Or we'll both have to swim ashore.'

He vanished, to reappear some time later in dry clothes which, Bella judged, had belonged to Mr Hill, for they were rather loose. Lambert had been weedy. The unknown Mr Hill must have been considerably fatter.

'There's food in the cabin. Presumably that which Lambert collected from his home. I am feeling decidedly hungry. Will you join me?'

They brought it outside, neither wanting to sit in the tiny, claustrophobic cabin, and sat side by side on the deck. Bella was ravenous. There was newly baked bread, ham and cheese, and some sweet, early apples. There was one bottle of wine which they shared.

'They must have been anticipating a long stay if they needed more supplies,' Lord Dorney commented as they cleared away the impromptu picnic. 'I wonder if they intended making a voyage? Or taking Mary somewhere else?'

'I've no doubt that miserable worm will tell us if we ask. And try to lay the blame on Amelia Stockley. Oh, how I want to go back to her card parties and see whether I'm right about their wanting to cheat me! If they do I'll – I'll take out an advertisement in *The Times*!'

He laughed. 'I didn't think you were so vindictive!'

'I hate being cheated! Just because I have more money than some other people doesn't mean I like to squander it.'

Lord Dorney looked at her for a long moment. 'Bella, why did you follow us?'

'Sir Daniel told me Lambert had taken guns from the house. A rifle, and a fowling piece. You wouldn't know, so I came to try and warn you.'

He smiled. 'Somehow I suspect that is typical of you. Instead of sitting and wringing your hands you have to take action, don't you?'

'Anyone would, who cared!'

He changed the subject. 'Dan's feeling better, then?'

'Sore, and his head aches, but he was coherent. He told me Lambert had been to the house. He might still have been there when Sir Daniel called, and guessed we'd followed him.'

'You could have been shot at, even captured like Mary was.'

'I had to try and warn you, or you'd have been the one shot!'

'Bella,' he said, and paused. 'I want to apologize. I've been pig-headed, too influenced by my brother's experience.'

'His wife, you mean?' she asked softly.

'Yes. I thought all heiresses would be like Selina. You've heard about her, I suppose?'

'A little,' she admitted.

'She had to change Dorney Court, which I'd loved as a boy. It was my home, and I thought nowhere else could be as perfect. Robert loved it too, but he couldn't gainsay her. She made it very plain it was her money. She didn't love him, only his title. Even that couldn't keep her faithful. Within a year of the marriage she was openly living with another man.'

'How could she!' The pain in his voice was not just for his child-hood home. It was clear to Bella that he as well as his brother had felt betrayed and disillusioned by Selina. Tentatively she reached out her hand and laid it on his. He turned it to grasp her fingers in his.

He shrugged. 'He was weak, my brother. Like my father, who gambled away much of his inheritance. But Robert couldn't bear the shame of it, so he called the fellow out. He wasn't a good shot, but he was beyond reason. He felt humiliated.'

'I heard he killed the man.'

'So you've heard some of the gossip?'

'In Bath. But that has nothing to do with you.'

'Robert was fortunate. He killed the man, but he maintained it was a freak shot. Certain malicious gossips who had predicted a different outcome tried to lay the blame on me, as I'm a much better shot. I think it was Selina who started the rumours. But soon she was with another lover. Robert, meanwhile, could not live with what he'd done. I think he'd hoped either to be killed or to wound the man.'

Bella squeezed his hand. 'And then he killed himself? I'm so very sorry. It must have been so dreadful for you.'

He looked down at her. 'Do you know all my family's history?'

She shook her head. 'People love gossip. And because it was you, I wanted to hear. Not because I was gloating, but I needed to know all about you.'

'I found him, hanging in the stables.' He sighed, remembering.

'Oh, you poor man. How awful it must have been!'

'It's in the past. But it made me wary of all women for a long time. Bella, my dearest, I tried to forget you, but I couldn't. I was deter-mined not to marry, after Robert's disaster. Especially I hated the idea of marrying a rich woman. That time in Bath, I forgot all my resolutions.'

'And then Salway revealed that I'd been lying,' she said, the bitter-ness against him still strong. He'd caused so much unhappiness.

'Yes. Oh, I was an insufferable prig. I understand now – I think I did at the time, but wouldn't admit it – your reasons. Do I have any chance? Could we start again?'

Bella stared at him, wondering whether she was dreaming. 'You mean – what do you mean?'

'If I offered for you now, would you at least consider it?' he asked.

She was speechless. This was something she'd longed for, but since that time in Bath had begun to think would never happen.

'Bella? Did I give you such a disgust of me you can't even consider it? I will wait for your decision.'

'Oh, no! I'm not disgusted,' she said hurriedly. 'There's no need to consider. That is, yes, I'll consider it, but do I have to? Can't I just say yes, please?'

For a moment he stared at her, then, smiling, pulled her towards him, and she went into his arms. She raised her face and he covered it with kisses, delightful, feathery kisses which grew more and more intense. Then he captured her mouth and Bella felt as though she was floating on air. When, breathless, they broke apart, she could scarcely believe that it had happened.

'Why? I mean, I'm not pretty, and I'm plump. There are hundreds of girls better looking than me.'

He laughed, a trifle unsteadily. 'Are you trying to deter me?'

'No! Of course not, but you could have anyone.'

'You're beautiful to me, and you are not plump – just a delicious armful. Why should I want a beanstalk whose bones would stick into me when I held her close?'

Bella giggled. 'You can't accuse me of that.'

'I think I fell in love with you when you challenged Lambert at that inn. No other girl would have had the courage. Then, in Bath, you were so outspoken against what you saw as injustice, whether it was a dog or a child, even children you'd never seen.'

Bella kissed him. 'Rags will enjoy it at Dorney Court,' she said provocatively, and he laughed. 'You refused to take him before.'

'You'll have to come with him. But Bella, why me? I've been so difficult, I must have hurt you so much.'

She frowned. 'I don't know. There are men more handsome than you—'

'That puts me in my place!'

Bella tapped his arm. 'Don't be a fop! I just knew, when I first saw you. I'd never felt like that before, for any man. I could scarcely believe it when you began to pay me attentions.'

Once more he drew her into his arms.

A long time later they began to talk. Bella told him all about her plans for housing orphans, and he told her more about the depredations his sister-in-law had caused at Dorney Court.

'I have begun to put it in order, and it will be ready for you. When can we be married? I'll have to come and see your father. And Bella, you are not going to spend your money on me or my house.'

She smiled and kissed him. 'It would be my house too. Can I not spend just a little? I want to help. But I promise you most of my money will be spent on my orphans, and on persuading other people to help support them. As well as Trahearne House. You would like to spend some time there, wouldn't you?'

'With you, anywhere,' he murmured, kissing her again.

Some time later, as they sat, arms entwined, talking and making plans, they felt the boat give a slight lurch. They sprang to their feet and looked over the side. Bella began to laugh helplessly.

'Oh, no! The tide has gone out, and we're marooned! I wonder if we can walk across the mud?'

They heard a shout from the shore, and saw Alexander riding towards them, leading two horses. He dismounted, tied the horses up, and came cautiously down to the bank. As soon as he stepped on to the mud he sank up to his knees, and staggered hastily backwards.

'Didn't you see the tide was going out?' he called.

'I don't know what we could have done about it if we had,' Lord Dorney replied, laughing. 'If King Canute couldn't control the sea, what hope would we have had? In any event, we were too preoccupied.'

Alexander frowned. 'You'll have to wait until the tide turns, which will be hours yet.'

'We have food,' Lord Dorney said. 'We'll just have to find ways to keep ourselves occupied.'

Bella giggled. 'You'd best go back to the inn, and come back for us when you can launch the rowing boat. We'll have to wait.'

Alexander looked disapproving. 'It's getting dark. You'll have to spend the night here. But don't worry, we won't tell anyone. Your reputation will be saved, Bella. No one knows you are here, and none of us will give the game away.'

'You mean I might be compromised and Richard will have to marry me?' Bella asked, trying to keep the laughter out of her voice.

'Yes. Richard? You don't mean—?'

'You can wish us well, dear boy. Before Bella has been compromised.'

'Oh, that's famous! Well, I'll leave you now, and come back in the morning, when the tide's turned.'

He waved and rode back towards the village. Lord Dorney took Bella into his arms. 'I warn you, my dearest love, that I shall be impatient, I don't want to waste another day before I marry you.'

'Nor I,' she said softly. 'It's my dream come true.'

You can return this item to any library but please
note that not all libraries are open every day.
Items must be returned on or before the due date.
Failure to do so will result in overdue charges.
Items may be renewed unless requested by
another customer, in person or by telephone, on
two occasions only. Your membership card number
will be required.
Please look after this item – you may be charged
for any damage.

Headquarters:
Information, Culture & Community Learning,
Town Hall, Bournemouth BH2 6DY

Bournemouth
Libraries